KU-208-098

ENON

By Paul Harding

Enon

Tinkers

ENON

Paul
Harding

WILLIAM HEINEMANN: LONDON

Published by William Heinemann 2013

2 4 6 8 10 9 7 5 3 1

Copyright © Paul Harding 2013

Paul Harding has asserted his right under the Copyright, Designs and
Patents Act, 1988, to be identified as the author of this work.

This book is sold subject to the condition that it shall not, by way of trade or
otherwise, be lent, resold, hired out, or otherwise circulated without the publisher's
prior consent in any form of binding or cover other than that in which it is
published and without a similar condition, including this condition,
being imposed on the subsequent purchaser.

First published in the United States in 2013 by Random House, an imprint of
The Random House Publishing Group, a division of Random House Inc., New York.

First published in Great Britain in 2013 by
William Heinemann
Random House, 20 Vauxhall Bridge Road,
London SW1V 2SA

www.randomhouse.co.uk

Addresses for companies within The Random House Group Limited can be found at:
www.randomhouse.co.uk/offices.htm

The Random House Group Limited Reg. No. 954009

A CIP catalogue record for this book is available from the British Library

ISBN HB 9780434020850
ISBN TPB 9780434021727

The Random House Group Limited supports the Forest Stewardship Council®
(FSC®), the leading international forest-certification organisation. Our books
carrying the FSC label are printed on FSC®-certified paper. FSC is the only
forest-certification scheme supported by the leading environmental organisations,
including Greenpeace. Our paper procurement policy can be found at:
www.randomhouse.co.uk/environment

Book design by Susan Turner

Printed and bound by CPI Group (UK) Ltd, Croydon, CR0 4YY

ENON

1.

MOST MEN IN MY FAMILY MAKE WIDOWS OF THEIR WIVES AND orphans of their children. I am the exception. My only child, Kate, was struck and killed by a car while riding her bicycle home from the beach one afternoon in September, a year ago. She was thirteen. My wife, Susan, and I separated soon afterward.

I WAS WALKING IN the woods when Kate died. I'd asked her the day before if she wanted to pack a lunch and go to the Enon River to hike around and feed the birds and maybe rent a canoe. The birds were tame and ate seeds from people's hands. From the first time I'd taken her she'd been enchanted with the chickadees and titmice and nuthatches that pecked seeds from her palm, and when she was younger she'd treated feeding the birds as if they depended on it.

Kate said going to the sanctuary sounded great, but she and her friend Carrie Lewis had made plans to go to the beach, and could she go if she was super careful.

"Especially around the lake, and the shore road," I said.

"E*specially* there, Dad," she said.

I remembered riding my rattly old bike to the beach with my friends when I was a kid. We wore cutoff shorts and draped threadbare bath towels around our necks. We never wore shirts or shoes. We would have laughed at the idea of bike helmets. I don't remember locking our bikes when we got to the beach, although we must have. I told Kate, all right, she could go, and she told me she loved me and kissed me on the ear.

KATE DIED ON A Saturday afternoon. The date was September 1, three days before she would have begun ninth grade. I spent the day wandering the sanctuary without any plans. Enon had been in a heat wave for a week and I had been up late the night before watching West Coast baseball, so I took it slow and mostly kept to the shade. I thought about Kate going to the beach so much over the summer, working on her tan, suddenly conscious of her looks as she'd never been before. The milkweed in the sanctuary had begun to yellow, and the goldenrod to silver. The edges of the green grass were about to dry to straw. Silver and purple rain clouds rolled low across the sky and piled into towering massifs. The slightest wind pushed ahead of the weather, eddying over the meadow, lifting dragonflies from the high grass. Bumblebees worked on the fading wildflowers. I hoped for rain to break the heat.

Chickadees wove around one another, back and forth between the bushes along the path. I hadn't brought any seeds to feed them. I remembered telling Kate about the first time I'd fed the birds from my hand, when I'd been in seventh grade, with my grandfather. We didn't have seeds because he'd forgotten about the birds. When he remembered, he and I stood still on the path, with our hands out, and the birds came to us anyway. The episode had happened so long ago, and I'd told it to Kate so many times, since she'd been a little kid, that I thought it might be fun to try it again, just so I could tell her and bring up the story about my grandfather. (Kate said once, "I never met Gramps, but you talk about him so much I feel like he's somebody I know.") It was getting late and I still had to run to the market to buy food for dinner. Carrie's coming home with Kate, I thought, if they're both not too tired from being in the sun and the bike ride. I decided to buy salmon and asparagus and a lemon and potato salad, and the corn Kate had asked me to get. I figured that if she was hot and tired, she'd want something light. Susan'll like that, too, I thought. I'll get a carton of lemonade, pink if they have it. Kate always said it tastes sweeter, less tart than the yellow kind, although I could never taste the difference.

I had almost reached the end of the boardwalk, at the boundary of the marsh, where the path took up again through the trees and led back to the meadow, where by then swallows would be lacing through the sky, feeding. Although I felt like I didn't have the time, because I didn't want Kate to have to wait too long to eat, I stopped and stood still and held out my empty hand, like I had twenty-one years earlier, eight years before Kate was born, fifteen years before I brought her there. It suddenly seemed lovely, the thought of standing there, coaxing even a single bird, if only for a fluttering instant, just so I could go home and cook dinner and when

Kate came out to the picnic table, fresh out of the shower, her hair still wet, maybe even staggering a little to be silly, groaning and saying something like "Argh, I'm so *tired*," I could say, "Hey, I tried to feed the birds without any seeds, like that first time with Gramps, and it worked!" In the two or three minutes I allowed myself, one bird approached my hand and pulled up short and rolled off back into the bushes when it saw I had no food. I decided that that was close enough and hurried toward the car, glad at the prospect of making Kate a good meal that would comfort her after a long day.

I came out of the woods and hiked up the path alongside the meadow, which was studded with a grid of numbered birdhouses where swallows nested every year. The sun blazed behind the towering thunderheads and backlit their silhouettes. The sky above the clouds was a bright, whitish yellow. The birdhouses and goldenrod and milkweed were suffused in granular, golden, pollinated light, and the swallows spiraled through it, catching insects on the wing. I reached the gravel parking lot and smiled at a woman urging her young son the last few yards to their car. He looked about three or four years old. He tottered and whimpered. The woman stopped pleading and picked him up and murmured something soothing to him and squeezed him to her and kissed his cheek and carried him. I walked across the lot to my station wagon and when I reached it I dug into my pockets for my keys. I saw my cell phone on the passenger seat.

Stupid—lucky no one took it, I thought, but then laughed at the image of a mild, pale birdwatcher in a sun hat and khakis smashing out a window with his walking stick and making off with the phone.

Lightning forked into the meadow and thunder blasted over the field and parking lot. The little boy and his mother shrieked. Rain poured out of the sky as if from a toppled cistern.

I unlocked the door and ducked into the car. The rain sounded like buckets of nails being dropped onto the roof. The backs of my legs felt tight, as they always did after hiking. The screen on the cell phone showed there was a voice mail from Susan. I dialed for the message and wedged the phone between my ear and shoulder so I could unscrew the bottle of spring water I'd left in the car. The water had warmed in the heat so it tasted stale and slightly impure. The phone sounded the sequence of tones for the voice-mail number. I screwed the cap back on the water bottle and tossed it onto the passenger seat.

"Blech," I said, irritated, and took the phone in my hand. I put the car into reverse and twisted around to back out of the parking space. Susan's voice came over the phone. It was hard for me to hear what she was saying over the noise the rain made as it hit the car.

"Charlie, Kate was killed. She was on her bike, near the lake, and a car hit her and killed her, Charlie." Susan's voice broke. A car honked its horn behind me and a woman yelled. My car was moving backward. I stomped the brake. A woman out in the rain, with her hair pulled back in a ponytail, still wearing sunglasses for some reason, pounded on my window.

"What the hell do you think you're doing? Are you *crazy*?" she yelled at me. "You nearly ran that mother and her kid over!" Susan's voice started speaking again, telling me to get home, that she was there with two police officers. The woman in the rain looked ferocious, water soaking her hair and her clothes and her expensive training sneakers and streaming down her face. I felt as if I'd been struck on the head and could not shake my brain back into place.

The woman pounded on the window again. I looked at her, and even as I understood what Susan's voice was telling me on the phone, even as I was already thinking, No, no, no, this can't be true, I thought, Aren't *you* determined to get your pound of flesh.

The woman stomped her foot in the muddy gravel, yanked her glasses off, pointed her finger at me, and yelled, "Roll down your goddamned *window!*" and spit away the rainwater running over her mouth. I cranked the window down and looked her in the eye. Rain poured through the window into the car, spattering the steering wheel and dashboard, drenching me. The woman must have seen something in my face, because she did not launch into the tirade she'd clearly intended. I held up the phone, allowing the rain to pelt it, as if it might be an adequate explanation.

"My daughter," I said. "This—that's my wife saying my daughter just died."

The woman frowned and her face went slack and she slapped at the car door. She slicked her hair back and pointed her forefinger at me and dropped it.

"Oh, God," she said. "You'd better not be—Oh, God. Go; *go.*"

I have remembered many times the sight of that woman in the rearview mirror, standing in the rain and looking at me, clearly unsure whether she'd been duped or I had told her the truth. That was the first thing I remember seeing as I was thinking, I had a daughter and she died.

THE MORTICIAN WHO TOOK care of Kate's funeral was the son of my grandparents' next-door neighbors. On the day Susan and I went to make arrangements for Kate's cremation and funeral, he wore a charcoal gray suit. He had close-cropped, receding hair that had turned mostly white over the course of the four times I had met with him in my life: when my grandfather died, when my grandmother died, when my mother died, and now when my daughter died. He smelled faintly antiseptic. He held his hand out and I shook it. His hands were very soft and clean, as if he regularly scrubbed them with pumice. His nails were manicured.

"Hello, Susan, Charlie," he said. "Come right into the office. Would you like anything to drink, coffee, spring water?"

"No, thank you, Rick." I was embarrassed to call him Rick. The family had always referred to him as Ricky, as if he were still a little kid, the son of the neighbors, Ricky Junior. I didn't know what name he went by as an adult. It occurred to me that I had no idea what name I'd called him when my mother had died, which was the first time I had dealt with him directly, as the person making all the decisions about services and burial. When my grandfather had died, my grandmother had made the arrangements, and when she had died, my mother had done so, calling Rick Ricky, I remembered clearly, but as one adult speaking familiarly and affectionately to another with whom she had shared some of her childhood.

"Please, sit," he said, waving his hand at a burgundy-colored leather sofa. Susan and I sat.

"We have taken care of everything. I just need to ask you about an urn, and if you could bring us something loose-fitting and comfortable for Kate to wear, pajamas or something similar, for the cremation."

Susan said, "She liked to sleep in a T-shirt and cotton pajama pants—I don't know what you call them. Ha, they're those things the kids wear to bed but to school, too, if you let them."

"Yes, yes, I know all about those. Lounge pants." I didn't know whether Rick was married or if he had children. There was a gold wedding band on his left ring finger. If he had children, they'd be my age. So, I reasoned, if he knew about kids wearing pajama bottoms and fleece slippers to school, it would be because he had grandchildren Kate's age or even older. I nodded. I had no idea what to say. Susan continued.

"And the slippers, too. Fleece-lined, open-back things. She tried to wear those to school, too." Kate's favorite clothes to sleep in had been a white pair of pajama pants with different flowers and their Latin names written under them in black, and a thin, soft T-shirt silk-screened with the word SUPERGIRL on it, both of which I knew must be on the floor next to her bed, because she'd been wearing them the night before she died, when she'd come downstairs to use the bathroom between three and four in the morning while I was watching a late Red Sox game. She'd have changed out of the pants and shirt and into her bathing suit and denim cutoffs and bright green, short-sleeved polo shirt, the clothes in which she'd died, it occurred to me, and in which she must still be dressed, unless the morticians had removed them.

"Can she wear the slippers, too? Can we get her slippers?" Susan asked. "We'll go get the clothes right now."

"Yes, of course, Susan. That's fine. And we can talk about the urn when you come back."

"Great. That'll be great. Perfect."

Susan and Ricky stood up, and I followed. They shook hands and I put my hand out to Rick and took two steps in his direction. He stepped toward me and put his left hand lightly on my shoulder for a moment and shook my hand.

"Very good, Charlie. Just let me know whatever we can do."

"Thanks, Rick. I'm sorry, I can't really talk. I really don't know what to say—"

"It's okay, Charlie. That's fine."

When we arrived back at the house, Susan went to the basement to get the clean laundry from the dryer. She said she'd washed Kate's underwear.

"Will you go and get her T-shirt and pajama pants?" she asked.

I went up to Kate's room. There were some flowers for pressing on her desk, chicory and a magenta-colored zinnia and an orange tiger lily, and some seashells she must have picked up at the beach. I opened the middle drawer of her bureau. I looked at her small, colorful, neatly folded T-shirts and my knees gave out. I almost dropped to the floor. I squeezed the edge of the drawer and closed my eyes for a moment and took a couple of deliberate, deep breaths and opened my eyes again and took a top and a bottom from each pile, without looking at them more than to confirm that neither had cartoon characters or some other inappro-

priate design on it. What could be inappropriate, though? I
thought. What's appropriate? Who at the funeral parlor's
going to undress and dress her? Rick? Some guy in a rubber
smock and gloves? There might well be health codes or laws
about what clothes people can be cremated in. Ricky might
have been humoring us and he won't even put Kate's slippers
on, just throw them out. Who, I thought, is going to trundle
my daughter into the fire? Then my legs really did give out
and I sat down on the rug in the middle of Kate's room. I sat
with my legs under me and the clothes I'd chosen for her in
my lap. My body shook and I could not hold myself up. I lay
down on my side until Susan found me, fifteen minutes later.

"What are you doing?" she asked.

"I can't do anything," I said.

"We need to, Charlie," she said. She came into the room
and knelt next to me. She'd been crying. She combed her
fingers through my hair. "We have to do all this stuff."

"I don't think I can, Sue. I want to, but I can't even get
myself to move."

SUSAN'S PARENTS AND HER sisters were gigantic Finns from
Minnesota. Sue herself was tall, but not as tall as her parents
and siblings. Her dad was six foot five and her mom was five
foot eleven. Both of her sisters were nearly six feet tall. Sue
was the shortest in the family, at five nine ("Five nine and
three-quarters, Charles," she'd remind me), and that was still
two inches taller than me. Her family skied and biked and
hiked together and looked people straight in the eye and
were in intimidatingly good physical and moral health. They

were always affectionate toward me but I was certain they were disappointed that their daughter had taken up with me. I felt like I must look puny and sound as if I did nothing but mumble to them. My deeply ingrained habit of proceeding by irony was lost on them, and when I was with them I deliberately had to make an effort to be straightforward. Luckily for me, Susan was just enough unlike them to want to keep a loving but firm distance. When we visited Minnesota or they came east, they mobbed her and tried to get her to go off on some alpine excursion or other. Or so it seemed. Her sisters, both of whom looked like Olympic athletes, would get on either side of her and take her by the elbows as if they were going to whisk her away to a ski lodge. "Sue," they'd say, "you look pale; you need to get some oxygen in your blood." Susan's father, a tree of a man, with a white mustache and a white halo of hair running from ear to ear and a perennially sunburned and freckled bald-topped head, used to look around at my stacks of books and maps and say, "The scholar. Charles Crosby, you need some exercise, too. You'll get water in your lungs." He'd give me a pat on the back with his huge hand that felt like being belted with a wooden oar.

When Kate died, Susan's family stayed for three nights at a hotel off the highway two towns over. They came to the house the day before the funeral. Susan and her mother and sisters sat on the couch and went through the shoe boxes of family pictures we had and chose the ones she liked best so they could make a display for the funeral. Susan sat in the middle and her mother and sisters pulled stacks of photos from the boxes and shuffled through them and showed them to her.

"Look at this one, Susie. She's so cute in this canoe."

"What about this one, hon? Which birthday is this?"

"Look at the face she's making here. Jesus, she looked just like you."

Susan's mother remained composed. It seemed she felt she had to, because she was parenting her daughter again, in a way that she had not done in a long time. Perhaps she had never had to help Susan through a tragedy. Susan had never told me about any deaths in her family. Her sisters wept and talked while they went through the photographs. They wiped their eyes with tissues and rubbed off the tears that dropped onto the photos. Susan's father paced back and forth in front of the bay window in a discreet but vaguely military manner, as if awaiting orders.

"We should have two boards for pictures," he said at one point. "No? One for either side of the urn?" Susan's mother and sisters stopped riffling the pictures and looked at him.

"Yes. Yes, I think that's right."

"I'd better go get them, then. I saw an office supply store off the highway."

Susan's family debated about what sort of display board they should buy and with what to stick the pictures onto the board. While they weighed the advantages and disadvantages of cork and thumbtacks, they stole looks at Susan and had a wordless conversation about her over and above the discussion about picture arrangements. My impulse was to rescue her. Had it been my own family, I'd have felt overwhelmed. I'd have felt the need for quiet and solitude. The practical trivia of double-sided tape and making sure the photos could be mounted and taken down without damage was meaningless static. I suddenly had the urge to scream, to make all the prattle stop. It all seemed like a flimsy curtain of noise yanked in front of the silent void of Kate's absence.

"Sue," I said. Her family stopped talking. I tried to sound soothing, calm. "Sue, do you want to take a little break, go upstairs and lie down for a little?" Both of Susan's sisters put their arms around her and leaned their heads against hers.

"Yeah, Susie. You need a break?" her younger sister asked.

Sue wrapped an arm around one sister and put her cheek against the side of the other's face.

"No," she said. She took a deep breath. "No. This is good." She looked at me. "I'm okay, Charlie. Thanks. I'm good. Come help us. You took so many of these. Help us figure out what we should put up."

Susan's father said, "Okay, then. I think I've got what we need. I'm going. Want to come, Charles?"

"No," I said. "No. I think I need to lie down a little myself. Thanks. I just need to go upstairs and lie down a bit."

I BROKE MY HAND five days after Kate's funeral, three days after Susan's family flew back to Minnesota. I woke up that Sunday morning on the living room couch after having spent most of the night sitting in the dark, exhausted and unable to sleep. It was one in the afternoon. I experienced again the impossible grief of remembering that my daughter was dead after the little sleep I had managed had cleared my mind of the fact. Each time that happened, I felt more worn away, less able to suffer the weight. I was curled up in an old afghan and turned toward the back of the couch.

"You need to get up, Charlie," Sue said. I couldn't see her, but I could tell from her voice that she was in the doorway leading to the kitchen. "It's one o'clock. I've been trying to be quiet all day, but I need to do things. I need your help."

I stared at the green velvet upholstery, which Kate and I had always agreed was the color of new ferns, and said, "Everything is shit because Kate's gone." Susan remained silent.

"Do you know what I mean, Sue?" I said. I turned myself over to see her. She was leaning against the door frame, hands at her sides. Her face was pale and swollen and her eyes were bright red and had black circles under them. She shook her head.

"Yes, Charlie," she said. "I know what you mean, but I need you to help." She walked through the room and out the other door, into the front hallway, and went upstairs. I sat up then and walked across the room after her. I meant to help her. I meant to follow her and explain how I meant to help her and to be stronger but that I didn't have any choice, that it was like I'd been withered, sapped of spirit. Susan moved around in our bedroom upstairs, opening and closing drawers. I meant to call up to her. I meant to go upstairs and to ask what she needed me to do. Even better, I'd find something essential that needed doing that she hadn't thought of and tell her I was going to do that.

That was when I broke my hand. Everything failed inside me. Something snapped in my stomach and I cried out and put my fist into the wall of the stairway landing. The old horsehair plaster pulverized and poured from the wall like hourglass sand but I struck a stud behind it and broke eight bones. I vividly remember crying out, because that was something I'd always consciously stifled whenever I had hurt myself around Kate, so I wouldn't upset her. I'd sighed and laughed out loud at my own foolishness in front of Kate when I'd pounded my thumb with a hammer, or had a pebble ricochet off a shin while mowing our lawn, or once had a two-by-four drop on my head when I was rebuilding the steps on the side porch and had to drive myself to the emergency room for stitches. "Your dad, the genius," I'd said as I'd fetched the first aid kit and wrapped a handful of ice cubes in a facecloth. But the pain when I broke my hand was something else altogether. It obliterated my will and I remember gasping in awe at how much it hurt and how neatly I had felt the bones in my fingers and hand snapping. I dropped to my knees, holding the wrist of the broken hand with my good hand, suddenly wondering how in the world I could tell Susan what I'd just done. I had obviously knocked myself half senseless, because the punch had sounded like someone trying to go through the wall with a sledgehammer, and Susan had lunged out of the bedroom and to the top of the stairs, as if the punch had released the ratchet locking a coiled spring, the way an angry parent might pounce when she heard her kid knock over a lamp after she'd told her six times to knock off tossing the tennis ball in the living room. She held one of her crewneck shirts in front of her by the shoulder seams, and clutched it to herself as she looked down at me kneeling on the hall floor.

That image of Susan, at the top of the stairs in her bathrobe, her face ravaged and pale, holding the shirt—a fitted white T-shirt with a pattern of flowers and vines embroi-

dered in black around the neck and sleeves and a small yellow
bird embroidered just above the left breast—seemed like a
photograph from a movie or a play that you see in a magazine you're leafing through while waiting to have your teeth
cleaned or have blood taken, and you think to yourself, Oh,
I remember *that* scene; that's when it all comes apart; that's
when he puts his hand through the wall and she runs out of
the bedroom and stands there at the top of the stairs, like she's
a parent about to yell at her kid, but she sees him down on
his knees at the bottom of the stairs, gasping, and he's gray in
the face, in a cold sweat, and he's holding a hand up and the
fingers look all mangled, and you can tell just by the expression on her face—it's so well done—that she's acted from
reflex, that she's still conditioned, still habituated to parenting
her daughter. But it's true: her daughter is dead, still and always and even though her mind still makes these little loops
back in time to before her daughter died if she lets go of the
fact for even a moment, and every time it's like hearing for
the first time all over again, *Your daughter has been in an accident,* and that is the moment she realizes, It's all over and I'm
going back to my parents' house, and I'm going to stay in my
old bedroom, even though it has been my mother's sewing
room for nearly twenty years. And whether or not she really
believes that that is what she will do, that spare corner room
with no rug and no curtains or shades and a chair and a table
with a sewing machine on it and a lamp bent down over the
machine and a single framed piece of embroidery of a red-
headed moppet wearing a sunbonnet with a basket of flowers
hooked on her arm and a rabbit at her feet, which used to
be her room when she was a girl, is the concrete picture her

mind makes of the certainty that she must go away, and that is the moment he realizes that that's what she's thinking.

When that instant passed, whether it was between us or in my mind alone, Susan said, "Let me get some clothes on," and rushed back to the bedroom.

Susan drove me to the regional hospital and sat with me in the emergency room for two hours, crying. My hand hurt terribly and I was exhausted and I felt humiliated for us. Not only did we have to bear our only child's death, but we had to do so in front of a room full of miserable strangers. I tried to comfort myself by looking at the faces of the other people in the emergency room. There was an old couple holding hands. The wife had a mask over her face, with a tube running from it to an oxygen tank. Her skin was gray. Her husband held her hand and stared at the floor. There was a young kid, maybe fourteen years old, with what looked like his older brother, or maybe a young uncle, who was holding a bloody dish towel to the top of the boy's head. The brother or uncle kept asking the boy how he was doing, saying the doctor was going to see him soon. The boy was woozy and said "All right" every time his brother or uncle spoke to him. I tried to think about whom it was these people had lost. What mothers and sisters and best friends. Susan was slouched in her chair, her clenched left fist pushed up against her mouth. Her breathing was rapid and shallow, like she was trying to breathe fast enough to keep ahead of sobbing. She gazed across the emergency room through the glass doors to the roundabout where people were dropping patients off. She shook her head as if she were saying no, no, no over and over. Tears drained from the corners of her eyes. She wiped her face and looked at me. I smiled at her but she didn't smile back. She shook her head no again and put her fist back to her mouth.

IT TOOK THREE MORE hours at the hospital to have X-rays and get my hand set in a cast. I spent the next day lying on the living room couch, trying to sleep but unable to. I could not sleep that night, either, despite the painkillers the doctor had prescribed, and left our bed for the couch, where I sat semiconscious in the dark, having nightmares from which I periodically started, only to find the waking world worse than my dreams.

Susan's older sister called at nine the next morning and they talked for half an hour. When the call ended, Susan came into the living room.

"How do you feel?" she asked.

"Oh, you know," I said. "Awful."

"Do you think you can get up today and maybe help me with some things?"

"I'll try. I didn't sleep at all. My hand is killing me. What'd your sister have to say?"

"She—they—my family—wants us to go out there and visit."

"What'd you say?"

"I said I'd talk about it with you."

It was Tuesday morning, when I normally would have been mowing lawns and Sue would have been at the elementary school in Salem, where she taught reading. A heavy wind rumbled outside, through the trees, and broke against the house in gusts. The mailman came up the walkway and I heard the squeak of the mailbox opening and closing.

I knew it was all wrong, that I was snipping the single, thin thread by which our marriage was barely still suspended. But I felt it was my obligation. I'd spent the week since the funeral lying on the couch in a daze. I'd lost my mind and punched a hole in the wall and broken my hand so that I couldn't work or do much of anything that needed doing. I thought, Poor Sue. She shouldn't have to deal with me. I'm no good for her, I thought. She's being loving and gracious because she has a good heart, but I just can't ask her to stick this out.

"Well," I said. "How about you go? I can't. I feel like I have to stay here. But you've got another week's leave. Why don't you go?"

Sue stared at me for a moment. It's the last time I remember the two of us looking each other in the eye.

She said, "I need to think about it."

The teakettle whistled in the kitchen. Susan went to make herself tea. I remained on the couch and listened to the cupboard door open and the mugs clink against each other as Susan took one out and the door slap shut and another door open and the rustle and scrape of her opening the box of tea bags and that door slap shut and then the utensil drawer opening and Susan getting a spoon.

"Sue, I think that's good," I called to her. "Your sisters and your mom, and your dad."

SUSAN HAD A BENIGN aloofness that made her irresistible from the moment I saw her. She was a mystery and remained that

way for the duration of our marriage. We were at school the
first time we met. She and three of her friends visited the
house I had just moved into with four other guys because she
knew one of them. We all sat across from one another in old
flea market chairs and a couch left out on the curb that we'd
carried home. It was a rainy, late, luminescent August afternoon and I chain-smoked cigarettes and we talked about
music and art and books and I exaggerated my enthusiasm
for anything Susan mentioned that I liked, too. She poured
red wine from a green jug into a blue glass. When she raised
the glass to her mouth, the daylight lit the glass purple and it
seemed as if her eyes turned the same color. When she lowered the glass, her eyes returned to the silvery turquoise of
her scarf. She wiped the wine from her top lip and smiled at
what I'd just said, but more to herself than me, and I knew
that I'd never get through to her, really, fully, and that if I
did it'd dispel what was already enchanting me anyway, and
that made everything impossible, but it also—or especially—
made her all the more attractive. When she stood up to leave
with her friends a couple hours later, she stretched her arms
over her head and looked out the window and her eyes
turned the gray blue of the thunderclouds gathering over the
vacant fairgrounds across the street.

Since I'd been a young kid I'd loved books and read constantly. I loved mysteries and horror stories and books on history and art and science and music, everything. The bigger the
book, the better; I deliberately found the thickest novels I could,
for the pleasure of lingering in other worlds and other people's
lives for as long as possible. I borrowed six books a week, the
limit, from the library and devoured potboilers and war stories

and histories of the Apollo space program and Russian novels I could make neither heads nor tails of and it was all thrilling. What I loved most was how the contents of each batch of books mixed up with one another in my mind to make ideas and images and thoughts I'd never have imagined possible.

School was another matter. I was a terrible student and regularly failed assignments and wrote pathetic essays and missed due dates. The only college I was accepted to was the state university, and that just barely. When I met Susan, I'd been on academic probation for a semester, and I dropped out the following fall. Susan and I moved in together while she finished her degree and I painted houses and mowed lawns and shoveled snow.

We moved to Enon when Sue graduated. By then, she was already three months pregnant. I went to work painting houses full-time for one of my grandfather's neighbors, a guy named Louis, who'd hired me for summers in high school. Louis had moved into a converted boardinghouse across the street from my grandparents with his wife and four kids a few years earlier. My grandparents had been friends for decades with the woman who'd lived there and let rooms before, mostly to Enon's bachelor civil servants: firemen, cops, mail carriers. When she died and Louis bought the house, he renovated and repainted it by himself. My grandfather liked to stand around in the side yard and pass the time talking about the neighborhood while Louis replaced shingles or primed the doors. Louis always called my grandfather "Mr. Crosby" and shoveled his driveway and the footpath to the front door whenever it snowed, "Because we're neighbors now, Mr. Crosby, and that's what neighbors do."

Louis paid me well, but I had to work with an old ex-con named Gus, who bragged and complained and spewed vulgarity without pause all day, each day, and nearly drove me mad.

"Shit, Louie's a dumb wop, but I owe him," he'd say. "You don't know fuck-all, kid. I *killed* a guy down in Florida. I bought his old lady some fancy drink with a fucking *umbrella* in it and he pulled a knife. On *me*? You got to be *kidding*. You pull a knife on Gus and you are *fucked,* pal; you got that? I threw him right through a plate-glass window and the glass went right through his neck and he bled out like a fucking *pig.* Ha! And *you*? Are you *kidding*? I'll kill you right here, right now, no fuck. I'll drown you in this bucket of *paint*. You *look* at me funny and I'll throw you right off this roof, and then I'll *laugh*. And then you know what? I'll take a big drink of paint and go back to work and whistle a little tune called 'I Just Killed That Little College Prick Louie Stuck Me With All Fucking Summer.' I will because what do I have to lose? What? I'll tell you what I have to lose—*fuck-all,* that's what. And *I* love paint. It's in my blood, you little shit. My *blood*. If you cut me open right now, *paint* would come out. Do it; cut me. I'd like to *see* you try. That would be funny, you college *fuck*. You do not know fucking *shit* about paint, kid. I love the way it smells; I love the way it feels; I love the way it *tastes*. I used to paint fourteen hours a day, seven days a week, and then I'd go home and me and my old lady would hop into the sack and smoke a joint and watch dirty movies until dawn, because *I do not fucking care*. Shit, it's hot up here. I'm not going to bust my balls and have a heart attack for *Loo-ee-gee,* that dago dick squeezer. Fuck it; I'm taking five."

Gus would work himself up into fits about Louis, that "skinny guinea who knows *fuck-all*," and we'd climb down off the plank we'd run between two ladders across the front of the house we were painting, and Gus would cover his head with a wet towel and complain and threaten me. (Later, we painted with a guy named Frankie Shuey, who got paint all over people's roofs and driveways, and Gus took to threatening to murder him instead of me.) I'd smoke a cigarette and think about the envelope of cash I'd get at the end of the week, and about Kate being on the way, and how strange it was to think of her, a little newborn girl, and Gus over there, all greasy and sweaty and decrepit, and to try to picture him as having been someone's baby, once, to try to think of him as a newborn infant. I imagined Kate at about ten years old, wondering about me at work and what I actually spent my time doing and with whom I worked. I used to do that with my grandfather, when I was in school. Instead of paying attention to geometry, I'd wonder about what he was doing at that exact same moment—whether he was in the basement, in his workshop coat, dipping clockworks into an ammonia bath by a wire hanger, or in his black windbreaker and black Greek fisherman's cap, driving one of his station wagons (he and my grandmother always had two matching station wagons, for which he always paid with cash that he took from one of the deposit boxes he had around the North Shore) to different banks, so he could cash the checks his customers paid him with where they had their accounts, so he didn't have to report the income, a practice one of his neighbors, an accountant for the IRS, had taught him.

I used to think about Susan, at the room we rented then,

in Matt Gray's house. Matt Gray was the chief of the Enon police. My grandfather and grandmother knew him well because they had been friends for many years with his father, Matt Senior, who had been the police chief before Matt. I used to sit on the lawns of the houses I painted, smoking cigarettes, drinking cans of soda, Gus spewing his dreadful jive talk, and try to think about what Susan was doing at that very moment. I imagined her, in the cool, damp summer morning light, maybe doing the couple of dishes we hadn't got to the night before, maybe folding some clothes and putting them away in the bureau we shared, maybe deciding to take a walk to the library to see if there were any books that interested her. She liked to read mysteries while she was pregnant with Kate. I'd get worried sometimes, thinking about what she was doing, because here she was, living with me, in a single room, in the police chief's house, in her boyfriend's hometown, with no job then and no money and me painting houses and her six months pregnant and summer getting hotter and hotter, and it made me half panicked to think of her being unhappy, maybe, and me being the cause of her feeling disappointed that her life wasn't going as well as she'd always hoped and that I was a big part of the reason that the plans we'd talked about at the kitchen table all those nights weren't working out, instead of being the reason they all came true.

ONE AUGUST NIGHT WHEN Susan was six months pregnant with Kate, she couldn't sleep and so we went outside to see what it was like and it was clear and beautiful and there was

a cooling wind flowing up in the trees and there were fire-
flies in the meadows and we took each other's hand and
started to walk together.

"Susan," I said after a while, "I can't wait to meet our
kid." I touched her stomach through her maternity blouse.
"Who are you in there?" I asked. "I'm your dad," I said. "Me
and your mom can't wait to meet you and see who you are
and find out about what you're like." Susan took my hand
from her stomach and kissed it.

"Whoever it is, she's going to make us better people, isn't
she?" Susan said. We never checked the gender of the baby.
Susan knew it was a girl from the moment she learned she
was pregnant.

"She is, Sue." I started to try to say something to her
about how I was sorry I wasn't as good a husband as she deserved, or as good a partner, or as successful or ambitious.
"Susie, you know, I'm sorry, sorry that—"

"Don't, Charlie," she said. "It's funny and sad, and a little
scary. But it's okay, too." She stopped walking. We stood where
one of Enon's oldest roads splits in two, one branch turning
toward the center of the village, the other leading to the section called Egypt. Four small neat, old houses, each with a
small barn, faced the intersection. A single streetlight stood at
the divergence and moths and other insects swarmed around
it. Susan took both my hands in hers. She leaned toward me
and kissed me.

"I know I'm no bargain, either," she said.

"Tut tut! Not another word yourself, my dear. I understand. Let's just walk some more and be happy about the little
cosmonaut on her way." It felt like Susan had been just about

ready to lie to try to make me feel better, and that seemed awful. She wished better for us and that was like a blessing, in that moment, like love itself, if a little sideways, but that was enough.

"My legs feel restless even when I'm walking." She pressed the heels of her hands against the small of her back and arched and grunted. "Whew," she said. "This is some thing, Charlie, having a baby. Let's head home."

We walked home and I held the door open for Susan and moths followed us in. I took two bowls from the cabinet and two spoons from the drawer. I grabbed a carton of ice cream from the freezer and scooped some into the bowls and we both sat at the table savoring the cold sweet sugary crystalline ice cream while the moths bounced and plinked against the ceiling lamp above our heads.

The summer grew hotter and Susan grew larger. We could practically see Kate in outline. Whenever Kate moved, her elbows and knees and head and behind projected themselves in relief against Susan's stomach. Susan had a terrible time at night and could not get comfortable. I spent the last three weeks of the pregnancy sleeping on the couch in the living room. Whenever the box springs creaked more than once or twice or Susan groaned, I'd bring her a glass of ice water and see if she needed me to rearrange her pillows or get her a book or just stay with her for a little and sympathize. Sometimes I'd fall asleep sitting up and rouse to find Susan still awake, frowning and trying to settle into a comfortable position.

When Kate was finally born and Susan saw her for the first time, the faraway look in her eyes vanished. Kate brought

Susan wholly and fully into this world. She made the tenuous threads that had held Susan and me together before obsolete. Kate's birth seemed to stop our drift away from one another, a process I had often contemplated before the news of Kate's arrival with the kind of melancholy one feels at an upcoming and inevitable sorrow. Kate bound us back together. Or, really, we were each separately fully bound to Kate and thereby to each other through our single, cherished daughter, and that was fine by us. After all, we did have a sort of real love for one another, or I did for Susan and she had a deep affection for me.

WHAT AN AWFUL THING then, being there in our house to-gether with our daughter gone, trying to be equal to so many sudden orders of sorrow, any one of which alone would have wrenched us from our fragile orbits around each other. Susan took her tea up to the bedroom. I went to the foot of the stairs and called to her. I said I thought it was a good idea that she go by herself to be with her family. I raised my broken hand and fit it to the hole I had punched in the wall, as if to insert a casting back into its mold. I withdrew my hand a few inches, imagining the hole filling back in and broken bones mending. Stop pretending, I thought. Face facts.

"Susan," I said. "How does that seem to you, you going to see your family?" I lowered my hand. I felt like an actor in a play, the house a cutaway set, the first floor the living room and hallway and foot of the stairs, the second floor the bed-room. The husband stands at the foot of the stairs, calling up to his wife. The wife moves around the bedroom, putting piles of clothes away but also selecting pieces that she makes into a separate pile on a small armchair—a hand-me-down, clearly, upholstered in an old-fashioned pattern of faded pink and blue bouquets of hydrangeas and roses and leaves and branches of berries. As the audience watches the husband, the actor playing the husband, the actor playing the husband struggling to figure out what to say, as if he strains to author his own lines, as if he is struggling to compose his own words, it becomes apparent that although the wife does not respond to her husband, the clothes she is setting aside are all hers and are what she is packing, or thinking she'd pack, for going back to her family. The audience already knows she will go and some members already know or suspect she will not come back, but the husband and wife must play the full scene, of course. The audience already knows that she will pack the clothes into a suitcase, something she does not quite yet know; nor does he. They are a young couple who had a single child young and who lost the child in an instant of combustion and are straggling around their home in shock at the child's death but nonetheless trying to spare each other in at least some slight degree the full blow of the end of their fragile marriage by acting as if it isn't the end for just a little longer, by spreading the blow over just a little more time so it does not fall on them all at once.

Time is mercy, I thought. Knowing that did me exactly no good and there I was at the foot of those stairs, part of me wishing I could just say out loud, "It's okay, Susan. You can go and I know it's done and let's just get it over with," but the rest of me struggling with what I should say next, so that the inevitable would play out in the fullness of time. Even in the midst of so much pain, an impatience overtook me, and for the first time I imagined the cemetery, the headstone on the slope, the Norway maples and the granite crypts and the gravedigger's shack and the spigot and plastic jug for watering the flowers, and sitting behind and above Kate's stone and thinking about her, talking with her. I imagined the set of the house, with Susan and me moving around in it, revolving to reveal another set, of the cemetery. The actor playing the husband could go through a trap door in the set of the house, while it rotated, and up a narrow ladder, to a hatchway cut into the top of the cemetery set. He could open the hatch, climb onto the artificial cemetery lawn, close the hatch, and find his mark as the set turned toward the audience's view.

"Sue?" I asked. "I don't know. This is all so, so shit-ass *crazy*. But maybe it's something you should think about doing." Listen to the husband, I thought. Listen to the actor, how he takes the line and delivers it with a kind of strangled levity, imparting the truth that, even as he speaks the line, he realizes that the tone of his voice only intensifies the tragedy of what he says, rather than alleviating it, as he intended.

Susan left for Minnesota the next day. I was too groggy from the painkillers to drive her, so one of her coworkers from the school picked her up. Before she left, she went shopping and bought food she thought would be easy for me to prepare for myself, bread and cold cuts and jars of peanut butter and jelly and a dozen cans of soup. I told her to call me when she got there and to say hi to her family and to send my love and regrets, my embarrassment, at not coming along. We

hugged each other and I kissed her on the forehead and said I
was sorry. I said hi to her friend from work, whose name I
didn't know, and I put her suitcase in the backseat of the car.
I kissed her again and she got into the car and the car pulled
out of the driveway and drove off and that was the last time I
saw her.

2.

KATE LOVED FEEDING THE BIRDS IN THE ENON RIVER SANCTU-
ary. The first time we went was because my grandfather,
George Crosby, had taken me there once, when I was thirteen or fourteen. I had walked to his house from school,
probably restless, probably bored, and he'd said that there was
a wildlife sanctuary a couple miles away where we might
walk around for an hour. We found Enon River, chose a random path, and followed it through a meadow to a boardwalk
that crossed a marsh. It was early October, and the sun was
low and behind the trees to the west. The cold that had collected itself up in the pines during the day had begun to flow
back out into the footpaths. As soon as we stepped on the
boardwalk, a small troupe of chickadees began blipping about
in the bushes and lower tree branches around us.

"I'll be damned," my grandfather said. "Hey," he whispered. "I think that if you put your hand out, you can get them to come to you here." We didn't have any seeds with us, but we stood next to each other, still, hands held out, palms up. The birds circled in tighter and tighter radii, until they nodded and curtsied toward us off the tips of the bushes, no more than an inch from our outstretched hands. When the first chickadee hopped onto the ends of my fingers, I startled at the grip of its scratchy, weightless little claws, and it wheeled off back into the bushes.

My grandfather whispered, "Heh! You've got to stay vary steel, so the leedy birdees dond get scared," in one of his weird, vaguely Slavic, vaguely vaudevillian-sounding accents. We must have been a sight—a short, potbellied old man and his thirteen-year-old grandson, already several inches taller than him, but still a kid, still skinny and thin-voiced and still interested in toy soldiers and plastic tanks and blowing up his model trains with firecrackers, standing side by side on the boardwalk, facing the bushes, each holding a hand out just past the tips of the branches, standing still, squinting into the shadows and light, occasionally whispering back and forth, the old man urging the boy to keep still, but in a funny voice that kept making the boy laugh and say, "*Stop* it, Gramp."

Another bird flew onto my fingers. It was above my head, on a branch perhaps twenty feet up. It tipped headfirst off the branch, wings tucked at its sides, and dropped like a bobbin straight toward my palm. It flicked its wings out six inches above my hand, spun itself upright, and dropped onto the tips of my fingers. This time I did not startle. The bird looked at my empty hand, gave me a couple bemused, sideways looks, and sprang off.

I never returned to the sanctuary with my grandfather, and the experience sifted away in my mind for years, until it emerged again one afternoon when Kate was seven years old.

"Hey, Kate. I just thought of something really cool. It's kind of a mystery, something I remember from way, way back when *I* was a kid."

"What is it, Dad?"

"Well, let me just show you, okay?"

We drove to the sanctuary and I walked her down the wide grass track that ran downhill alongside the meadow, high with milkweed, and the grid of swallows' houses until we reached the edge of the woods and entered them through a leafy archway. The path turned to packed dirt and stone, with steps made out of the trunks of trees spaced every fifteen feet or so. The hill leveled out at the edge of several miles of marsh and interconnected ponds. We crossed a boardwalk hedged by spicebush and willow. Birds began to chirp and call and zipped back and forth in front of us. We stepped off the boardwalk and onto a sandy path exposed to the fumy heat and bright, open buzz of the marsh, swarming with insects. The path led past a low section of stone wall at the edge of the marsh. Clumps of speckled alder grew on either side of the wall.

"So," I said. "The cool thing is that if you put some seeds in your palm and hold it out, the birds might fly to you and eat right out of your hand."

"Yeah?" she said. She wore jeans and pink sneakers and a green T-shirt with a cartoon monkey on it. Her hair hadn't darkened to brown yet and was still bright blond, and long, and not, as I remember, especially well combed. It was snarled and looked a little wild, like vines.

I opened a plastic sandwich bag that I'd filled with black sunflower seeds.

"Take a handful and stand with your hand out, right near those bushes, and be very still, and very quiet." She scooped some seeds from the bag.

Kate whispered, "Dad!" A trio of chickadees had come to the alder near where she stood. They hopscotched around in the branches at the back of the tree and made their way to the front in a series of formations that looked choreographed.

"Stay still!" I whispered.

"Dad!"

"Don't worry," I whispered. "It's okay; they're more nervous than you." That wasn't true. The birds were tame and used to being fed by people. Kate turned sideways toward the branches. She hunched up and covered the side of her head nearest the birds with her shoulder, as if to protect her cheek and ear. Her fingers started to curl shut over the seeds.

"Open your *hand,* Kates. It's okay; I promise." The lead chickadee perched on the tip of the nearest branch and leaned out. It feinted toward her and she yelped and snatched her hand away. The bird wheeled back up into the branches and chirped twice, indignant.

"It's okay, my love. It's a little startlish. You don't have to do it if you don't like."

Kate kept her eyes on the springing birds. There were now five of them in the tree. She held her hand up. The lead bird made its way to the end of the near branch again, and this time when it launched toward Kate, she didn't move and it dropped down, clinging to the tips of her fingers, beaked around at the seeds until it found one it liked, and whirred off into the tree.

"Dad, Dad! Did you see?"

"I saw, I saw. Keep still and you'll get a ton of them." And so Kate stood there, almost like statuary, as a flock of chickadees took turns going back and forth between the alders and Kate's hand. A screechy, manic quartet of titmice arrived. They managed one or two seeds each from Kate—which she didn't like; she said they were scratchy and hurt a little—but they mostly just fluttered around in a tizzy behind the chickadees. Two nuthatches scrambled up and down the trunk of a nearby dead pine tree, *nyuck*ing and waiting patiently for the chickadees, who were bossy and would not allow any other birds near while they were still feeding. Wilder birds that would not be hand-fed were attracted by the activity and orbited around us—cardinals and blue jays in the trees, sparrows and wrens in the underbrush. When the chickadees finally had eaten all they wanted, the nuthatches dropped down and took some seeds.

Just before Kate's arm gave out, a tiny yellow bird emerged from the reeds in the marsh. It perched on top of a cattail that ticked back and forth like the pendulum of a metronome. Kate looked back at me and whispered, "Is it okay if I'm done, Dad?" Just as she spoke, the little yellow bird looped up onto the tip of Kate's forefinger.

I pointed and jabbed. "Tsssst, tssst."

Kate looked back at her hand. The bird did not seem to notice the seeds. It was smaller than any I'd seen before, save for hummingbirds. But it was not a hummingbird. It was not a finch or a warbler or a wren. I'd never seen a bird like it, in the woods or meadows or in a book. Kate looked at the bird and smiled. The bird sang a liquid, silvery little phrase that was so clear and so limpid it seemed without source, trilling in the air for an instant and evaporating without a trace. (Afterward, whenever Kate and I talked about her first time feeding the birds, we ended our recollections by talking about the little yellow bird and the little silver phrase it sang that neither of us could have said quite for certain we had actually heard, but for the fact that the other seemed to have heard it as well.) The bird remained on the tip of Kate's finger for another moment and whirred back into the reeds. I tried to sight it with my binoculars but could not find it again.

We crossed the boardwalk, walked up the log steps in the woods and into the milkweed field, which was full of swallows zinging around catching insects on the wing in the sunset.

Kate rubbed her arm and said, "Oh, man, I must have fed like a hundred birds. That pretty little yellow one was the best. I couldn't even feel it on my fingers."

WHEN I WAS A kid, we followed the Memorial Day parade from the Civil War memorial in the center of the village, down Main Street, to the cemetery. The veterans and cops and firefighters and dens and packs of Boy and Girl Scouts and the high school marching band formed a semicircle around a portable podium with a built-in microphone and speaker, which was never loud enough, set up once a year for this occasion in front of a file of uniform headstones belonging to a group of Revolutionary War veterans, each with a small United States flag poked into the ground next to it. An officer in the army or navy reserves would give a speech, which, translated through the podium speaker, sounded like a garbled distillation of every Memorial Day speech ever given in every small town in the country, the words of which were not as important as the spirit in which they were delivered. When the day was sunny and blustery, the wind would pop and roar through the speaker along with the speech. When it was overcast or rainy, the speech would sound nearly subterranean, as if it were channeled through the officer at the podium from one of the soldiers in the ground behind him. Villagers sat on the hill overlooking the podium or meandered among the headstones, searching for the oldest dates, or stood behind the crowd with toddlers in strollers. Kids ran around playing tag or hide-and-go-seek and were shushed by whatever nearby adults when they squealed too loudly. After the speech, the first trumpeter in the marching band played taps. When he was finished, the second trumpeter played it again, from behind a maple tree at the back of the cemetery. Three veterans from the National Guard fired three rounds of blanks from their rifles and the Cub Scouts scrummed at their feet for the shells. The parade re-formed, the drum line started a march, and the procession headed back to town, where it ended with another short speech in front of the town hall.

I played drums in the high school band and dreaded the Memorial Day parade because I had to spend the day among everyone I knew dressed in a shiny blue polyester suit, with a white sash, white bucks, and a blue plume sticking up from the crown of my white vinyl shako. After high school, I never thought about the parade until I moved back to Enon and had Kate.

Kate was born in November, on the Monday before Thanksgiving, but the next May, when she was six months old, I found myself taking her to the parade and following alongside the band with her in her carriage. I took her to the parade every year until she was old enough to join the Brownies, after which she marched in the parade, and I followed alongside her troop, taking pictures. She didn't continue into Girl Scouts because by then she was preoccupied with tennis and running, but I was still able to lure her to the parade the two years before she died, although the last year, the spring before her death, she ran off with three of her friends and they all sat on a stone wall along the route, sucking on lollipops, knocking side to side off each other's shoulders, laughing and yelling at their friends in the parade. I took their picture and they all mugged it up, making funny faces, and we kept the photo on the refrigerator until Kate died and Sue moved back to Minnesota and took it with her.

THE FIRST NIGHT I spent alone in the house after Sue left I lay on the couch in the living room, in the dark, resting my broken hand on my chest. The hand was swollen and my black-and-purple fingers stuck out of the cast. The doctor had given me a prescription of thirty what she called instant-release painkillers and I'd been following the directions on the prescription bottle to take one pill every four to six hours. I took a pill and my brain felt slightly rubbery. But my hand hurt so much that I began to resent the pain for distracting me from Kate. I found myself having a debate between thinking about Kate and concentrating on the pain. The argument became one of those tedious, seemingly never-ending dreams that irked and provoked me but from which I could not rouse myself, even though I was not, properly speaking, sleeping.

I had known lots of guys over the years who took pills and mixed them with other drugs and alcohol. I thought, A second pill won't kill me; it'll just sand the burrs off the pain and cool down these voices, these antagonists who haven't the decency to leave me in peace. I need a break, some rest. I'm just so cooked, so cracked up and crooked. If I get some time out, if I can just step back a little, get my feet back under me, let this hand heal a little, stop killing me so much, I can figure out how to get hold of myself.

I sat up and took another pill from the bottle and swallowed it dry. I was thirsty. My mouth stuck together and the pill seemed to adhere to the back of my throat. Instead of getting up for some water, I lay back down and rested my hand on my chest and closed my eyes and whispered, "Just have some mercy, please just have some mercy."

I surfaced into consciousness four hours later, sweating and parched. I rose and lurched to the bathroom and ran the cold water tap in the sink until the tepid water in the pipes cleared and the chilled water from underground poured out. I filled the red plastic cup Kate had used for rinsing her mouth when she brushed her teeth and gulped the water down and filled the cup again. I stood for a moment in the dark. What if Kate and Susan could just be upstairs, sleeping?

I thought. Couldn't I just be down here going to the bathroom and getting a drink of water, or having a couple Toll House cookies and drinking milk from the jug in the light from the refrigerator, the door propped open against my hip, and pulling back the shade on the kitchen door a couple inches to look out at the moonlit yard, to think for a second about all the animals out there, hidden, going about their business, to think that that was eerie but also taking some comfort in it and going back upstairs and peeking in on Kate to make sure she wasn't hanging half off the bed like she often ended up and climbing back into bed next to Susan, and maybe even worrying about money or work for an hour before I fall back asleep? What a comfort that would be, worrying about money while my daughter slept.

Going back to sleep upstairs in Sue's and my bed, next to Kate's empty room, appalled me, so I went back to the living room and picked up the bottle of pills and shook it. I tapped a dozen pills into the palm of my hand. I pinched up two painkillers and put them in my mouth and washed them down with the rest of the cold water in the red cup.

I WOKE AT TWO the next afternoon and struggled to make a pot of coffee with my good hand. My broken hand hurt dangling at my side, so I held it up near my cheek. Out of habit I looked for birds in the backyard. We'd bought a couple of feeders and Kate kept them filled. She tried to get the chickadees to eat from her hand, but they never would. The feeders were empty by the time Kate was buried. I couldn't bring myself to refill them, so I fetched the bag of seeds we kept in the bottom drawer of an old bureau in the garage. After cranking open one of the windows in the nook, I removed the screen and scooped up a bunch of seeds in an old plastic juice pitcher that had faint traces of a family of cartoon bears painted on it, and tossed them out into the yard.

The empty house held its silence like a solid volume. There was weight to it. The hosts on talk radio sounded brash and insipid and oblivious. The music on the classical station sounded like music for a dentist's office. Rock music sounded lurid and insincere. I tried to read a newspaper but the bad news made me feel more hopeless and the good news seemed invented. I wanted to call Sue's parents' house and ask if she'd arrived okay and ask if it felt better to be there, but I knew that that would be the wrong thing to do. Sue had called at some point the night before. I remembered hearing the message on the answering machine, and from the tone of her voice that she'd arrived without any problems. I already felt bad, not having answered her call, not having already called back, as if I'd missed my one slim chance. I couldn't bring myself to listen to the message and I unplugged the phone. I checked my cell phone and saw that she'd left a message on it as well. I slid the backing off the phone and removed the memory card.

By three o'clock, it was unbearable to be in the house anymore, so I went outside and started to walk. I didn't want to walk along the road, on the sidewalk. Someone might see me and stop and offer condolences or deliberate small talk. I imagined myself walking down the sidewalk and a woman pulling over and asking if I was doing okay and other people driving by and seeing me and knowing I was that grieving father and separated husband, and the exposure and embarrassment and humiliation being too much to take. But, since the Fairfield estate had been subdivided into a development twenty years earlier, it was no longer possible to cut through the fields that had originally been called Wild Man's Meadow, when Enon had first been colonized, at least during the day. As conspicuous as walking along the road felt, cutting through the meadow would have drawn more attention, if only for the strange and sorrowful fact that in the thirty years there had been houses set around it, I had never seen anyone, adults or kids, in the meadow, no one exploring or stalking through the high summer grass or marching through winter snows. Whenever I passed it, I recalled swiping my way through the tall, buggy grass and being half terrified that the wild man, after whom the area had originally been named and about whom I had been told by some older neighborhood kids, was scrambling toward me with unnatural speed and aim from somewhere along the line of trees bordering the meadow. My terror was greatest in broad daylight, because of a sense that the wild man was so terrible and so wild he did not even need the cover of darkness or creeping stealth to claim his victims in his realm. I told Kate about the wild man one day when we were walking by the meadow. She must have been seven or eight—old enough to be told the story and be thrilled instead of frightened. But she had not been thrilled or frightened in the least.

"That's just people's backyards," she said, and just like that it was true; her understanding of the landscape unseated my

own—the mythical wild man of the meadow simply disappeared or, simply, had never existed for her and would never
be grafted into her impression of the place.

Scooting past the meadow, I felt so panicked that someone was going to pull over and talk with me before I reached
the woods that twice I nearly stopped and turned around and
ran back to the house. When I reached the West Enon playground, I hurried off the sidewalk and past the empty basketball courts to where an old path entered the woods at a break
in a stone wall. I sat on the wall for a moment and half-
sobbed in relief at reaching cover. My broken hand ached
terribly. The blood pulsing through it hurt. I took one of the
six painkillers from the breast pocket of my flannel shirt and
swallowed it.

The path in the woods dated back to the Revolutionary
War, and I thought that only animals and kids must have used
it for many years, deer and coyotes and the dogs of the village,
which were allowed to roam with complete freedom, Enon
never having had a leash law, and kids, at least when I'd been
young, always having been given the run of the village by the
time they were nine or ten years old. My friends and I had
used the path when we were kids. I realized that I'd never
shown it to Kate and that I had not walked it in over twenty
years. As I recalled it, a quarter mile into the woods the path
crossed in front of the ruins of an old cabin engulfed under
thickets of bittersweet. The cabin was harmless but eerie. I
had been inside only a couple of times, when I was a boy, on
dares, during the day; otherwise, I always skipped into a half
run to get past it. It lent the sense of some forsaken soul lying
in a bed in the back room, someone who had been ill and

semiconscious for two hundred years, his limbs and body wrapped in the bittersweet, too, who sensed me passing by out on the path, and who wanted me to come into the house and snip the vines from him and take his hand and put a cloth soaked in cold water on his forehead. But his hands would have been hairy with roots and would have crumbled away like dirt when I cut the vines from them and took hold of them, and his old striped shirt would be rotted and full of spores that would have made me cough, and his old body would have been packed dirt that had half-rotted through the bedding, and the entire room would be full of a noxious suspension that had been fermenting for over a century, since the dying man had been quarantined and forgotten, exiled in an obscure dead water of time, the sort of which Enon is full, if you observe carefully enough.

There was no trace of the cabin where I remembered it being. I ranged up and down the area where it should have been, looking for a pile of logs or tangle of bittersweet that somehow might have digested the cabin, but there was nothing.

"There was an old cabin here when I was a kid, Kate," I whispered out loud, still scratching a little at the underbrush with my foot, half-looking for a threshold. "But it's gone, just disappeared, like it never even existed." I turned back to the path and resumed walking.

I walked all afternoon through the woods and hidden meadows of Enon. The sun went down and dusk spread and darkness began to fall. At one point it occurred to me that I had not eaten anything, but I felt neither hungry nor very thirsty. I reached the western shore of Enon Lake as the last

light left the sky. I knelt down by the water and raised my
broken hand above my head so it wouldn't get wet and cupped
some in my good hand and took a couple sips. The water was
cold and clean-tasting, fine, mineral. I swallowed two pills
with another mouthful, then jogged across the street and into
the trees on the other side of the road, at the edge of one of
Enon's two nine-hole golf courses. The cemetery was a quarter mile away, back toward the village. It lay between the two
golf courses, along the flank of a large hill. The golf courses
and cemetery begin on flat tracts directly off the old Post
Road to Boston, which then steeply elevate in a succession of
rises. I crossed the near golf course and stepped over the stone
wall into the upper part of the cemetery. Kate was buried
below, toward the front, in the family plot, next to my grandfather George Washington Crosby and my grandmother
Norma Crosby and my mother, Betsy Crosby, and where I
will be buried when I die. My great-grandmother Kathleen
Crosby is also buried in the cemetery, in another section.

It was just superstition, but I did not want to pass in front
of Kate's grave. I felt the way I would have had she been alive
and I on as many drugs as I'd taken over the course of the day.
Without having paid attention, I realized I had taken at least
twice as many pills as I ought to have, and maybe more. It
almost felt as if I were levitating when I stopped walking and
stood still and looked down through the shadows to where
Kate's stone was. The moon was out and there was a beautiful
view from the top of the cemetery. Deer browsed on the golf
greens below to my right, and the tombstones made of white
marble glowed. A corner of the lake was visible below, past
the road, beyond the trees, sparkling.

I sat and surveyed the land, and looked down the hill, toward the Norway maple under which my grandparents and my mother and my daughter lay. A stupor fell over me and I floated without direction for some time, possibly hours, until I was roused by the voices of two young girls. They were sitting fifteen yards away from me, to my left, cross-legged, face-to-face, hidden from the road behind an enormous rectangular white headstone, on the other side of which, as I knew from my many trips to read the inscriptions on both the cemetery's prominent memorials and its modest ones, lay a family of six, named Smith, all of whom had died during an epidemic in 1839. The girls shared a cigarette and swapped a bottle of wine. They both bent forward to examine something on the ground between them. One took a drag from the cigarette and passed it back to the other and opened a small book she had in her lap.

The girl with the book held it close to her face and fingered through the pages until she said, "Here it is."

"What, *what;* what *is* it?" the other girl said.

"Give me a second, will you?" The girl examined the book, then dropped it into her lap and stared at her friend. She said, "Dude, this deck is *whacked,* it's always so right. This card is that you lust for someone you know is evil."

The other girl blew smoke out of her nose and clapped herself on the head, her forearmful of bracelets and trinkets clinking and twinkling in the moonlight, and groaned, "Oh man—that's freaking *Carl!*"

Both girls had long, very dark, unkempt hair, which I assumed was dyed black but could not tell for sure. They both had pale skin and heavy black eyeliner on, and very dark lipstick, which might have been black or a very dark shade of purple or red, and they both wore all black clothes. I guessed they were a couple years older than Kate. I liked them immediately, and imagined Kate being their friend and going through a safe and uproarious adolescence with them. I even found myself wishing that they might do what they did in front of Kate's stone, so that Kate could hear them and have the company, although she was too close to the road, and the girls would have been overheard by someone walking his dog, who would probably have called the police on his cell phone. I lay still where I was for half an hour, while the girls sipped wine and smoked and used their tarot cards as prompts to talk about what was important to them. Their conversation was endearing, although I was embarrassed by a good deal of it, and embarrassed that I was eavesdropping on them. But I did not want to try to sneak away or attempt to rise and act as if I'd stumbled on them by accident. I did not want to frighten or upset them. So I let them chatter and laugh and enjoyed the smell of the smoke from their cigarettes and looked up at the stars and tried to see if I could detect their movement through the sky, and thought about Kate watching the whole scene and being amused by it and teasing me about it when we both returned home.

Toward midnight, one of the girls said, "Man, it's almost twelve. I got to go; my parents will be home soon and get all over me if I come in later than them."

The other girl said, "Yeah, me, too." Both girls stood up and stretched and brushed off the backs of their skirts, their bracelets jingling. I heard the cork squeaking back into the mouth of the wine bottle. The girls walked back down the hill, past my family, still talking, but more quietly. They passed under the light of a streetlamp and into shadow and were gone.

THE CARETAKER OF THE Enon cemetery was named Aloysius Shank. He talked through a voice box wrapped around his neck with a cord. There was a hole in his throat, from an operation for cancer. He smoked a pipe, though, and told me once about having smoked four packs of cigarettes a day for fifty years, since he'd been eight years old.

He bubbled away at his pipe and said, "But I quit to smoking when I got that cancer."

Although I'd hardly ever spoken with Aloysius before Kate died, I'd known about him since I could remember. He had always simply been the man at the cemetery. I remember asking my mother once, when I was a kid and had already seen him countless times, for years, as we passed the graveyard in our car, "Mom, who's that guy who's always in the grave-yard?"

She answered, "That's Aloysius Shank." She chanted, *"God help Aloysius Shank! His shack is cold and dank! He pays no rent, his head got dent, and one of his legs is a plank!"* That was a rhyme she had learned as a kid during recess at the Bessie Boston Elementary School, the same school I went to, was probably going to, in fact, when I asked her about Aloysius, sitting on the massive, maroon vinyl back bench of the wood-paneled station wagon my grandfather, her dad, had given us—as he would continue to do with all his station wagons until he died, and the last of which was still sitting in my driveway, and still worked, fifteen years after his death, ten after my mother's, and two weeks after Kate's—no seat belt on, windows open, wind roaring, sun pouring in, on our way to poke around the Woolworth's five-and-dime store—she the clothes and knickknacks, me the records in the store's tiny music section—and after go to the drugstore lunch counter, where she'd get coffee and a blueberry muffin and I'd get a chocolate honey-dipped doughnut and a chocolate milk in a paper carton. When I asked her who'd made the rhyme up, she said that she had no idea, that everyone just seemed to know it.

It was true that Aloysius had a prosthetic leg. The original had been wooden, but it was plastic by the time I knew him, paid for collectively by the members of the Enon Fire Department, who all chipped in for it because he had been a mascot or honorable member for as long as he'd been the caretaker at the graveyard. (All the members of the Enon Fire Department were buried in the same section of the cemetery, of which Aloysius always took special care. There was a brigade of two dozen souls in the section, reaching back to the first official members of the department when it had been established, in 1821, with the purchase, by subscription, of six ladders and three hooks, according to the local histories.) He told me that he'd lost the leg when a Japanese kamikaze plane had struck the deck of the transport ship he'd been an ensign on in the Pacific during World War II. His left leg had been torn off at the knee by a chunk of white-hot shrapnel.

"Lucky it was heated," he said, pursing on his pipe. "Cauterized the wound before I even hit the water." (He'd been thrown overboard by the blast.) "Would have bled out right there and been fish food otherwise."

It was also true that Aloysius had a dent in his head. "Crease" is a more accurate description. A shard from the same exploding plane had propellered its way into his forehead, just above his left eyebrow.

"When I woke up on the hospital ship, the metal was still stuck in my head. They were afraid to pull it out, were afraid it would kill me, that it was the only thing keeping my brain from spilling out of my head," he said. "I told them take it out, I didn't care, because living with that saw blade of a piece of Japanese metal stuck in my crown made me feel like a traitor, or like some sort of secret weapon they could hear through and send radiation waves through or something, and it gave me a terrible headache right behind my eye. So they took it out and patched over the hole with a piece of tin or something or other and that was that. The only thing that was different after is that now I can't smell anything and green looks red and sometime I forget who I am for a minute."

Aloysius had the habit of running one of his forefingers up and down the crease when he was concentrating. It was impossible to tell whether the injury had done anything else to his personality. He did belch, fart, and pick his nose freely, in front of anyone who happened to be nearby, no matter what the occasion—funeral, Memorial Day speech, or smoke break. Sometimes, when I thought about the plate in his head and his old wooden leg, which I fitted in my mind with rusty metal hinges and braces, and even that piece of shrapnel, which appeared in my imagination as a table-saw blade sticking up out of his head like a steel rooster comb, it seemed

that Aloysius was in fact some archaic military experiment
gone awry. He was like a vacuum tube Frankenstein. When
the Japanese had tried to make a double-agent robot to sabo-
tage the enemy, they had succeeded only in creating a pipe-
chomping gravedigger who saw the lush green lawns of the
cemetery as blood-red and who had an abiding love for firefighters.

My mother got to know Aloysius when my grandfather
died. After my grandfather's ashes had been buried, my
mother walked the two and a half miles from her house to
the cemetery so that she could put her hand on top of his
stone and talk with him. She wiped pollen and dirt off the
top of the stone with the tissues she kept in her purse. Every
spring, she planted red geraniums in front of the stone, in
time for the Memorial Day parade. She overwatered the
flowers, but since the grave was several feet up a slope, the
water drained away and didn't drown them. My mother had
spent her whole life in the town, so she knew many people
in the cemetery. Besides her father and mother, her paternal
grandmother, Kathleen Crosby, was buried there, as well as
both of my grandfather's sisters, Marjorie and Darla, who had
followed my grandfather down from Maine and lived within
a quarter mile of him until they died (Marjorie of lung cancer, Darla of a stroke, although my grandmother always said
that it was a stroke if by stroke you meant gin). Many of the
people with whom my grandparents had been friends when
my mother was young were buried there, too. My mother
could offer a census of the old neighborhood; she knew
where every person from her parents' group of friends was
buried, and once my grandfather was there, and soon after

my grandmother, too, she regularly planted and tended flowers at their stones as well. Since she spent so much time in the
graveyard, she and Aloysius got to know each other. When
she died, Aloysius planted geraniums in front of the headstone for the first Memorial Day parade after her death. I felt
embarrassed, and when I saw him at the ceremony, I thanked
him for remembering my mother and for planting the flowers, and said that I'd make sure to plant them the next year.

He said, "We all end up here sooner or later. Your mother
was a nice lady."

I BEGAN TO WALK the length and breadth of Enon every day,
as late summer turned into early autumn, wandering paths
and the old railroad line, where deer grazed and coyotes
sometimes commuted. Since I'd broken my hand so severely,
I'd been able to refill the prescription for painkillers. In order
to conserve the pills, I got into the habit of taking one in the
morning, when I started my walk, then two or three at once
later in the afternoon, and abstaining from taking any at
night, drinking whiskey until I fell asleep, to get me through
to the next day. After wandering all morning, at noon I would
sit against the trunk of a hemlock or chestnut tree and eat an
apple and a chocolate bar, or whatever I had found scaveng-
ing through the increasingly bare cabinets at home, and drink
rusty-tasting water from an old tin canteen. A breeze would
rise and I'd fall asleep watching the traces it made among the
ferns. I would awaken curled up on my side, warm against
the ground but chilled down my back. I would curl up tighter
but be unable to warm myself. It would be late afternoon and

the warmth gone from the sun, and the sun's light would
knife through the trees sharp and gold. As chilly as it might
be, I did not want to return to the house. The idea of returning to the house, cold, too, my steps echoing through its
empty rooms, the plates and glasses in the sink clanking as I
lifted a dirty bowl from the pile and swabbed it with a dirty
dish towel and poured stale corn flakes into it and poured
water from the tap onto them because the milk was sour and
looked for a spoon that didn't have old food cemented on it
and couldn't find one and so just tossed the bowl of cereal
into the sink, where it split in two and shattered a juice glass,
and so on, until I had swallowed enough pills and drunk
enough whiskey to get past the rightful despair at the condition of the house and myself in it, that idea—the idea of that
sequence of acts—was intolerable.

   Susan had been gone for more than a week. I wanted to
call her, to hear her voice. The idea of hearing her became a
little like being able to call Kate, wherever she was, and hear
her voice and be comforted by it. But I didn't call. Poking the
numbers on the keypad and hearing the ring on the other
end of the line and having Susan or Kate answer would have
split something that had already begun to skin over. The idea
of hearing Kate's voice was already an instance of the kind
of daydreams I'd begun to give myself over to. (What if there
were to be a phone somewhere in the woods, a chthonic hot-
line made of dark horn, resting on a bone cradle, that patched
me through to Kate in her urn?) Calling Susan seemed increasingly impossible, too, though, because after she said hello,
after she had answered the phone, or her mother or father
had, which, I thought, might even be worse—having to say

hello to her mother, for example, and having to ask if she could get Susan to come to the phone, when maybe she wouldn't, when maybe the phone call would even end with that, with her saying, "No, Charlie, I don't think that would be good for Susan right now," or something equally gentle and negative—after Susan had answered the phone, and there was that open sound coming over the handset, that white noise that old phones pick up from the ambient commotion of the planet, what would I say? What could I say? What word could I utter into that rushing silence that would change things, that would bring Susan back to Enon, that would bring Kate back to the both of us?

OUR HOUSE WAS RAMSHACKLE and had old plumbing that smelled ammoniac in hot weather and heating that clanked all night in the winter and ancient horsehair plaster on the walls that crumbled if you tried to tap a picture hanger into it. We'd bought it just after Kate's third birthday, with help from my grandmother and my mother and some from Susan's parents out in Minnesota as well. It consisted of two smaller structures, neither originally built on the site, joined end to end. The back part of the house had been a seamstress shop originally located a mile away, at the crossroad in West Enon, where two hundred years earlier it had stood facing a one-room schoolhouse and the long since demolished home of a man named Ebenezer Cross, who'd acted as the caretaker of the school. It had been constructed in 1798 and had low ceilings and small windows, and when we first moved in and I was poking around in the attic space above the kitchen, I

pulled back some of the old lathing and found it insulated
with crushed seashells and balled-up newspapers from 1807.
The front part of our house had originally stood a mile away
in the opposite direction, on the road north to Hillham. The
man from whom we bought the house, a widower named
Roberts, told us that the front part of the house had been
built by a young husband for his wife and child—a young
family like ours—in 1880. When they had raised a family of
three boys and four girls and the husband and wife passed
away, both within a month of each other, in 1950, the farmer
who owned all the orchards around the property had the
house moved to its present location, along with the old seamstress shop, which had belonged to one of his great-aunts.
The front part of the house had high ceilings and tall, drafty
windows that Susan and I both loved because they let in so
much light. There were two rooms on the first floor—a dining room and a living room—and two bedrooms on the second floor. The two halves of the house were connected by a
single low doorway between the kitchen in the old part and
the dining room in the newer part.

     Houses retain traces of the people who have lived in
them and I feel those traces immediately whenever I step
into one. When Susan and Kate and I looked at the few
houses within our price range in Enon, there were times
when my stomach soured and my head ached before I had
walked through two rooms. A given house would seem like
a repository of misery, a deliberate prison in which succes-
sions of families had huddled and cowered from one another
for decades. It seemed criminal for the real estate agents to
talk up such miserable wrecks, as if they could ever be homes

again for reasonable, peaceable souls, as if they should not have been demolished and the land on which they stood rededicated in special, purgative ceremonies. The agitation I felt in those tomblike buildings felt like contagion, as if the frequency and amplitude of the woe vibrating through the boards and pipes and wires of the house immediately began to affect the synapses in my brain and interrupt the beat of my heart. Susan experienced this, too, and the two of us passed silly, exaggerated looks behind the real estate agent's back as we allowed her to give us the complete tour, having agreed after the first time this had happened that we were too self-conscious to stop the agent short because the house had bad vibes. Susan would squinch her nose, as if she smelled turned milk; I'd hunch my shoulders and limp like Quasimodo; she'd put her hand to her mouth and nod a couple times, miming laughter; I'd raise a fist and tilt my head, roll my eyes back and loll my tongue, mimicking the hopeless father who had hanged himself in the basement.

KATE AND I SOMETIMES took walks along the Enon Canal. We reached the canal by a dirt access road that ran between my old friend Peter Lord's house and the estate of a widow named Hale. I had met Mrs. Hale twice. The first time was when Pete and I were boys, maybe eleven or twelve, and had been sledding down the hill on her property, which was called Hale's Hill and was the third-highest hill in the village, and the highest down which a sled could be run. We had not asked permission to be on her property. She must have seen us from one of the third-story windows of her mansion, just visible over the east slope of the hill. When we saw her marching across the deep snow toward us, we thought she was coming to scold us. Being brought up in Enon, neither of us had the inclination to run away. We were well used to taking scoldings from elderly women. Mrs. Hale was tiny, barely five feet, and as lean as rope.

When she was within a few yards of us she said, "You sled like girls."

She reached us and grabbed Pete's sled from him.

"This is how you do it," she said. She dropped the sled, knelt, and lay belly down on it, face-first.

"Push," she said. I leaned down and took the sled by the backs of its runners and inched it toward the brink of the hill.

"A real shove," she said. "Shove me right down the thing." So I gave her a heave and down she went. The snow was packed and hard where we'd been making our runs, so it was like an ice chute. Mrs. Hale went down the hill as fast as if she were on a luge. There was a swamp at the bottom, full of trees and shrubs, and we always bailed off our sleds before the ends of our runs, so that we would not be dashed against a tree or shredded up in the briars. Mrs. Hale must have seen us flopping off our sleds before we hit the swamp and been galled by it because, when she hit the bottom of the hill at near-Olympic speed, she simply rocketed ahead. We lost sight of her past the tree line, but we heard the racket of the sled as it clattered among the trunks and frozen tules. We ran after her, convinced that she lay broken and dead, headfirst among the bulrushes and alders. But before we were halfway down the hill, she staggered out of the swamp, dragging the sled behind her, hat askew. She stomped up to us and handed Pete the tether.

"*That* is how you sled," she said and limped away back to her big house behind the hill.

The second time I met Mrs. Hale I went to her house with my grandfather to fix one of her clocks. Her house was the sort about which I have always had dreams. Maybe hers is the house that prompted them.

When my grandfather was alive, and whenever I had a hard time during college making enough money to pay rent or bills or to buy groceries, he paid me to help him with his clock-repair business. He had been a machinist at a shoemaking factory for years when he'd been young and then taught mechanical drawing at the vocational school the next town over. He cut new gears for broken clocks in his basement workshop and used a slide rule. I had no aptitude for numbers and was useless when it came to making real mechanical repairs. But I had a pretty good feel for taking the works apart and finding out what was wrong and then putting them back together and oiling the pinions after my grandfather had done the skilled work and I had cleaned everything in an ammonia bath in the ultrasonic cleaner.

Whenever I worked for him, my grandfather made me get to his house by seven in the morning. I'd find him at his kitchen table reading *The Wall Street Journal,* because he had a few shares in a couple of utility companies, and my grandmother clearing his breakfast plate and coffee cup.

"Behold!" he cried when he saw me. "The flower of Enon village!" I groaned, sleepy, and tried to smile. He folded his paper and rose from his seat and said to my grandmother, "Well, never mind the wood, Mother."

I finished, "Father's coming home with a load," and we all laughed and my grandfather and I went down to the basement and went to work, him at his old school desk that, in order to get it into his basement, he'd had to cut into pieces and reassemble, and me at the workbench, puzzling out the guts of a carriage clock.

One morning I found my grandfather already dressed in his windbreaker and Greek fisherman's cap.

"Leave us go, Lucky Pierre," he said.

"Where?"

"We are going to *Mrs. Hale's* house," he said. "She has a tall clock she wants looked at." Whenever a customer had a grandfather's, or tall, clock that needed repairing, my grandfather made a house call to see if he could fix the problem at the home, so the clock's works would not have to be removed from the case and transported.

My grandfather and I drove to Mrs. Hale's in his station wagon. We brought a stepladder and a tackle box and an old leather physician's bag full of tools. As we came around the last turn in the driveway, the house rose and spread across the view in front of us. My grandfather whistled.

"I guess you know what she spends her time doing," he said.

"What?"

"Counting her money." I pulled the stepladder and tackle box out of the back of the car, and my grandfather took the physician's bag. We walked to the main door and my grandfather lifted the brass knocker—a pheasant—and tapped the rhythm to "Shave and a Haircut." One of the things of which my grandmother remained most proud her whole life was that my grandfather had never used the service entrance to any home where he did work. "He always used the *front* door," she said many times.

Mrs. Hale, as slight and lean as I remembered, with her white hair pulled back, appeared in one of the sidelights. She did not acknowledge us and vanished from the window. A moment later, she appeared around a far corner of the house off to our left.

"Come through here," she called.

She showed us into a hallway that seemed to connect two wings of the house. "Good morning, Mr. Crosby. Haven't had that front door open in years. This one is closer to the clock anyway."

Mrs. Hale led us into the main part of the house, past elegant, dimmed rooms and long hallways to a broad, uncarpeted wooden stairway. The clock stood on a landing halfway up the stairs. It was seven feet tall and wholly without ornament. Its hood was a simple, beautifully constructed box of wood and leaded glass. Its dial was ivory white with slender Arabic numerals painted around its circumference and nothing else, no illuminations, no decorations. Its case was narrow and plain, the wood seasoned and dull with age.

My grandfather whispered, "Well, I'll be *damned.*" Mrs. Hale raised an eyebrow and looked at my grandfather for an instant and resumed her impassive demeanor.

"I guess you know this is one hell of a clock," my grandfather said. "Simon Willard. If the works are what I think they are, this is the only one of these he ever made."

"Mr. Willard made it for my grandfather," Mrs. Hale said, by which she meant her great-great-great-great-great-grandfather. "There are some clockwork roasting jacks in the fireplace in one of the old kitchens, as well, that he made for Mr. Revere when they were in business together."

The house enchanted me. I felt a mix of awe and longing and embarrassment at the awe and longing. I wondered how many kitchens there could be, whether the huge outer house contained several others, nested one inside another, like Russian dolls, each smaller and more primitive than the one immediately encapsulating it, until, arriving at the center, one would find a mud hut, and in the middle of its earth floor a charred depression in which sat ashes, dead to appearance, but from which the gentle breath from someone kneeling in the dirt and putting his face to them, close enough to whisper a confession, would arouse an orange ember, crystalline, nuclear, at the very heart of Enon's greatest virtues and its innermost corruptions.

"And there is the orrery, of course," Mrs. Hale said. "Mr. Willard made it for my grandfather, for Christmas 1799, the year there was so much snow." She talked about and among the generations of her family and their acquaintances as if they were all alive and their doings recent or, if not recent, remote but personally recallable. "That is in my grandfather's study. One of Mr. Willard's brothers—I think it was Aaron—made several orreries, but Simon made just the one, for my grandfather, as a token of his affection." Mrs. Hale stopped herself abruptly, as if catching herself in the sin of demonstrativeness, offering so much information. It occurred to me that she must be lonely. I looked from Mrs. Hale to my grandfather.

"What gives, Captain?" my grandfather asked.

"I don't know what that is," I said.

"An orrery is a mechanical model of the solar system," Mrs. Hale said. She seemed pleased at the opportunity to instruct somebody.

"Oh. That sounds wonderful," I said and smiled, at a loss for the correct response.

"Yes, it is quite wonderful. What do you think about the clock, Mr. Crosby?"

My grandfather said, "Well, let's take a look and see what's what. Set that ladder right in front there." I opened the ladder and stood it in front of the clock. My grandfather climbed up and the two of us removed the hood together and I placed it on the floor at the bottom of the stairs. My grandfather looked at the clock's works and whistled again. He said, "This is it, boy. Boy, is this ever *it.*"

"I'll leave you two gentlemen to your work," Mrs. Hale said. I smiled and nodded and she walked off into the reaches of the house.

"Open the case and take the weight off," my grandfather said. He handed me an old-fashioned key he'd taken from the front ledge of the hood before we had removed it. I inserted the key into the keyhole and opened the door. The old air fell out of the clock, dry, held in the cubic shape of the case for who knows how many years until I opened the door and it collapsed out into the contemporary atmosphere, distinct and nearly colonial for a moment and then subsumed, and I wondered how old it was, if it contained any of Simon Willard's breath. I lifted the lead weight and unhooked it from its pulley wheel. It felt like removing the heavy heart of the clock. I laid the weight on a rug at the foot of the stairs. It thudded onto the wool like an object from another, outsized planet with twice the gravity of our own. A heavy lead heart, I thought. That has to do, too, with the burning ember in the center of the house.

"Get that flashlight," my grandfather said. "Shine it down right there and let's see what's what with this tricky little *zon of a beetch*." I stood at the foot of the stepladder with the flashlight held above my head, pointing down at the works and the chains depending from them, while my grandfather fiddled around, pulling and poking and muttering and humming to himself. I looked at the furniture and the paintings and the rugs and the sconces. I tried to see through doorways into other rooms.

"Hey, who turn out da lights?" my grandfather said in the French-Canadian accent he used for jokes. I had aimed the flashlight beam away from the clock, looking at Mrs. Hale's house. I pointed the beam back onto the dull, dusty mechanism, which, I noticed for the first time, was especially simple.

"I let go this bear's ass, you find out who turn out da lights!" I said and pointed the light back at the clock.

"Now you hold that steady, Junior, right there, and leave us find out just what the hell . . ." My grandfather's voice trailed off. He inserted a long, slim flathead screwdriver into the works and stuck an arm down into the case of the clock and tugged on the chains from which the weight had been hung. The works clicked for a second, but then the chains seized.

"Ooh, you tricky little *bastard*," my grandfather said. He spoke to clocks like that when he fixed them—as intimates, as if they were both adversaries and patients against whom he had both pitted himself and to whose well-being he had sworn an oath. My attention wandered again. A window I could not see threw a crosshatched apron of light across the floor at the far end of the hallway through which we had come to reach the clock.

"Now you just wait one sweet, precious *minute* . . ."

"You got it, Gramp?"

"Jesus, Leviticus . . ."

"Is that it?"

"Julius, Augustus . . ." My grandfather used the screwdriver shaft as a fulcrum and bent some part of the works a little and pulled on the weight chains and they didn't move and so he bent a little more and pulled again and the chains moved and kept moving. He stuck the screwdriver in his back pocket and pulled the chains with both hands like a deckhand hoisting a sail.

"Ha *ha*!" he barked. Mrs. Hale reappeared almost as if on cue.

"Have you met with success, Mr. Crosby?" she asked.

"I can't say for sure," my grandfather said. "But I think we are cop-a-*cetic*." He patted his forehead with a folded tissue. "That clock is something else. I'd have hated like hell to take it apart." In fact, he'd have loved nothing more than to have taken the works home and mounted them on one of the six-foot wooden frames he used for repairing tall clocks, for the sheer pleasure of having such a rare—in truth, unique—piece in his home for a month or six weeks. But he also knew that this was not an artifact with which to trifle, and the less fiddling with it, the better. "We'll leave it for now and see how it does. If it stops, you just ring me and we'll come back and take another look."

I put the tools back in the physician's bag and folded the stepladder and rehung the weight in the clock and replaced the key on the ledge of the hood.

"Between this clock and those jacks and that orrery, I suppose you know you've got a regular museum here," he said to Mrs. Hale.

"You may see the orrery, if you like," Mrs. Hale said. She and my grandfather looked at me.

"Oh, I'd love it," I said.

The orrery stood on an oak dais in the middle of a room that had been the study of probably eight generations of Mrs. Hale's forefathers. Four brass legs supported two horizontal brass dials connected by vertical posts, in between which was a series of coaxial shafts, stacked with telescoping gears, and a long brass hand crank with a wooden handle. A kettle-sized brass sphere, set above the middle of the upper dial, represented the sun. Its surface was so polished and reflective it not only threw the room's light back out, as if generating the glow itself, but also seemed to possess depth, as if one might be able to plunge into its fish-eyed fathoms, into another brassy room. The planets and their moons were made of proportionally sized ivory balls. Each was fixed at the end of a brass arm. My grandfather and I stood looking at the marvelous machine in silence.

Mrs. Hale said, "Master Crosby, you may turn the handle once or twice if you'd care to." I looked at my grandfather.

"That means you," he said. I stepped forward and grasped the handle.

"Clockwise," Mrs. Hale said. I turned the crank and there was a pleasing resistance against it and as I found the right amount of pressure to use, the wheels and gears began to revolve. The machine was nearly silent. Its precision was such that the planets tilted and turned on their axes and their moons spun around them and all of the arms revolved around the diameter of the disks with a fine, low whir so apt I thought I could hear it harmonizing with the roar of the real universe. The earth and moon turned on a third disk, into which had been etched the seasons and night and day and the moon's phases. As the arms and disks and spheres turned, I looked at my reflection in the brass sun and thought, This is a part of it, too—the ember in the pit, the clock's lead heart, the brass sun in its corona of wires and gears and ivory moons.

"I suppose Harvard or some such place would like this someday," Mrs. Hale sighed. She seemed about to say something else but left off. "What do I owe you for the clock?"

Every time I hiked past the house I imagined the old clock and orrery and the fantastic rooms. With Kate or by myself, I imagined sun-drenched salons with open double casement windows of leaded glass, some panes stained to pale summer tints that took up the tendrils of light twirling through the draperies of the linden trees outside; walnut libraries with first fires lit more against the idea of autumn frosts than their actual nick, in order to please and add comfort to the contemplation of books; hibernal innermost parlors at the heart of the house, with deep chairs set before small, hot fires, the heave of winter winds and piling snow telegraphing through the timbers, pointing up the good for-

tune of well-being; bare, clean, cold, high white rooms filled
with sun and wide views of crocus beds and back lawns
greening in the rain; the massive orrery, oiled and polished
and potent, ready to replicate the symphonic whirlings of the
pale minor bodies around our pale minor star.

That was the thing about Mrs. Hale's house. It loomed so
suggestively in my imagination and my dreams that its essence changed almost every time I thought about it. It seemed
as if its nature, its architecture, had been made to accommo-
date those very whims, as if its very construction in fact required that, for example, the notion of the jeweled orange
ember at the center of the house be transformed into the
brass and ivory orrery, and that in turn converted into the
next dream, all somehow having to do with the heart of my
home village.

Mrs. Hale's house prompted my deepest desires to pro-
vide for Kate, as well as my deepest resentments about
wanting such material wealth. There were evenings when,
returning from an afternoon walking along the canal, tired,
hot, sweaty, thirsty from our hike, Kate and I would cross
Mrs. Hale's cracked and weed-shot tennis court and sit in the
grass on the side of a rise overlooking the estate, a copse of
darkening fir trees looming at the top of another rise to the
right, and the house half sunk behind another rise on the
left, beautiful in the oncoming dusk—dim, solid, so white it
glowed blue in the gloom, huge, one or two windows lit and
glowing the color of the wood of the floors and walls, the
colors of the Persian carpets, the colors of the glass lamps that
lit them. We'd sit and recline next to each other and the shadows would advance over our heads like a canopy and clouds

would spread out over the sky from the west and Kate would braid stalks of grass and I'd watch the sky and point out the evening star and the crescent moon as it arced up from behind the dark firs and the bats would begin fluttering after insects and we'd each take one last sip of the last of the water in the canteen, tepid and metallic, holding some of the day's earlier heat in it, and we'd cool off and rest a little beneath the wide pavilion of night before setting out for home. And I'd tell her about the secret clock and the secret solar system deep in the house, the solar system elegant and outrageous almost, almost indecent in its elaborations, almost, I could hear Mrs. Hale saying to my grandfather and me, ornamental, and the secret clock, elegant and simple and enduring and itself also almost ornamental, or worse, but worse because it was secret, because it was hidden away from everyone, but preserved, too, because it was hidden away from everyone (*almost secret,* I thought, because I know about it, and my grandfather did, and Kate knows about it now, too, but hasn't seen it, hasn't been into the inner rooms, the sanctum of the temple, and seen the ark, seen the actual wooden case hung with the simple mechanism and fitted with the simple, clear dial painted with the simple, clear unadorned black Arabic numbers and nothing else) and not donated to some Harvard and degraded to being another anonymous plank in its hoard of bric-a-brac, stuck in a corner of a room where faculty members and committees meet in order to resolve on more meetings and committees and faculty members and so maddeningly exclusive and precious both and incurably so. And the incurable pull inside me that Mrs. Hale's house and the clock and the orrery exerted was impossible and yet so and sometimes even made me want to sob and I felt ashamed to be taking my daughter back to our little house, which seemed those times dingier and more poorly kept than ever, its table-tops piled with newspapers and bills and shoes and laundry and crumbs on the counter, its cheap, hand-me-down furni-ture, more like a den for little animals than a house for hu-mans, and hot and stuffy instead of cool in the summer, and freezing and drafty instead of warm in the winter. And some-times on those nights I lay awake in bed haunted by Mrs. Hale's house, there in what felt like the dead center of the village, almost Enon's essence itself but not quite, more its trope, its idiom, its veil, prosperous and merciful, bland and trivial, wicked and fallen, and I across the way in my little shack, alien, native, insomniac, and enthralled.

3.

I USED TO WAKE UP BEFORE KATE AND SUSAN ON SUNDAY mornings. I'd get a pot of coffee going and fetch the Sunday paper from the end of the driveway, wondering each time why the delivery guy couldn't just chuck it farther toward the back door. When it was warm, I'd pour a cup of strong coffee with some milk and sit outside at the table on the side deck, under the umbrella, in one of the cheapo, stackable green plastic chairs I'd bought on sale at a hardware store. I'd smoke a cigarette and flip through the paper, looking at the sports pages first, then the book section, then the real estate listings.

Kate would usually come down half an hour later, in sweat shorts and a three-quarter-sleeved baseball shirt, her hair snarled, her eyes a little puffed, with a sleepy half-smile. She'd plunk herself into the chair across from me and swivel sideways in the seat and dangle her legs over one armrest and lean her back against the other.

"Hey, Dad."

"Hey, kid. How you doing?" She made little swimming kicks with her legs and yawned. I stopped myself from warning her about how tippy those crummy chairs were. She knew and I'd told her a hundred times and anyway she never once toppled in one.

"I'm good," she said. She arched her back and stretched her arms behind her head and yawned again. I could never get really comfortable in those chairs and I wondered at how easy Kate seemed in hers. I realized that her comfort came not from the chair but from being young and limber and strong. Jesus, I thought, what a beautiful kid.

"Can I have a sip?" Kate said. She sat up and half-reached for my coffee. I didn't like the idea of her drinking coffee but I liked the idea of her wanting to. I guess it seemed like a nice, safe sort of way for a kid to push a bit at the doors of adulthood. It was a little ritual we had.

"It's like mud," I said. "Gravelly."

"I know, I know; it's your *rocket* fuel." She took the mug and looked in it and crinkled her nose at the grounds floating on the surface and took a sip.

"Blech." She handed it back.

"Told you."

"Mah, mah," she mimicked. "Are there any yard sales?"

"Check it out," I said, and pulled out the classified section and tossed it to her. That was a ritual, too, her asking me about the yard sales and me having her check the paper for us. I deliberately never looked before she woke up. She opened the paper and laid it out across the table, leaned her face close to it, and followed the listings with her index finger. I wondered whether she might be farsighted.

"Junk, crap, junk, junk," she said as she worked her way down the list. "Hey, an estate sale, over off Ash Street."

"That might be good."

"Books and records for you, maybe."

"And maybe you'll find Hector's brother, or one of his cousins," I said. Kate liked to search yard and estate sales for curiosities. The strangest thing she'd ever found was a translucent amber-colored bowling ball in which a dead rat had been preserved. The name "Hector" was etched in the ball, above the finger holes. Kate had wrangled the ball for two dollars.

"Alas, poor Hector!" Kate said. That had become our refrain whenever we mentioned the ball. It's what I'd said when Kate had first shown the ball to me at the yard sale, after she'd bought it.

"So, Ash Street then?" I said.

"Ash Street," Kate said.

"Okay. Let me get my sneakers on. Why don't you fill up a water bottle."

"Aye, aye, sir. What about Mom?"

"We'll let her sleep in."

BEFORE KATE DIED, I loved studying the history of Enon. I read things like mimeographs of the minutes from old town meetings, and the four books that had been published about the village's history, the earliest of which had been written in 1823, on the occasion of the town's bicentennial, and the latest of which had been written in 1973, for the village's three hundred and fiftieth anniversary. Over the years, three of the village's historians had drafted maps of Enon at different times in its history, with little drawings of individual houses and the perforated lines of extinct lanes and paths, and the disused names of every rise and cleft and meadow and tuft of land sticking out of the western swamp, like Birch Plains and the Thick Woods and Pigeon Meadow, and Hemlock, Grape, and Turkey Islands. The hills were named either after their original colonial owners or the fact that their summits were capped with bare granite. There was Cherry Hill and Cue's Hill and Moulton Hill, and there was Bald Hill and Barepate Hill and Stone Crown Hill. I imagined the hills as the exposed heads of giants standing asleep in the earth, older than the colonies and the Indians and the kettle holes and drumlins carved by the glaciers, the earth having risen around them and buried them during their eons of slumber, and that they might someday stir and scratch the tops of their boulder skulls and upend the whole village. I had also bought survey maps of the village from the government geological service and fitted them together like a puzzle and tacked them up on one of the walls of the back room. Kate and I occasionally plotted our walks beforehand, standing in front of the maps, sometimes inspecting them with a magnifying glass or taking rough estimates of distance with one of my grandfather's old metal shop rulers, or tracing some arbitrary radius around our house or the day's destination with one of his compasses. I kept a dozen of his drafting tools hung from tacks I'd stuck in the wall next to the maps. Even though Kate and I only ever fiddled with the compass and the ruler, there was also a slide rule and a micrometer and a protractor, a divider and three or four other tools for which I did not know the use. (I had wanted to take apart the old clockworks I'd kept in a box after my grandfather's death and somehow or other fit them together with his tools and make a kind of sculpture or machine, but nothing ever came of it.)

I loved summer, and my perfect weekend days were spent lying on the couch in the living room, with the windows wide open and the sunlight flooding everything, and the perfume from the flowers Susan planted in the beds outside the windows drifting into the house with the breeze. I'd read a few pages of a book I'd picked off one of the piles stacked around the house (which provoked Susan to fond exasperation: "Arrgh, more books! They're *everywhere*!" she'd yell from the bathroom or the bedroom) or a reprint of a pamphlet about Enon's centennial celebration of 1723, or I'd look over a quadrant of a survey map with a magnifying glass and float off, riding the updrafts of whatever interesting scrap of local history or theory of thermodynamics or description of Scottish moors I'd just read, my senses intermingling in half sleep, and read the topology of Enon with my fingertips like Braille, tracing brown hills, aqua swamps, curved blue lattices of streams and rivers, the bright moss green of its meadows, dozing, hearing Susan ask Kate upstairs for all the whites out of her hamper or Kate ask, "What's for dinner?" and Susan answer, "Dad's grilling. Want him to make corn?"

ANY GOOD-SIZED GRANITE STONE you come upon in Enon, and by good-sized I mean large enough to step or climb on without it rolling, has at one time or another in the past three hundred and fifty years had a sermon preached in front of, on top of, or from behind it. Such stones are scattered all over the area. Several have bronze plaques bolted to them commemorating local, formerly less obscure occasions when a minister, usually itinerant, usually involved in the Great Awakening, preached the Word to the local farmers and merchants, often to electrifying effect, if old accounts are to be believed. There's Pulpit Rock in Rowley, and Whitfield's Rock in Ipswich. Enon has Peters's Pulpit, which is where Hugh Peters preached the village's first sermon, in 1642, presumably on John 3:23 and the surrounding verses. Peters later returned to England, where Cromwell appointed him a chaplain and he was beheaded on Tower Hill after the restoration of Charles II. Peters did not preach his sermon by the rock that now commemorates the occasion. The site is located on the northeastern shore of Enon Lake, in a patch of meadow. There is no path to the rock or sign indicating its existence. Donny Leavitt and his two helpers in the DPW, a pair of hangdog older guys who usually stand around over a pile of dirt or wheelbarrow full of hot asphalt chain-smoking, mow the meadow every two weeks, although not a soul outside the village knows of the site, and no one from the village ever visits it. There was originally a hill on the site, with a broad, moderate slope and a granite brow. Peters preached to the villagers from the top of the hill. I imagine that little group of people, gathered in a small clearing in the middle of what was then wilderness, full of wolves and dismayed, abraded Indians, on a blustery Saturday morning in October, perhaps with clouds gathering and rolling across the horizon behind Peters on the summit, banking and releasing the light, intermittently spattering the trees and the grass and the rock and the congregation with fat drops of rain, and Peters on high, exhorting, perhaps even using the weather as an occasion to emphasize the verses he preached, about the darkness that men love because they are wicked, and the light of God coming into the world being its condemnation, and how this small brood of souls must lift up the serpent in the wilderness, must lift up Christ on His cross in this wilderness and flood its shadows with glory and light.

The hill was leveled in 1839 to build an icehouse for the Enon Ice Company. Eighty-four years later, in 1923, Rebecca Fisk, a descendant of John Fisk, who had assisted Hugh Peters in his ecclesiastical activities during that first year of Enon's existence and subsequently established the first church of Enon after Peters had returned to England, donated the money to the town to buy, as her original instructions, on file in the town clerk's office, read, *A large, appropriately sightly rock, a bronze plate, and the inscription thereupon, for commemorat-*

ENON 77

ing the introduction of God's Word to Enon by Hugh Peters, martyr, to be placed as near as can be determined to the original location of Peters's Pulpit.

Kate and I used to ride past Peters's Pulpit once in a while on our bikes. I never had a good bike when I was a kid. Neither my grandparents nor my mother knew or thought much about them, and I remember how frustrated I used to get trying to convince them how important a good bike was, for getting around town, for hanging out with my friends. When I was maybe seven or eight, I persuaded my mother to let me buy an old bike off one of the older kids in the neighborhood, a guy named Doug Draper. His parents had just bought him a new bike that looked like a real dirt bike. He pitched his old bike like a used car salesman.

"This kind of banana seat is the best; you can fit two people on it and the guy on the back can lean back against the sissy bar. And these ape hanger handlebars are the best; if you move them up, then you can stand up and lean way forward when you pedal and go wicked fast. Or you can move them down and lean way back and just cruise around, like a chopper. This is the best kind of bike except for my new one."

The bike was a shiny brownish orange. I begged my mother for the money for a week, until she gave me the four dollars Doug wanted. I paid Doug and hopped on the bike and started toward my grandparents' house, across the village. Less than halfway there, the air had leaked out of both tires and the handlebars had come loose because the bolt that held them in place was stripped.

My second bike was a red three-speed with a saddle seat

and a metal emblem of Robin Hood on the handle post. I was too big for it and all my friends called it a girl's bike, but it worked and I used it to get around the North Shore for four years.

I was not especially traumatized by those experiences. It exasperated me, though, that no one in my family could figure out how to patch a tire or tighten a pair of handlebars or raise a seat, especially my grandfather, who had a basement and a garage full of tools.

When Kate was four, I was determined that she would have a good, solid, well-maintained, and new bike for every stage of her girlhood. I took her to a bicycle store in the next town over, called Black's. Black's was located on the corner of a block of local shops, in between a cobbler and a locksmith. The three or four guys who worked there wore short-sleeved, button-up shirts with gray pinstripes and kept their glasses cases and pens and receipts in the breast pockets. They wore dark green work pants and Hush Puppies shoes, had army-induction haircuts, and looked like they should be teaching mechanical drawing at the vocational high school. But they knew all the bikes as if they'd designed them themselves, and the store carried only the most straightforward, unadorned, solidly built brands. There were no tassels or decals of cartoon characters or fake plastic motorcycle engines clipped onto the frames. The first time I took Kate there she was uninterested until we walked through the door and she saw the bikes arranged in two long rows down either side of the store, men's and boys' on the left, women's and girls' on the right, smallest to largest. Kate let go of my hand and dashed to the girls' bikes. She stopped and stood in front of a bright blue bike fitted with training wheels.

"Look at this one, Dad!" she said. There was a salesman on duty at the back of the shop, working on a bike clamped to a repair stand.

"Hi there," he called. "Can I give you guys a hand with anything today?"

"Well, this is Kate and we're looking for a bike for her," I said.

"Well, hi, Kate. That's a good thing," he said. "Looks like it's about the right time." He tossed the hex wrench he was using into a tool tray and wiped his hands with a handkerchief from his back pocket. "What kind of a bike do you think you're looking for?"

Kate pointed to the blue bike. "This one."

"That's a great one," the salesman said. "I'd say that one or one of these other two would be good for you, too." He drew the blue bike out into the aisle and two others, one sunflower yellow, the other nail-polish red. Each was fitted with training wheels. Kate barely looked at the yellow and red bikes.

"This one," she said. I was surprised by how adamant she was. My first reaction was to think she was almost being a little rude to the salesman, but I realized that it was more like conviction, a kind of intensity in her I'd never seen before that the blue bike seemed to activate.

"I like that," the salesman said. "You know just what you want. Now, I can get you a helmet that goes with that blue color too, if you want," he said.

"You want that, love?" I said. Kate came out of the little

spell the bike had her under. She looked at me and beamed and said yes, she'd like that.

"Well, hop on it and we'll get the seat adjusted for you," the salesman said. Kate looked at me, suddenly shier, blushing.

"It's okay, sweetie," I said. "Get right on." She grabbed the handles and put a leg over the bike.

"Here," I said. "I'll hold it still so you can sit." I held the middle of the handlebars and Kate wiggled herself up onto the seat. She put her feet on the pedals and leaned forward and made a serious face, as if she were racing, and made a sound like rushing wind with her mouth.

"It's going to be really cool," I said to her.

"Yeah," she whispered. "Really cool. I'm going to go *fast.*"

A sound, working bike, with properly filled tires and an oiled chain and tight handlebars, had always seemed impossible when I'd been young, and I tried to imagine the feeling of being a little kid in possession of such a treasure.

"We can go all over town," I said to Kate. "Every night after I get home from work, if you want. All over."

"And we can race!" she said.

The first bike trip Kate and I went on, I was too ambitious and we barely made it to Peters's Pulpit. We ate the lunches I'd packed. Kate asked me what a sermon was and I stood behind the rock and pretended to bang it with my fist and threw my arms up and cried, "Ah, Sister Kate! Unless my name be *not* the right, ah, Reverend *Borrowed Moment,* then allow me, ah, to shout about how we are, ah, *blessed* to be, ah, *together,* ah, like *this,* under the, ah, sun, and, ah, down by the clean clear, ah, *waters* of Enon, ah, *Lake*—yes that *water,* child, where so many good things *happen!*" I felt impious about my imitation of a preacher, but not about being blessed to be together or about the water.

We tried to ride our bikes back home but Kate tired and was close to tears after a hundred yards. I called Susan to come get us and we leaned our bikes against an old fence and Kate sat on a stump and twirled a stalk of chicory between her fingers and hummed to herself. Susan wasn't long, but I felt a genuine sense of rescue when I saw the familiar white station wagon round the corner a quarter mile away. I thought to myself, We have each other.

Susan pulled over and opened the car door and stepped out and rested one elbow on the car door and the other on the roof and smiled at us. "My two cyclists are bushed!"

I winked and nodded my head in Kate's direction. "I think we both need an ice cream, Mom."

"I think we all do," Susan said. She came around and hugged Kate and kissed her head and Kate hugged her back, her hair matted and damp. "Okay, my Kat. Let's pack up the gear and go to Dick and June's for an ice cream." She wheeled Kate's bike to the car and I put it in the back with mine. I hopped into the passenger seat and kissed Susan on the cheek and said, "My undying appreciation and loyalty to you for rescuing us, milady."

Susan rolled her eyes. "'Twas nothing, *milord.* Let's go get a frappe."

Susan pulled the car onto the road and made a U-turn and headed toward the ice cream place. I looked at Enon Lake and thought about what pottery and arrowheads and people must be under its silty floor.

"That stand of beech trees, right over there? That's where the icehouses used to be," I said to Susan.

"It seems so crazy that they shipped the ice to England," she said.

"We're being bad," I called back to Kate. "We're having ice cream for dinner. What flavor are you going to get, babe? Maple walnut? Strawberry?" Kate didn't answer. Susan looked up into the rearview mirror and nodded for me to look, too. I turned around and saw Kate curled up on the back seat, her hair trailing over her face, asleep.

IF YOU LOOK AT the side of the hill between the sixth and seventh holes of the Enon Golf Club, west of the cemetery, you can still see traces of the foundation of the town's only windmill. The windmill burned down in 1661. Farther down the hill, by the road, near the putting green for the tenth hole, stood the house of the father of Sarah Good, who was condemned as a witch and hanged down the road in Salem in 1692, and who famously told her accuser that God would give him blood to drink. I wondered if the girls I had seen in the cemetery knew this. I imagined it would please them, that they'd feel an immediate kinship with her, like Kate always had from the first time I told her about the witch trials, perhaps one that ran deeper than their usual teenage sense of persecution. I read about Sarah Good in an old history of the town, published in 1823, for the town's bicentennial. It was striking that at that time the author of the book, a man named Barnet Wood, already considered Sarah Good a part of the town's remote history. I liked to think about the fact that he wrote his book one hundred and seventy-five years before I read it, and that Sarah Good met her fate one hundred and thirty-one years before he wrote it. Sarah was hanged in Salem, but there were nights when I passed through the center of the village and imagined Sarah swinging in the wind from a gallows where the Civil War memorial is, which was originally a green used for common pasturage. The statue standing atop the pediment of the memorial is modeled after a man named Benjamin Conant, who fought in the Union Army and was famous for the grapevines he kept, and who repaired shoes before and after the war out of a small shack behind one of the larger houses along Main Street; the shack is still there and is now used as a tool shed by a dentist. Benjamin Conant's statue was erected in 1870, while he was still alive, forty-seven years after Barnet Wood published his book *A History of Enon, on the Occasion of Its Bicentennial,* one hundred and seventy-eight years after Sarah Good was hanged in Salem, thirty years after the first Crosby settled in Enon, and one hundred and thirty-five years before my daughter was buried half a mile up the street. In fact, Barnet Wood and Benjamin Conant are both buried in the cemetery as well. I don't know where Sarah Good was buried—maybe in Salem. I never looked it up. But the woods of Enon are full of very old unmarked graves and hers may well be among them, along with the bones of animals and citizens: sheep and dogs, fathers and brothers, oxen and horses, mothers and aunts, pigs and chickens, sons and daughters, anonymous cats and owls, Puritans and Indians, and unnamed infants, getting their bones mixed in the currents of soil and groundwater, migrating beneath the foundations of our houses and the fairways

of the golf courses, trading ribs and teeth and shins and
knuckles, commuting under baseball diamonds and the beds
of streams, snagging up on roots and rocks, shelves of granite
and seams of clay. There are certainly more citizens of Enon
beneath its fifty-four hundred acres than there are above it.
Just beneath our feet, on the other side of the surface of the
earth, there is another, subterranean Enon, which conceals its
secret business by conducting it too slowly for its purposes to
be observed by the living.

IT WAS EASY FOR me to imagine Kate living in an Enon that
existed in the past, though, where all the citizens from all the
village's history lived among one another. I could see her
newly arrived, walking alone down Main Street, between the
cemetery and town hall—the Memorial Day parade route, I
guessed. I saw her as having come from the beach a mile
away, not from the sunbathing she'd done with Carrie right
before she died but from a landing, a disembarkation after a
trip across another Atlantic.

Kate has dried in the breeze but her skin is salted and her
hair, clothes, and beach towel brined. She is pale and still
wobbly on her feet from the weeks of the rise and fall of the
trip across the ocean, and still feels nauseated from the seasickness she suffered most of the way. The details of the shore
and the dark boat that brought her are imprecise, beyond the
boundaries of this other Enon. I knew that the boat turned
back after its crew saw Kate safely ashore and that by the time
she entered the village it had sailed beneath the horizon to
fetch more pilgrims.

Main Street is unpaved and called the Turnpike. A dog, a terrier, trots out onto the road from the high corn that grows in a field belonging to the farm opposite the cemetery. It approaches Kate and barks and grins.

Kate crouches down and says, "Hi, boy," to the dog and scratches it behind the ear. The dog is small, a descendant of the first terriers the villagers must have kept in order to help control rats. Kate takes a corner of the hard yellow corn bread she has rolled up in the beach towel and offers it to the dog. The bread must be old and stale and salty, the last of Kate's rations from the crossing. The dog sniffs at the bread, looks up at Kate, yawns, shakes itself, and trots off, toward a low brown house with a high roof and small windows fitted with diamond-shaped panes of leaded glass. The house stands alone, behind a stone wall running along the road. The front door of the house is closed, and when Kate gets to it and knocks, no one answers. She walks around to the back of the house. There is a dirt yard and a garden planted with Good-King-Henry and purslane, smallage and skirrets, and other obscure herbs dotted with black and midnight purple flowers that have prickly, hairy leaves the color of bats' wings. Kate does not recognize any of the plants. There is a pile of wood stacked against the back wall. Kate turns from the house and looks up the hill, which appears to be used for pasturage. It is late afternoon and shadows are long. A quartet of goats are making their way across the summit of the hill, slowly, in single file, and their thin shadows stretch at oblique angles ahead of them in parallel lines down the length of the hill, as if they are puppets being marched along the crest of a stage at the ends of long black sticks. Halfway up the hill, there is a girl, two or three years older than Kate, sitting on a stump, with her elbows on her knees, one hand curled into a fist, on which she rests her chin, the other hand extended and open, palm up, in which a small yellow bird is perched, eating this-tle seeds. She wears a black dress that Kate finds archaic and beautiful, and black leather shoes with wooden heels. Kate knows the girl from all the town history I've told her over the years, stories that bored her in themselves but that she loved to hear because she loved that I loved them and that I loved telling them to her. Despite the girl's later, infamous role in local history, after she had grown up and found herself homeless and spent her days scolding her neighbors for being uncharitable, Kate was loyal to her from the first time I told her the story and always remained so, convinced that theories about her hysteria and madness were the kind of humbug-gery that always suppresses and deforms the spirits of strong young girls. Kate knows that the girl has seen her, or at least is aware that she is there, even though the girl has not moved. Kate knows, too, that the girl does not move or gesture toward her because she already knows that Kate will ap-proach her. Kate walks across the yard and into the pasture and up the hill and stands in front of the girl, who looks up, squinting in the light of the late, low, orange sun. There is a cooling, gusty breeze that makes the flowers and the long, stiff grass shiver. The pasture smells like grass and open earth and, faintly, dung.

Kate says to the girl, "You are Sarah." The girl raises the little yellow bird in her hand to her lips and whispers a syl-lable to it. The bird nods and flies away, behind the hill, toward the setting sun.

The girl says to Kate, "And you are Kate." Kate suddenly understands that she and young Sarah Good are together in a suspended moment, a small eddy or niche set aside but within all the compounded times of Enon, which are always confluent and permeative. Sarah stares at Kate, in a manner that is patient and deeply familiar, and that frightens Kate. Kate begins to cry, and Sarah reaches out and takes one of her hands in both of her own. Sarah strokes Kate's hand as Kate sobs, but her expression does not change, and even her hands stroke Kate's in a perfunctory way, as if she is consoling someone else, and it feels to Kate like Sarah is looking into someone else's eyes, not hers, and that terrifies Kate all the more. Kate startles and tries to draw her hand out of Sarah's grasp. Sarah does not let go.

Kate sobs to her, "Sarah, let me go."

Sarah says, "It is all right, my dear friend; everything is all right." But again, it feels to Kate as if Sarah Good is speaking to someone else, just beyond her, maybe just behind her, or just to the side, she cannot tell where, but just outside of her awareness. Then Kate catches a glimpse of whom Sarah is talking with. It is Kate after all. There is a rushing sensation of relief, similar to what it feels like to regain consciousness after nearly drowning or passing out from having the wind knocked out of oneself. Kate gasps and there is a flooding of herself back into herself, and she looks at Sarah, who now is clearly looking right at her, was looking right at her all along, and who is once again Kate's dear, cherished old friend, born, grown, scapegoated, accused, condemned, and hanged, and Kate is once again herself, also born, also grown, beloved, struck down, and killed three centuries on, tomorrow, just this moment, ages ago, on the very road laid out below them. Kate kneels down in front of Sarah and rests her head in her friend's lap.

Sarah runs her fingers through Kate's hair and says, not much louder than a whisper, "Sometimes, it's hard to remember."

4.

WHEN I WAS A KID, MAYBE TWELVE OR THIRTEEN, WHAT I MOST wanted was to be outside somewhere, in the woods or crouching in the high grass in the fields of Mrs. Hale's estate, next to my friend Peter Lord's house, late at night, almost dawn, and knowing that my friends were scattered about the field, too, stalking one another but mostly alone. There were revelations that occurred only at night. Some were horrors, like the muddy corpse of a dog, its gums pulling away from its teeth. But there were other secret, nocturnal processes that I observed and could ponder days later, failing to fall asleep on a weeknight, say, dreading school and the regime of home-work. I'd think about being crouched in the field, dilated, tacky with cool, mineral damp, inhaling the fumes of the grass and soil and hearing the wind move up behind the hill and come over it and swirl through the pine trees and stick to the pitch leaking down their trunks and push across the field in waves through the long grass, all beneath the stars and the pink moon, the flower moon, the strawberry, buck, and hunter's moons, and the clouds lit up in silhouettes, their outlines turning and cresting and collapsing so intricately that I could never recall their true extravagances days later when I lay sleepless in my bed.

My friends and I scattered and hunted one another with flashlights across fifty acres of woods and meadows. The rules for hiding and searching were few and vague and seemed years later to have been kept so in order to preserve the respective solitudes of both those in their hiding places and those trying to find them, while still tethering us all within loose, shifting constellations along the stone walls and clefts, atop hillocks and across the fields. If being alone in the dark unsettled a hider, he was free to crash around and be found. If a hunter decided to turn his flashlight off and stalk the hiders in silence and frighten them to near fainting by pouncing on them where they hid, it was fine. No matter how deeply you crawled into the thickets or the muddy reeds in the swamp or how high you clambered up into a pine tree, if you fell and broke an arm or got spooked by the stars suddenly getting brighter or the leaves stirring without any wind or a voice grunting a single syllable a few yards away, you could always call out and be heard by at least one of your fellows.

When each round of the game exhausted itself—through fear or antagonism or boredom—we would find ourselves convened in some remote copse or break in the miles of granite stone walls that not only bounded current property lines but also ran through all the woods where the ghosts of old farms and the foundations of former houses mingled with the forests and clearings and streams we explored, and we would report to one another about the night—there was Jupiter; there was a dancing light we all saw but none seemed to have made; there was the corpse of Freaky, Mr. Jones's mutt who after years of chasing cars and losing his tail, then an ear, then an eye, then a leg, now lay split open in the uncut grass of the ditch between the silent road and Mr. Jones's orchard, his coat matted with gravel.

"Jesus, it's Freaky."

"What?"

"It's Freaky, man. Dead as *shit.*"

"I'm going to bury him."

"Are you crazy?"

"I'm going to. Out of respect. He was the guardian spirit of Cherry Street."

"Bullshit."

"Yeah. And look at him. He's all fucked up."

"And he smells *nasty.*"

"Go home then. I'm getting a sheet and a shovel and I'm going to bury him."

"Hey, Wader, I'll give you ten bucks if you eat a mouthful of his guts."

"Lord's right. We've got to bury Freaky. Out of respect."

"Out of respect."

"Out of respect."

How different we were at night, out from under the tyrannies of due dates and gym classes and school bells, luminescent faces in a circle, telling one another what we'd seen and heard, what we'd found (Algonquin arrowheads and flints would still turn up now and then, when one of us scratched at a patch of sand), making small adjustments to the rules for the next dispersal, fetching Peter's dad's old GI-issue spade and spending the rest of the night taking turns digging a grave for a dog.

WHEN WE CAMPED ON Peter Lord's front yard we always stopped whatever game we had been playing in the meadow just before the first fletchings of dawn and stood in the high grass for a moment or two, scratching bug bites, wiping our noses with the backs of our hands, raking our dirty fingers through our sweaty hair, murmuring a quiet, conclusive word or two.

"Something big moving in the pond tonight."

"Huge."

"Full moon's why."

"Bullshit."

"Look it up."

"Look *what* up?"

"He's right."

"Owl took half Watt's hair."

"Screamed so hard his balls fell off."

THE LAST CARS OF night had driven past hours ago on Cherry Street, beyond the fields, past the stone fences. The first cars of morning had yet to come. We thrived in that nocturnal kingdom, which emerged from the fields like a pop-up world in a cardboard book and collapsed back into the grass as we kicked one another to jittery sleep. You could almost hear it folding itself back up just ahead of the sunrise, outside the nylon walls of the tent. We were careful never to be outside when it disappeared, in case one of us tripped on an over-turning corner and was gobbled down into the throat of that old earth, into the cross sections of years and centuries and generations, folded up into the curled layers of prehistoric winters and antique summers where we had no business being after dawn, and getting coughed back up into the right night onto the right front lawn might be a one in a million or even slighter chance, and the rest of us finding a rope in Peter Lord's garage and lowering it into the eons and lassoing our friend and hauling him back up through the constellated gears and pinions of eras and epochs was something we couldn't get a grasp on, couldn't plumb, didn't have whatever tool, whatever rare sextant or theodolite was required for sighting the lines along which we could pull him back to the here and now without him being hoisted from the ground a dead Puritan or quadruped fossil.

THE SPRING BEFORE KATE died, she decided that she wanted to make the girls' cross-country team when she started ninth grade at the regional high school. She did track at the middle school but disliked just running around in circles, as she called it, on the course behind the school. She was at that age where a lot of kids appear to be and more or less are in shape no matter what they do, but, as limber and slim and athletic-looking as she was, I still could not believe how swiftly she could run the first time I watched her at a meet. She woke up early on a Saturday to start her serious training and I got up, too, intending to accompany her. I supposed I could manage the mile or two that I figured she was capable of, and I wanted to reconnoiter the route she'd told me she meant to use to make sure she wouldn't have to cross any dangerous intersections or go for any stretches where she wouldn't be within yelling distance of a house—even though I knew every stride of the route she'd described, having walked or ridden my bike on it, alone, since I'd been four or five years younger than she was.

As in shape as I thought I was from all the raking and mowing and bushwhacking, I was winded after half a mile. Kate's legs were longer than I'd ever noticed. She took long, seemingly weightless strides, and appeared propelled not by her own exertions but by the graceful strength of her legs themselves. She hadn't broken a sweat nor was there any trace of breathlessness when she asked me if I was already pooping out.

"Not pooping out, Kates; just warming up."

Without breaking stride, Kate looked at the digital runner's watch Susan and I had bought for her previous birthday. She pushed a button and the watch beeped twice. She undid the elastic band holding her hair in a ponytail, pulled her hair and twisted it up tighter against the back of her head, wound the elastic back around it at the base, looked at me and smiled, and said, "Okay, Dad."

I knew that I was slowing her down, and that she wanted to run on her own, much faster and much farther than I was capable of.

"Just to Peters's Pulpit," I said. "Just to the Pulpit, and then I'll let you do your thing, okay?"

"Okay, Dad. That's okay," she said.

Peters's Pulpit was another half a mile. I intended to say something funny or nostalgic about the times we'd ridden our bikes there and had our impromptu picnics of chips and juice, but when we rounded the bend that gave way to the meadow with the rock in its middle, I felt Kate accelerate rather than pull up, so I veered off into the meadow and ran toward the rock, crying, "Help me, Hugh Peters! Help this sweaty old tub of guts!"

I kept running toward the rock and didn't turn back toward Kate but waved my hand high in the air and shouted, "Go on! Go on! Save yourself while you can! I'm done for!" like in the old war movies we'd watched together late at night when she had had a tough time getting to sleep—all those corny John Wayne and Audie Murphy films.

Kate shouted, "Bye, Dad," and lunged into a pace half again as fast as we'd been running together and disappeared around the bend. I half-sat against the rock, gulping breaths, and looked out across Enon Lake. The water near the shore was like sheer blue glass, transparent, filled with light, the lake floor lined with clean sand and smooth pebbles. Breezes etched themselves across the surface farther out, toward the center. I saw my reflection in the water and it angered and embarrassed me. I looked just the way I imagined I would: closer to middle-aged than I wanted to admit, a little heavy in the chops, sweaty, winded, my hair wet around the edges, the rest stood up by the breeze and salt in my sweat.

The name Enon, spelled Aenon for the first four years of the village's existence, is from the Greek *ainon,* which is from the Hebrew *enayim,* which means double spring or, more generally, a place of abundant water. It is mentioned in the Gospel of John. The evangelist baptized in Enon *because there was much water there.* The best of Enon's water is in the lake, which is spring-fed and famous for its clarity and taste. Whereas five years before, I would not have hesitated to scoop up a handful of water and slurp it down, to show Kate how pure it was, while telling her about its history, about the Indians who'd fished it and the colonists who'd exported it (although I would not have let her drink any, "Because your nice young guts might still get grumbly from the stuff in it," I'd have said to her, or something like that), now I worried that something in the water might worsen the queasiness I felt from running and lead to some humiliating intestinal predicament as I headed back to the house. This made my mood worse, and I walked home cursing the lake and its clean water, and all the half-bullshit history I'd told Kate over the years, for no better reason than that she'd been a kid.

When I got back to the house, Susan was in the kitchen taking dishes out of the dishwasher and putting them away.

"That didn't go so well," I said. I felt embarrassed, not so much at being out of shape and foolish-looking in my old tennis sneakers and sweat shorts, but by how inexplicably angry I felt. I had always anticipated the day when Kate would suddenly seem not like a little kid anymore but like a young woman, or like someone I didn't know. It wasn't that I was surprised that she could run faster than me or that she wanted to run on her own without me. It was that it had happened so abruptly and taken me by surprise, even though I felt like I'd prepared myself for it a long time ago.

Forty-five minutes later, I had showered and was sitting

outside with a cold beer when Kate came running up the
road. She made a last leap across the seam between our driveway and the sidewalk, her finish line, and checked her time
on her stopwatch.

"You *suck.*" She cursed herself with real anger, with an
insular, personal seriousness that had become more frequent
in the last months.

I knew that she would be provoked by anything that
sounded like consolation, but I said, "Don't worry. You'll set
a better time tomorrow. I screwed your concentration up,
coming along, is all."

"My concentration was fine, Dad. It had nothing to do
with you." She let the screen door slam behind her and
stomped up the stairs.

I forced myself not to follow and try to make her feel
better or explain why she shouldn't take her training so seriously. There was a childishness in my impulse to dissuade her
from placing such value on and devoting such effort to getting a better time on her run, or to excelling at her schoolwork, because I had not cared about such things in my own
adolescence but had suffered the same degree of frustration
with myself and the world, had found myself angry or sad for
no reason. The beer had gone warm, so I tapped a couple of
railroad ties in the retaining wall along the driveway, like I
was checking them for rot, then poured the last couple of
swigs behind the yew bush and went back inside.

5.

My grandparents and my mother died when I was more or less fully grown. That's the way I imagined things should be. I never knew my father; nor did my mother. (He and she spent a night together at a college homecoming weekend she'd gone to with friends. He didn't tell her his name and they both left the next day and that was that.) I had no siblings. So behind me were the ghosts I always expected to have there, looking over my shoulder. But after the accident, ghosts surrounded me. My whole family made a circumference of ghosts, with me the sole living member in the middle. Or perhaps I was at the end; perhaps my family was not a circle but a procession in which we all had our supposedly proper places but then my daughter ran ahead of me into death. My great-great-grandfather was the farthest spirit back that I could imagine in any detail, because he was my grandfather's grandfather and my grandfather had known him and remembered a few facts about him. He was a Methodist minister who'd had some kind of breakdown and been taken away and that's about all my grandfather could recall. Beyond him trailed a parade of phantoms. He would have told me that Kate hurrying ahead into death was a blessing, a mark of grace and mercy that I, myself a grandson of dear old fallen Adam, was not competent to see as such. I found myself having imaginary conversations with him, in which he tried to console me with that point of view. I imagined myself wholeheartedly agreeing with him, not because I actually felt that way but because it seemed that he would be so convinced of what he said, so certain it was providence, and his certainty would be a comfort, however slight. I never once felt that there was any deeper goodness or benediction in Kate's death, as easy as it was for me to imagine that idea, even accept its integrity. Because I understood that there are vastly greater meanings in creation to which I have no access did not mean that I could shed my sorrow.

Understanding that my woes were minuscule compared with the sum of the universe did not prevent them from devastating me. I knew that the anguish I experienced was presumptuous, that I pretended to absolute tragedy. If I claimed I was too weak to bear my daughter's death, didn't that mean I really had the strength? My persistence in feeling that Kate's death was the end of the world was an embarrassment, because I knew of people who had suffered the deaths of children from suicide and gunshots and falling from windows, the deaths of siblings to drowning and avalanche, the deaths of friends and lovers and spouses to fever, to falling, to ice, and to fire. I could have bought a plane ticket or rented a car or hopped on a bicycle or in some cases walked to those people's houses, knocked on their doors, sat in their living rooms, drank coffee, and talked with them about the override proposition or their vacation to Portugal and they would have done what people have always miraculously managed to do, which is carry on when there are so very many reasons why doing so should be impossible. I had a deep and abiding love for the idea that this life is not something that we are forced to endure but rather something in which we are blessed to be allowed to participate. But I felt no gratitude whatsoever for, and no relief from, the pain I experienced every waking moment, and this life felt like nothing more than a distillation of sorrow and anger. Even after Kate's death, when my prior, occasional despair became general, I still believed that giving in to it was a failure of character.

And yet. Wouldn't my sorrows have been the greater if Kate had never been at all? Wouldn't they? Wasn't it the case that her short and happy life was the greatest joy in my own? Wasn't the joy of those thirteen years its own realm, encased now in sorrow but not breached by it? That is what I told myself. The joy of those years had its own integrity, and Kate existed within that. She could not be touched by the misery caused by her own death. Sometimes I had the sense of her watching me and smiling because she saw me in my sorrow and anger and understood that it was a natural part of the comic tragedy of this life. I hoped that the reason she no longer felt sorrow or anger was not because she was inhuman but because she was now wholly human, even if I, yoked to this life, still had to suffer the joy of my life with Kate, unbreachable as it might be, in stark and ruinous contradiction to my life without her. That joy was the measure and source of my grief.

I REMEMBER SITTING AT our dining room table late one spring afternoon, with rain and wind blustering around in the side yard and through the maple trees. Susan was in the kitchen, finishing some schoolwork, while Kate and I played a board game called Sorry! at the end of the table nearest the windows. The rest of the table was piled with clean laundry that needed folding. Kate drew from the deck of cards placed on the middle of the board.

"Eight," she said. She tapped one of her playing pieces along, counting, "One, two, three . . ."

I drew a card.

"Move backward four," I said.

Kate said, "Sorry, Dad."

"That's half the fun, kiddo."

"Dad, who's my grandmother?" she asked.

"She was Grandma Crosby," I said.

"So who's my great-grandmother?"

"Nanny Crosby."

"I never met her."

"Yes, you did, but you were a real little kid, almost just a baby."

"Who's my great-great-grandmother?"

"Grammy Black, whose name, in fact, was Kathleen, which is kind of like Katherine, but we didn't name you after her."

"Why not?"

"Well, because she was what your Grampy Crosby used to call a *pisser*. She was a grump who lived in her bathrobe and bossed everyone around and complained all the time."

"Who's my great-great-great-grandmother?"

"I don't know that far back."

"Who's my great-great-great-great-great-great-*great*-grandmother?"

"Take your turn, wise guy."

"Okay, wise guy." Kate took another card and tapped out the spaces.

"Hey, you and I need to go to the garden store and get some red geraniums and go to the cemetery where Nanny and Grampy Crosby and Grandma Crosby and even Grammy Black are all buried and plant them in front of their stones, to make them look nice for Memorial Day. You know geraniums; you've seen them the times we've gone to the Memorial Day parade and stood near where everyone's buried while they talk and when they shoot the guns."

"And all the Cub Scouts run for the bullet shells."

The next Saturday the weather was mild and bright. Susan went out on the side porch and tipped the rainwater out of the seat of one of the plastic chairs and wiped it dry with a dish towel. She took her coffee and a stack of papers to correct and sat out in the sun. I dug up a couple of trowels from the mess in the garage and tossed them in the foot well on the passenger side of the station wagon. The wagon was the last my grandfather had bought before he died. It was rusted and decrepit but I had a great loyalty to it, an unabashed sentimentality about having ridden around in it with my grandparents before I had become a husband and a father. It was white and had a broken deck for cassette tapes and electric windows that worked only half the time and less than that in cold weather. The tires were bald and the chassis shook so violently when the car idled that it sounded as if the entire exhaust system were about to drop out of the bottom of the car. I felt like a bad parent every time I drove Kate around, but I also had a sincere if wholly unfounded faith that the car was charmed and that Kate would never come to any harm in it.

I said to Susan, "Kate and I are going to go get flowers and plant them at the cemetery."

"Okay, babe. Say hi to everyone for me," she said.

"Fun*ny*," I said.

Kate and I bought a tray of six red geranium plants at the garden center, then drove to the cemetery and yanked up the old plants from the previous year. Kate took the job seriously, telling me to make sure that we lined up the rows of holes for the new plants and spaced them evenly in front of the stone so that they would look neat. She pulled one of the plants from its pot and held it in front of her nose. She sniffed at the flowers, then at the root bundle and soil.

"Smell nice?" I asked.

"Kind of," she said. "I like the way the dirt smells better than the flowers, I think."

"It's the leaves that smell so strong. Cool how the roots stay in the shape of the pot, huh?" I said. "That makes it easy; you can just stick the whole thing right into the hole you made."

When we had planted all the flowers, I said, "We have to water them now. See up the hill there, the spigot—that pipe with the faucet like the one for the garden hose at home? There's a plastic milk jug by it. Do you want to go fill it up with water and bring it back down so we can water the flowers? Think you can?"

"Yeah, I can do it," Kate said. She started to march up the hill, zigzagging in between the headstones. She sang a song to herself that I didn't recognize. As she made her way up the

hill, her singing became fainter and I could hear only inter-
mittent notes carried back down on the breeze. The farther
up the hill she went, the more the headstones in between us
obscured her. I had a sudden impulse to follow her. The way
the headstones looked—almost like walls made of alternating
granite and marble and slate shingles—it seemed as if she
might lose her way among them, as if they were arranged in
narrow rows without exits or with dead ends, as if she were
walking through a maze suddenly.

"You see it, sweetie?" I called up. She turned around
toward me. "You *see it*?" I called up again, louder. She took a
step back toward me. I waved her back.

"Never mind; never mind; you're fine," I yelled. She
turned back toward the spigot. She bent forward and disappeared behind a row of three white stones and stood back up
with the plastic milk jug in her hand. When the jug was full,
she hauled it down the hill, bending and stepping sideways to
keep her balance.

"That was a bit more of an adventure than I thought," I
said. "You okay?"

"Yeah, I'm fine, but I'm *soaked*," she said. She set the jug
next to the headstone, dropped onto the apron of grass in
front of the plot, and lay on her back.

I sat down next to her and we were quiet, looking up at
the maple trees and their new, luminous shawls of foliage, and
at the blue sky and the clouds, which were gray with white
piping and silhouettes of gold light. Kate tipped her head
back far enough to see the headstone behind her. She whispered letters to herself, translating them from upside down,
and half-spelled the names on the stone. She stopped reading

and looked at the sky again and shivered. Her arms were
covered in goose bumps.

"Chilly?" I asked.

"Yeah," she said. "It's warmer standing up."

"You're right. Let's get up and water the flowers and go
get you changed. Our work here is done." I pushed myself up,
then gave Kate a hand and hoisted her to her feet. She poured
the water into the soil around the plants and it rose and broke
over the edge of the grass and streamed down away from the
plot, beading through the turf and shining like chrome.

I WOKE UP ON a Wednesday afternoon in October, nearly two
months after Kate had died and Susan had left, with what
sounded like the reverberations of some catastrophic, cosmic
organ chord clapping off the walls and rattling the windows
and dopplering in the blood of my ears. It took me a full two
minutes to remember where I was and who I was and what
the circumstances of my life were. Two minutes does not
sound long unless you cannot figure out where you are; then
it is a terrifying undertow out of which you desperately try
to paddle and inside which you cannot figure out what direction is up, and no matter where you try to put your feet,
they do not touch the sandy bottom of the upright world,
and for all you know you might be upside down, as much as
you feel that the surface of the water must be just above your
head. When I coordinated my senses, my panic gave way to
misery. The living room was littered with empty whiskey
bottles and dirty drinking glasses with dirty spoons and forks
in them and piles of old newspapers and magazines, books

ENON   105

and maps, and dirty clothes. Cigarette butts were piled in pyramids in two glass ashtrays and scattered across the coffee table and stubbed out in the glasses and in the bottles and on plates and even in the potting soil around the houseplants. I groaned and pounded the couch in frustration. Its cushions were filthy from my having slept on them for weeks, and stained and slick from having spilled beer and whiskey when I passed out.

I wobbled to the kitchen. The old stove, spattered with food, with its rusty burner grates and greasy, dented blue tea-kettle and greasy hood that had dust gunked up on top of it, seemed a concise sign of my devastation. I yanked the kettle off the stovetop, opened a kitchen window, leaned out, and dropped it into the weed-shot flower bed below, but carefully, as if I were placing it there to great purpose, so as not to appear erratic to anyone who happened to be standing in the rank backyard. The cabinets were all shellacked in grease and dust, too, and had stains running down the doors. What seemed like every dish and glass and mug and cup and utensil was dirty and piled up in the sink and on the surrounding counters.

I decided to clean the house. Unless I took a shower and ran a load of laundry, with half a cup of bleach in it, and shaved and combed my hair and dressed myself in a real pair of my old pants and a real, button-up shirt and clean socks and a nice pair of shoes, and mopped the floors and scrubbed the cabinets, and washed the dishes and opened the windows and scoured the counters, the engines of ruin could never be reversed. So I spent the day cleaning. Every task took twice as long as usual, because I had to do it all one-handed, hold-

ing my broken hand up or dangling it off to the side like a
wounded animal. Although I'd broken it seven weeks earlier,
my hand still ached most of the time.

Darkness had fallen by the time the job was done. The
house was not so much cleaned as ravaged. It still smelled of
garbage and old cooking, as well as, now, of bleach and disin-
fectant. I was drenched and exhausted. The spotless, purified
sensation I'd spent the day trying to achieve, had anticipated,
had hoped for more and more frantically, scrubbing caked
grunge from drawer handles with a toothbrush, swabbing
buckets of oil soap over the floors, which always looked dirty
anyway, even after they had been scrupulously mopped, that
sanctification I so much desired, the feeling of having scoured
and cleaned and purged the self-pity and druggy grit caking
my brain and clogging my heart, taunted me from just beyond reach, like a cloying, shiny mirror image of myself prim
and sober and at ease, sitting with perfect posture in spotless,
pressed clothes, my hair freshly cut and combed down, clean-
shaven, in an armchair upholstered with immaculate, ivory
fabric, a portrait of my smiling, beloved Kate on a table next
to the chair, a glass of freshly brewed iced tea glowing in the
sunlight streaming into the room from the windows, an an-
thology of inspirational verse in my lap, my forefinger keeping place at a poem in which a pastor consoles a father who
has lost his only child, which has quieted my heart and
brought me at peace with my daughter having been ground
up beneath the wheels of a car.

6.

I USED TO LOVE WORKING IN THE YARD IN NOVEMBER, ON SAT-urday afternoons. Even though I mowed and tended other people's yards during the week, taking care of my own had a different quality. I loved the last fall cleanup, when the trees were bare and I raked up the last of the leaves from the grass and among the bushes. There was something devotional about it. The sun began to set by four o'clock and traffic sub-sided on the road. The yard had a majestic, planetary feel to it. Groomed, it seemed like a preparatory offering to winter, which was headed toward the village, just over the horizon. Wind swelled through the bare trees and made deep chords I felt in my throat more than I heard. It carried a cardinal's chipping from the hedge and the neighbor's sparkly chimes. The brightness and warmth of working evaporated in a sud-den chill and I fetched my hooded sweatshirt from the picnic table. I raked all the yellow and scarlet maple leaves and the thatch from the grass and mowed and raked out the flower beds, too, and the yard looked clean and bare. I scooped up a last armful of leaves and twigs and pitched it into the orange wheelbarrow and teased the last dregs of the leaf pile from the grass with the rake and whisked them around, so they would blend into the yard. Except for someone using a chain saw half a mile away, and the occasional approach and passing

of a car out on the road in front of the house, there was a
sense of solitude. It was the hour when most everyone else in
the village had gone inside to prepare dinner.

I missed those final moments of the afternoon, the loamy
quality of light that illuminates the last of the day in its true
suspension, and that coolness and the freshly scrubbed earth,
that clean, satisfied fatigue, that savory anticipation of a hot
shower and a steak and, later, a whiskey and a game of cribbage with Kate before she went to bed. I taught her how to
play cribbage when she was eight, and she could beat me by
the time she was ten. My grandfather had been an excep-
tional cribbage player, and he and his closest friend, from
back when they had been boys in Maine together, Ray Morrell, taught me how to play one summer at Ray's summer
camp on Lake Winnipesaukee. I was never any good, but they
always let me play with them, and always gave me grief when
I lost, which was almost always, because if they hadn't let me
win sometimes, it would have been harder to be discreet
about their charity in agreeing to play me in the first place. I
had to relearn the game every summer when we went to
Ray's camp or went fishing up in Maine, for the most part,
because I never played it on any other occasion. I have
thought many times about what a strange and unlikely game
it is, what a strange set of rules it imposes upon a deck of
cards. There was something reassuring, and charming, in how
good Kate was at it, although when she began to beat me
regularly, when she was around twelve, and although she
teased me about it in the same gentle way my grandfather
and Ray had, I could also see how seriously she took the
game, how seriously she took winning and how upset she

got when she lost. I wished for her to be more lighthearted about it, but when I said something it only provoked her.

I thought about that on the night of what would have been Kate's fourteenth birthday, November 25. I sat on the couch in the living room, eating stale cereal dry out of the box, and it occurred to me that the cribbage board was in the buffet in the dining room somewhere, with its pegs still presumably where Kate and I had left them after our last and dramatic best-of-five tournament, which I had won by one point.

I SUPPOSED I COULD dig through the deep drawers in the buffet and find the board, which was made from an old bowling tenpin cut crosswise down the middle. There was a decal of a cartoon skunk at the top of the pin, above where the pegging holes had been drilled, and whenever it looked like Kate was going to beat me by at least a full street, she'd grimace and click her bottom and top front teeth together, tap on the skunk with a forefinger, sniff at the air, and say, "Oh, Fazher! I szeenk I szmell a szgonk!"

Kate had discovered the board at a yard sale we stopped at one Saturday morning, when we'd both gotten up early and had decided to walk together to the next town for coffee and doughnuts instead of driving. The woman selling the board wanted eight dollars for it.

I reached for my wallet, but Kate put a hand out and said, "Wait. Eight bucks for that crazy thing? How about two?"

The woman said, "I'll let you have it for six."

Kate said, "Four dollars."

"Five," the woman said. Kate looked at me.

I stuck out my lower lip and lifted my eyebrows and nod-ded my head, to signal that that was pretty good, and Kate said, "Okay, you got a deal," and I paid the woman.

As we walked away down the sidewalk, me holding the coffee and doughnuts, Kate carrying the board, I said, "You sounded just like your great-grandfather George back there, Kate. You're a bona fide Yankee skinflint."

Kate grinned and said, "I *love* this thing, but *eight bucks?*"

I washed a mouthful of the stale cereal down with a gulp of tap water from a jelly jar and thought again about how I could find the cribbage board in the buffet and bring it out and clear a space in the mess on the coffee table in front of the couch and look at the peg stuck in the dead man's hole and think to myself, Kate put that there. That's a little mark left in the world by Kate. I thought about how I might ago-nize for a while over whether I should ever remove the peg, or leave it and put it up on the mantel and make a little shrine out of it, maybe set a stick of incense in one of the empty peg holes and burn it and think about the last game we played together, ignoring the trivial, circumstantial an-noyance I'd felt at the time. I didn't want to do any of that, so I left the board buried somewhere in the layers of cloth nap-kins and trivets and decks of cards and candleholders and empty photograph frames and odd sheets of gift wrapping and silver steak knives, and looked for a moment out the side window in the living room at the light snow drifting in front of the streetlight onto the lawn and the driveway and the sta-tion wagon I hadn't used in months and whose battery I was

sure must be dead and wondered about what birthday presents Kate might have asked for.

I woke up on the living room couch one morning in the
middle of December. The autumn had been mostly wet and
mild until then. I had been taking long walks through the
woods on paths lined with wet, soggy leaves that felt like vel-
lum to step on, and up from the pagelike, pulpy folds of
which little white moths innocently spun into the wrong
season with nearly every step. But that morning the house
was freezing. I sat up, shawled in one of my mother's afghans,
irritated at having been half-wakened repeatedly throughout
the night because the afghan was too short and didn't cover
my feet and they were icy and because my dreams were full
of endless, foolish arguments and wrestling matches with
tireless antagonists. My breath steamed in the cold air. My
throat stung and my nose ran and I was certain I must be getting sick. Half of my brain lagged behind my head rising off
the couch, and I had to close my eyes and take a couple
breaths and wait for it to catch up and refit itself together.
The sunlight tracing the borders of the window shades deto-
nated bursts of purple and green hydrangeas in the foreground of my vision, and my head pounded. I reached for the
bottle of painkillers. I was too groggy to take any so soon, but
the fog from the previous night's pills and whiskey would
burn off in a few hours and, after a long afternoon nap, I'd
wake at dusk and want the night's first dose to soothe myself.
I picked up the bottle and put it next to my ear, smiled at the

idea of the sight of myself half-playing a burnout, and gave it
a little shake. It sounded like there were only two or three
pills rattling around. My wry—romantic, even—image of
myself evaporated and I shook the bottle again and listened
to the rattling and tried to guess the greatest number of pills
it could possibly indicate, as if the number in which I could
reasonably convince myself to believe before I looked might
influence the number of pills I found when I actually opened
the bottle. I thought to myself, Be careful, Charlie; this is very
tricky business, very fragile stuff you're playing with here.
One false move, one lapse of concentration, and you could
be very, very screwed. But that very thought was the lapse
itself, I realized.

My broken hand still ached most of the time. Even loaded
on pills and whiskey, I could always feel pain thumping
through it. The breaks were bad enough that I'd been able to
convince the different doctors I'd seen to give me two more
bottles of painkillers after the first. Since I had no health insurance, I saw whoever was on duty at the walk-in clinic.
One doctor, a woman I was startled to realize might be
younger than I, with freckles and what I'd always called a
boy's haircut, dressed in men's khakis and a man's blue oxford
shirt, told me I needed to get into physical therapy.

"Your hand's going to wither away if you don't do exer-
cises," she said. "You've got to stretch your fingers, flex them,
start squeezing a ball."

"I know it," I said. "The thing kills all the time, though,
still. I still can hardly even sleep with it." She held my hand
gently in hers and moved each finger in turn by putting a
very slight amount of pressure against the tip. I sucked my

breath in, because it hurt, but also to convince her that my need for more medicine was genuine. I lied, "I rolled over on it the other night and it felt like I rebroke it all over again."

"Well, here's some information about PT," she said. "You really need to get on it. I'm going to give you some more of the painkillers, but I also have some concerns about that. Do you think it's becoming a problem?"

"Jesus, I hope not," I said. "I'm scared half to death of those things—getting hooked on them—but it's really the only way I get any rest."

"Okay. Try not to take them unless you really need one. Try to hold out as long as you can each time. Push on your pain threshold. Try taking just half of one. Try aspirin or ibuprofen instead. You really don't want to get tangled up with this stuff. This should be the last script you get for them."

"Got it," I said. "And I'll call for the PT first thing next week. Thanks so much, Dr."—I looked at her name tag—"Dr. Winters."

I opened the bottle and found a pill and a half. I tried to count how many pills I'd taken the night before—the two to begin, and a third I had intended to take two hours later, and another an hour after that, and another half pill an hour later, but I thought maybe I hadn't split a fifth pill but had taken it whole, then maybe decided later that another half would be fine so long as I didn't drink the whiskey any faster—and I could not make a clear tally. It all just blurred together.

I reached across the couch and snapped on the lamp, which was a contraption assembled in someone's workshop sixty or seventy years before, by the look of it. It was a pewter tankard fitted with a cord and light socket and shade harp.

The lampshade was sepia-colored and printed with botanical drawings labeled in French: *Hypopétalie, 348. Anémone Hépatique, 304. Artichaut.* Some of the words were chopped off at the ends, where the paper they were printed on had been cut and fitted into the shade: —*orollie, svnanth*—. The drawings and tallies reminded me of the pajama bottoms in which Kate had been cremated. The lamp had ended up in our living room after my grandmother died. It wobbled and clanked whenever it was turned on or off, and I could never figure out how to tighten it. Susan and I had been convinced that it would surely burst into flames and incinerate the house some afternoon, when it had been accidentally left on for the day while no one was home. Despite our certainty that the lamp was probably lethal, we used it all the time, with low-wattage bulbs, because it gave a pleasant golden glow to the room, almost like a cheap surrogate for a fireplace. Susan sometimes said, "It just hides the dirt and makes the worn-out furniture look antique, but that's okay."

I cupped my hand around the pewter base of the lamp because the morning was so cold and I thought that the pewter would be cold, too. The cold pewter made me think of the tankard stripped of its lamp hardware and sitting outside in the frosted grass in the light of dawn. The tankard would have frost on it, too, and the pewter would contract in the cold, buckle and split and release a sharp, sour metallic odor. The tankard was silvery gray and the frozen grass looked blue, like pewter made with lead, and the clouded sky behind it looked like layers of pewter alloyed with copper and bismuth and lead. Pewter is mostly made of tin, and I imagined my great-grandfather for a moment, soldering the breaks in the clouds with patches of tin. And I thought of Kate's cremation urn, made of pewter, in the frost-tightened ground on the other side of the village. Choosing a pewter urn for my daughter's ashes might have been the persistence of a trivial family conceit, which I remembered my grandmother invoking with the refrain "We prefer the classic colonial furniture," which struck me at that moment as bearing witness against its own truth. The lamp now seemed surely to have been made by some company in New Jersey that manufactured cheap, ersatz colonial souvenirs, sold to credulous, working-class dupes on their crummy local weekend vacations to fake pilgrim villages, the sort through which I had suffered as a kid and romanticized as an adult. I felt terrible for my grandparents, and love for them, and deeper loyalty than ever to them for what they had given to my mother and me. And I felt both abashed and comforted by the fact that I had maybe deepened the connections between myself and my grandparents and my daughter, as best as I could, in an inadvertent, backhanded way, by having been susceptible to the notion of being a colonial son during the subdued sales pitch for my dead daughter's urn rather than the whelp of mongrels.

In the kitchen, I saw that I'd run out of fresh coffee, so I dug around in the freezer and found an old, half-full can from what must have been a couple years earlier. The can was so cold that my hand stuck to it. I wondered what sort of metal it was made from, whether it was tin or aluminum or something else, and that made me think of the pewter tankard and Kate's urn. Digging up the cold, grainy coffee with the yellow plastic scoop made me think of Kate's ashes and for a moment the coffee became her ashes and I was performing the suburban variation of a ghastly pagan ritual, abominable to all good folk, during which boiling water was percolated through the ashes of the dead, her essence imparted into the water and absorbed by the person who drank the cannibal tea. As outrageous as the idea was, as shameful and gruesome, it also seemed like something that, were I to read about it in the history of an ancient culture, or to see it in a documentary about an isolated population deep in the Amazon, might seem perfectly appropriate, profound even, even blessed, and I considered that, after all, the only thing missing to ennoble the idea from morbid daydream to sacred rite was my consent, my belief. I sat at the kitchen table listening to the coffeemaker burble and steam, and then I poured the coffee into the least dirty mug I could find in the sink. Foolish as it was, I could not bring myself to spoon any sugar into the coffee. I didn't have any milk, but that seemed as if it would have been blasphemous, too, and I swallowed the scalding drink black, strong and bitter.

The coffee helped clear my head and I thought about the pills. Dr. Winters would not give me another prescription. I did not want to get hooked but I was also not ready to wean myself from the schedule I'd adopted. As much as I conserved the pills and tried to use them to augment the alcohol, I began to panic at the thought of spending nights without the consolations of floating on that placid, narcotic-kissed ocean. I emptied the linen closet and the medicine cabinet and the cabinet under the sink in the bathroom, where I knew there was nothing besides the toilet brush and containers of bathroom cleaner, praying for some cough syrup with codeine in an impossible, crusted, brown plastic bottle from a long-ago bout of bronchitis, or muscle relaxants from a strained neck muscle, or painkillers from a root canal. I had the hope that my own simple will might be able to invoke the spontaneous appearance of a moldy pill or two, in some dark, dusty corner at the back of a closet or cabinet, as if it might be just a matter of concentration, as if, once I could take the idea and turn it in just the right way, to just the right degree, almost in the way a thief cracks the combination of a safe, can feel the tumblers drop with a minuscule twitch of the dial, I could transform the idea of a pill into an actual pill, could parlay my desire for a pill into the fact of a pill.

I spent the better part of the day crawling around closets and wriggling under beds and moving chairs and sofas, concentrating on the appearance of a miraculous dose. After scouring each room, I sat on the floor with my back against a wall, sweaty, more tired and more irritated. I'd eaten nothing all day except for the cup of ancestral coffee. But Kate was not your ancestor, I told myself. She was your heir. It must be blasphemy to assimilate the spirit of your own offspring. It should have been Kate, years from now, a grown woman, drinking the water steeped in *your* ashes.

By three-thirty in the afternoon, the sun was already lowering into the trees. The last of my hopes for finding drugs in the house evaporated with the day's light. The cold that had poured into the village from the north the previous night had settled in and the house snapped and popped as it contracted in the frigid air. You are just *not* going to *not* have your medicine tonight, I thought. Although I'd considered it three or four times, I lacked the nerve to rebreak my hand. I'd thought about laying it on the kitchen table and clobbering it with a saucepan or a rubber mallet, or even holding it under my butt and sitting down on a wooden chair as hard as I could, but whenever I decided to go get the toolbox or pulled out a kitchen chair and felt the hard wooden seat, I became queasy and my nerve failed. But where can you find some pills? Where? I asked myself. And I answered, You can get some from *Frankie*!

Frankie Shuey, a.k.a. Frankie the Dope, Hanky Frankie, Frankie Freak, or just Dumbass Frankie, was a kid I'd painted with one summer when I'd worked with Gus the ex-con and a few years later hired to work on a crew I put together myself. He was a tall, babyish, boneless-looking guy with long curly red hair that he let fall in front of his face so you couldn't really ever see his eyes, like a big sheepdog. He must have had adenoid problems, too, because he always had a stuffy nose and could apparently breathe only through his mouth. He was a slow, sloppy painter and ended every shift covered in paint. It got all over his clothes and his arms and his hands and his legs, and caked in his hair, too. He took a lot of grief from the other guys on the crew, but everyone liked him and he was a good sport about the guff he got. He also could get just about any drug anyone wanted, just about any time anyone wanted it. Three of the other guys on the crew moved back and forth from the North Shore in the summer to Colorado in the winter. In the winter, they went to Vail and skied all day and took jobs as dishwashers in restaurants at night. In the summer, they painted houses during the days and worked as crew members on the sloops that raced out of the yacht clubs on the coast on weeknights and weekends. They were intense, wiry guys anyway, but they all kept going by sniffing tons of cocaine and popping any kind of speed they could get their hands on. Frankie got them most of their coke and bagfuls of amphetamines, too.

Frankie's father had worked for one of the major airlines for years, as a mechanic, until he'd had an accident—falling off a wing or something like that, I never quite knew the whole story, and Frankie had a knack for being vague about it. Part of the settlement Frankie's dad had got from the airline, though, was that he and his immediate family could fly wherever they wanted, whenever they wanted, for life, for the cost of the flight taxes. Without his ever getting into particulars, Frankie "went to New Mexico" every other weekend and came back with whatever drugs anyone had ordered. It got so that the first and third Mondays of every month were more or less shot, because Frankie came to work with the stuff everyone had ordered the previous Friday, and before ten in the morning the entire crew was zonked on dope, speed, hash, and the cold beers they all kept in their lunch coolers. The guys would straggle to wherever we were painting a house at about eight-thirty, groaning and exhausted, smoking cigarettes, as often as not with black eyes or split lips from having gotten into fights over the weekend after their races, when they took the cash the rich bankers and doctors who owned the boats paid them for crewing and spent it on booze and mostly lost it playing cards and sometimes dice.

"Frankie, man, gimme the shit; my eye is *killing* me. Murph sucker punched me and I'm fucking *fucked*. I had blood coming out of my fucking eye all night. It was *sick.*"

"Sucker punched you? You called him an Old Town pussy and he laid you out with a little love tap."

"Fuck you, Rug. Murph was Airborne Golden Gloves. I

could get Blazing Bill to bust him for assault with a lethal weapon."

"Blaze'd kick your ass again and throw you in the tank, you pussy. Shut the fuck up and give the man the money."

And so on. The guys razzed each other and talked like that all the time. They gave Frankie all sorts of grief, especially by making him get them their drugs without payment up front, but he always managed to supply whatever they wanted. He even got their buddy Billy Kopecky, who was a cop in town, a sack of amphetamines once a month.

"Jesus, Roger Dodger, when are you going to pay me for that last eightball? You owe me like five hundred bucks."

"Come on, Frankie, don't bust my balls; you know I'm good. Just front me a gram until I get the bread from Tammy. She gets paid Wednesdays."

I could never figure out how it all worked, but somehow Frankie got the drugs and all the guys and he stuck together, like they all just happened to spend a couple summers working together with me as their titular boss by common consent so long as I got jobs for us and never did more than plead with them to work faster and more thoroughly and curse them out once in a while. But really it was me just passing through their world. When I thought of Frankie, I wondered if he would still be around Stonepoint. If he was, he'd be drinking at the Ironsides Tap Room.

A few weeks after Kate had died, a check for twenty thousand dollars had come in the mail from an insurance company. The amount was a pittance, what seemed like an insult. I hadn't any mind to pursue the matter, though, and had mailed half of it to Susan in Minnesota and cashed the other half for myself, which I kept in a shoebox under the couch. Before I went looking for Frankie, I counted out two thousand dollars in hundreds and twenties and crammed the nut of bills into the inside pocket of my jacket.

Frankie was just where I thought he'd be, sitting on a stool next to the waitress's serving station, smoking a cigarette and scratching at a lottery ticket with a nickel. There was a beer glass with a couple sips of beer left in it, an empty shot glass, and a red plastic ashtray in front of him. He wore a heavy green army coat over a frayed plaid flannel shirt, white carpenter's pants, and tan work boots. He was covered in plaster dust. It was in his hair and on his arms and all over his boots and pants and shirt.

When I sat next to him and said, "Hey, Frank," he recognized me but didn't use my name when he said hello. I realized again that although he'd been on my painting crew, I was an outsider to him and the other guys I'd hired those summers. I suddenly felt humiliated asking him if he could still get drugs.

I said to him, "Hey, Frank, do you still ever, ah, make those trips anymore like you used to?" He looked at me and didn't answer and went back to scratching the ticket. It struck me how suspicious it might be to him, me coming into this bar after not having seen him in probably ten years and asking him to score. He probably thinks I'm a cop now, I thought.

Before I said anything stupid, like *No, man, I'm not undercover; it's cool,* I just told him, "Frank, my kid died and my wife left me and I busted my hand and I'm stretched out pretty thin and I thought that maybe you might still be around and know something."

He stopped scratching the ticket and took a pull on his

cigarette and asked me what I had in mind. I told him and he told me an amount of money and when to come back to the bar. The money seemed exorbitant and I got angry for a minute that he'd fleece me in the condition I was in. But I had the amount he asked for, and I looked at him, sitting there alone, covered in dust, covered in ashes, just like me and just as worn out and worn down and as baffled at this life as everyone else and, really, I thought, worse off than me, and I thought, God help us all, and agreed to what he said. He'd told me to come back in a couple hours, so I wandered around the tightly huddled old captains' houses by the water and watched snow begin to fall over the harbor. I returned and Frankie had what I'd ordered and I gave him the money, right at the bar because no one but the bartender was there and he did not care. I bought Frank and myself a round of boilermakers and swallowed four pills with the whiskey.

"You got to get the aspirin stuff out of those before you take them," Frankie said.

"The aspirin?"

"It's not aspirin. It's some other stuff, some headache stuff. It'll fuck up your liver. They put it in there so you can't take too much of it and get high."

"How do you get it out?"

"You grind up the pills and put a little water in the powder and make like a paste. Then you put it in the freezer for like half an hour or a little more, just so it almost freezes. All the aspirin junk turns into crystal. Then you put it all into a coffee filter and squeeze out the liquid and chuck the crystal stuff. The liquid is the stuff you take. Best way to do it is get one of those syringes they use to give little kids medicine and stick it up your ass and shoot the liquid up there. You get way more fucked up."

"Up your ass, huh?" I said. "That's pretty weird."

"Works every time."

I talked with Frankie for twenty minutes about the town and who was still around and who had gone. I barely remembered any of the names he mentioned. As the pills started to work I shook Frank's hand and said how much he'd helped me out and thanks so much and could I come back again if I needed to. He said I could come back but that he was out of town a lot these days.

I said to him, "Okay, Frank, thanks again and I'll try here again if I need to."

I left the bar and walked the six miles back to Enon in a heavy snowfall that kept traffic off the road and quieted the world.

7.

LATE ONE WINTER NIGHT, AFTER THE NEW YEAR, WHICH CAME and went without my being aware of it for two weeks, after I had lost track of how much whiskey I had drunk and how many pills I had crushed and snorted, I lapsed into a blackout and awoke nearly frozen in the cemetery six hours later. I was

laid out on my side, stopped up against the backs of three
closely laid headstones, for three sisters, who had all died on
December 12, 1839, at eight, seven, and five years old. I was
sure that my toes and fingers had frostbite. By the wind and
the barest light in the east, I could tell that it must be after
five in the morning. The sky was still full of stars, but they
were not the limpid, tame stars of an early summer evening.
They were cold, wild, staring, and ferocious. They were stars
that had arrived in Enon's sky from the deepest trenches of
space, from terrible, unimaginable beginnings, their light de-
mocratized by the present moment, but in fact a vast, tangled
thicket of times, of ghosted universes haunting the hillside
with their artifacted light. Their light unsettled me the way
the open eyes of a dead person would—because it is impossible to believe that open eyes do not see. Their light blazed
in the eyes of Enon's dead for a moment in false resurrection.

I rose and convulsed from the cold and retched from the
poison. I looked over at the snow-covered golf course, where
kids sledded every winter, and imagined the dead having
sledding parties at midnight, on the back slope of the hill,
warming their finger bones in blue fires that they kindled in
granite urns, laughing when they held their hands inside the
flames. I imagined them melting clumps of dirty ice in a tin
bucket over the fire and drinking the hot muddy brew and
cackling with glee as it ran off the backs of their jawbones
and spattered down their ribs. I imagined them using headstones for sleds. The idea made me nauseated and I repented
of it. I had the urge to go to Kate's stone and kneel in front
of it and say, I'm sorry, over and over again, because no matter
how much I knew better, I could not stop myself from step-

ping over the same dark threshold, night after night, trying to follow her into the country of the dead in order to fetch her back, even though she visited me in dreams and never left my waking thoughts. Memories of her feeding the birds and practicing running and playing cribbage were not enough. I was ravenous for my child and took to gorging myself in the boneyard, hoping that she might possibly meet me halfway, or just beyond, one night, if only for an instant—step back into her own bare feet, onto the wet grass or fallen leaves or snowy ground of the living Enon, so that we could share just one last human word.

8.

KATE WAS WITH HER BEST FRIEND, CARRIE LEWIS, WHEN SHE was killed. They were riding their bikes, in tandem, along the curve the road made around Enon Lake. Carrie had been in front of Kate. The last time I had seen Carrie was at Kate's funeral. She was with her mother, Helen, and her dad, whose name I did not remember. She wore a black dress with her hair pulled back and no jewelry and no makeup. She cried so much and so hard that her parents took her away from the ceremony behind a tree a few dozen yards from the grave site to try to calm her. Her grief undid me all the more, because she, unlike me, had seen Kate underneath the car, mixed up with the wrecked bike. It was impossible for me to get the image of Kate's shoulders and the split helmet covering the top of her head, framed in bent metal, underneath the front of the car—what I imagined Carrie would have seen—out of my mind. I did not see Carrie at the reception after the funeral. I am not even sure that she came. I did see her mother, though, so maybe her father had taken her home.

Helen Lewis showed up at the house one afternoon in February. I never would have answered the door, but as it happened I was just leaving to walk in the swamp. I was not paying attention and had my head down, probably running through a calculation about how many pills to bring, and I didn't see the car in the driveway and Helen heading for the back porch. I was reaching for the doorknob when she knocked. She clearly saw me and I had no choice but to open the door.

"Oh, hi, Charlie," she said. "I'm so sorry to bother you—"

I had not seen myself in a mirror for weeks but it was clear from the expression on Helen's face that I was in bad shape. She was surprised, not because I looked horrible but because I looked more horrible than she had been prepared for.

"No, Helen. No," I said. "It's fine. I'm sorry I haven't called to see how—"

The conversation was already hopeless. It was obvious why I had not and could not have been in touch.

"No, Charlie, you shouldn't—I mean, it's okay. Carrie's. Well, it's been rough, but, I mean, you've been so much more—" Helen took a step backward and held out a baking dish covered in tinfoil. "I hope it's okay. I just brought a lasagna—" Idiotically, I raised the dish to my face and sniffed at the foil. I could not smell the lasagna.

"No, that's so nice of you, Helen. It smells wonderful."

"Charlie, can we do anything? We've heard—I mean, it sounds maybe like you could use—"

"No, not at all, Helen. I mean, I know. I'm a little worse for the wear, but I'm doing good, doing better." I could not look Helen in the eyes, but I could tell she was sneaking glances into the house behind me. I could tell that she saw the filthy, moldy dishes and the papers and tools and junk piled on the table and the counters and the stove and scattered all over the floor and I wasn't sure if it actually happened or was just a part of my horror but it seemed as if at that moment some foul gust exhaled out the door and enveloped us and Helen blanched. She took a step back.

"Charlie. I feel like—a few people feel like, that maybe you might need a little bit of—" I put my hands up, like a soldier in a movie surrendering. I realized that Helen was frightened of me. Not because I had been a violent guy or had a bad reputation but because she thought I might be mentally ill, I might be deranged, even capable of harming someone.

"Ah, Helen, you got me; you're right. It *has* been bad. Real bad, I guess. But I *promise* you, it's better. Corners have been turned. Susan's been gone, and it's been real rough. But I think she's coming back, and I'm coming back, you know, back *here*. And I know it looks bad—" I felt out of breath, and transparently full of shit. Helen had backed up toward her car. I lowered the volume of my voice, and lowered my hands, and said more deliberately, "I know it looks bad, Helen, but, please. I just can't."

"Okay, Charlie. Well, I hope you enjoy the lasagna," Helen said. She opened her car door and put one foot in. "We're around. Call if we can help."

I tried to smile and look upbeat, and said, "Will do!" and waved, but Helen was already looking over her shoulder, backing out of the driveway.

I WOKE UP EARLY one morning on the couch. I woke up every morning on the couch. It felt like the same morning all the time, or like an infinite series of nested dreams from which every day I imagined I awoke but I only ever really arose into another dream. When my mood was not pitch-black, I thought it would be interesting to come up with a Homeric formula for waking up on the couch, an invocation that would ennoble the act, make it more like poetry, less like a monotonous personal apocalypse. *The couch as a ship. The couch as a ship sailing to retrieve the lost daughter. Grieving Charles, Crosby Undaughtered, piloting the couch, sorrowdark and stitch-loosed, through all of Oceandeath, forever, until he spies golden Kate, shining and whole, hanging steadfast from the horn of a low moon.*

It was early spring or, I guess, very late winter—sometime in the second or third week of March. The sun had not yet risen but was about to. Light was beginning to flood earlier up the shores of the mornings and ebb away later in the evenings, accelerating as the planet pulled alongside the sun in equinox. Despite the gelatinous, nervy pain of the previous night's drugs, I felt the necessity of watching the sun rise, as if to roll over and tuck my head back into the corner of the couch and sleep through the dawn would be blasphemous even for a decrepit soul like me. There was still a thread, tenuous, strained, barely but still holding, connecting that drugged and bleary consciousness with the mornings when we were fishing in Maine and had to get up early in order not to miss breakfast in the dining hall and my grandfather, who had been up for an hour already, dressing in the cold, washing with cold water from the spring, singing, deliberately provoking me in my warm cocoon of sleep, would finally come to the foot of my bed and sing in his loudest buffo tenor, *Ringy dingy!,* just ahead of the actual ringing of the bronze bell in the dining hall belfry, and bang the bed's metal foot rail with the poker from the woodstove and yank the blankets from me, leaving me uncovered in the frost-shot morning. His gusto during those freezing sunrises angered and delighted me. I cringed almost in pain at how sleepy and cold I was, hunched up into myself on the bed, the chilled air piercing me. Sometimes I growled at my grandfather, which amused him more and made me even grumpier. But I admired his heartiness, the spirit he seemed to imbibe from the clean cold tonic northern morning. Although I had always been gentler about it, I had done the same thing to Kate on cold school mornings in our home—bright autumn mornings, dark winter mornings, rainy spring mornings—when it was then me who had already been up for an hour, drinking coffee, smoking a cigarette, and reading the morning paper in the quiet left behind by Susan after she'd gone to work. I'd enter Kate's room and pull the shades up in the windows and sit on the edge of her bed and pet her back and kiss her head

and singsong, *Oh, Ka-ate; it's time to get u-up!* She'd turn and
groan and screw herself up more tightly in her blankets. I'd
tickle her behind one of her ears and she'd unsheathe one of
her arms from within the blanket and swat at me and growl
for me to leave her alone and *Stop,* Dad. I know, my little
Katie-cat, I'd say. You're all curled up and cozy like a kitten in
a den. I know just how you feel. But it's a new day and life is
good and get up and get dressed and we'll get you some hot
grub. This was a gentler version of my grandfather's stagy,
gruff rousings. And I felt such love for my kid in those moments, such a sense of how good it was that she was safe and
warm and cared for and healthy, how charming it was that
within such larger goodness she was a little cranky, a little
feisty. I also felt in those moments how much my grandfather
must have loved me when he got me up those mornings for
fishing. And I wondered at how when his mother or father
had gotten him up when he was a kid it might have been
with a love that I and even less Kate hardly could have recognized, because getting up when he had been a kid often
enough had been so that no one would actually freeze or
starve to death.

   I wrapped the blanket around my shoulders and sat up
and looked for the cigarettes on the coffee table. They were
not there. I leaned over and looked under the table. The cigarettes were there and I fished them back with my big toe. I
grabbed the pack, but it was empty. This irritated me as much
and in the exact same way as before I'd lost Kate and slipped
so far into decrepitude. I went to the kitchen to make coffee.
There was no coffee. I considered running water through the
old grounds, but the water had breached the filter and the

grounds spilled over into the filter well and the coffee would be full of grounds and, Shit, I thought. Shit, *shit*.

Most days, I never would have walked to the convenience store half a mile down the street to get cigarettes and a cup of the lousy coffee they served there. But for some reason, the familiarity of my irritation at being out of smokes and coffee gave me just the boost of spirit necessary to make the trip. There was a speck of reassurance feeling that small but persistent emotion from the terrible Before, even as I felt a corresponding plunge of deeper despair at the thought of Kate's death being merely now a milestone of my life, because my life continued while hers had been canceled. It was just a matter of grammar on one level, I realized, but it still felt selfish and awful and disloyal.

I meant to splash cold water on my face and rake my wet hands through my hair and go. But the person I saw in the mirror looked ravaged and haunted and underfed. In the instant before I equated myself with the reflection, I thought, Look at how helpless that guy looks. I thought, That's the look of real grief, and my face changed to a frown as it looked at itself.

I stared at my reflection and said, "You're a wonder, Charlie Crosby; it's a wonder you don't fall apart."

There was a lozenge of soap in the gritty bottom of the bathtub near the drain. I scraped it up and rubbed it between my palms under the running water in the sink until it lathered and scrubbed my face and rinsed it. My hair was filthy but I felt revulsion at the idea of taking a full shower, something I had not done, I realized, since before the New Year. The idea of immersing myself in hot water and cleaning myself off made me feel as if I'd come out raw and vulnerable and exposed, like some animal that properly lives up to its eyes in mud for protection. I did strip off my four layers of shirts, though, all at once, and scrub myself with a wet washcloth and swab on some of Kate's old deodorant because I smelled foul. Almost miraculously, there were a couple of clean old shirts in the bottom drawer of my bureau, articles I'd told Susan not long before Kate died that she could give to charity.

My worries about feeling like an animal coming out of its hiding place were confirmed when I stepped outside and the sunlight felt as if it were scalding my eyes. I wanted to turn and scurry back into the darkness of the house, but my cravings for tobacco and caffeine compelled me.

The convenience store was called Red Orchard. It was one of the last two or three dingy franchises left from what had once been a near monopoly around the North Shore. When I was a kid, there had been a Red Orchard about the same distance from my mother's house as there was now from my own, and as I walked I thought about being sent there by my mother for a gallon of milk or by our neighbor Dolores—Dolly—for cigarettes when she and my mother got together on summer afternoons to gossip and play a dice game called Yahtzee. Most of the short walk, which couldn't have been longer than a third of a mile but seemed much longer when I was young, took me past a stretch of Enon Swamp that had remained undeveloped even after World War II, a few dozen acres of lowland that flooded in the spring and gave way to skunk cabbage and smelly mud in the summer. For me the trip was always fraught with perils.

Milk used to come in glass bottles and I dropped a half gallon once on the sidewalk and the bottle shattered and I ran home, terrified. Since the road we lived on was fairly busy, dead animals regularly materialized spraddled out against the curb— a raccoon or gopher or someone's cat. The bodies were usually intact except for some single, horrifying detail, like a green, vermiform length of intestine trailing out from under a woodchuck, or a tabby with its hind legs twisted backward, or maggots devouring a possum's eyes. My mother and Dolly told me horror stories, too, in order to frighten me into being conscientious near the road, about the Litchfield boy who jumped into the street after the basketball he'd been dribbling and got run over by one of Keener's oil trucks, or Kimmy Leach, who pirouetted right into Mrs. Abbot's Nash Metropolitan, which the widow never drove faster than twenty miles an hour, but that just meant it took Kimmy three agonizing weeks in the hospital to finally die. In between the nerve-racking odysseys to and from, though, there was the store itself, stacked with soda and stuffed with candy and comic books. Comic books were an unthinkable luxury, but when I was sent for milk or bread or Dolly's cigarettes, which were called Pall Malls and came in red packages and had no filters, and which I bought three packs at a time, Dolly's daily ration, I was given fifteen cents to buy a candy bar or a bottle of store-brand soda. The soda was a source of great frustration because it came in dozens of flavors, all of different, bright, alluring colors. I wanted so much for the soda to taste like what I imagined the colors should, but it never did, and I ended up nearly in tears so many times over, for example, how lousy the beautiful, almost fluorescent green soda, called Key Lime Rickey, tasted that my mother finally forbade me to buy any more.

When I reached where the sidewalk met the Red Orchard parking lot, I wanted to turn and flee again. Instead, I walked along the back perimeter of the lot. Half of the low, one-story building was a vacant storefront where over the years a succession of ill-planned businesses had come and gone: a store that sold nothing but soccer equipment, a haberdashery, a frumpy dress shop. When a barbershop had looked for a time as if it might thrive, the landlord had expanded the parking from its original half dozen spaces to twenty, where the men of Enon would park their cars every Saturday morning in order to get their weekly trims. The barbershop closed a year after the new lot had been completed (the owner, an ex-marine, only knew how to give flattops) and the space had been used since by the DPW trucks during snow-plowing breaks and the police for speed traps. I walked toward the back of the lot, along the border between the pavement and the weeds that were matted down and half buried in the road gravel that had melted out of the snowbanks over the winter, resisting the temptation to dive for cover beyond the verge, trying to appear as if I were studying some bit of botany. (I imagined seeing myself from a car pulling into the lot, a scarecrow of a man hunched over the twigs, scratching his chin and nodding expertly to himself about some soggy mirage of his own madness.) As it happened, I did see the pale tips of crocus buds rising from the mulch.

I walked along the side of the store and when I reached the front corner I peered around it. There was only one car in the lot, a big, expensive European sedan, empty and idling, straddling two spaces. I waited until the car pulled away and walked across to the storefront, deliberately avoiding looking at my reflection in the glass, pushed the swinging door, and went inside.

The interior was much dingier than I remembered. The fluorescent lighting was dim and fluttery and buzzed, the floor worn and scuffed. An old card table with two folding chairs was set up in a corner, facing a television set screwed into brackets set high up on the wall. Sets of random numbers flashed on the television screen. A plastic stand with paper forms and half a dozen stubby pencils had been placed on the center of the table. A couple of bright green lottery scratch tickets had been left in front of one of the seats, next to an empty coffee cup. The racks around the store seemed half empty, and the boxes and cans all looked like they'd been there for years, like they were props used to stage the appearance of a convenience store rather than real goods someone might actually buy. The magazine rack and wire carousel for comic books were empty except for what looked like real estate brochures and menus from pizza places. The store smelled stale and papery, but it was clean. There was no dust anywhere and the worn floor was well swept. I figured the store must do most of its business selling lottery tickets and coffee and newspapers, which were piled up in front of the cashier's island, and maybe still cigarettes, although no one seemed to smoke anymore. Six coffee carafe pumps were set on a counter perpendicular to the cashier's island, along with stacks of different-sized cups and lids and bins of sugar and artificial sweeteners and plastic thimbles of cream and milk.

The man at the cash register looked like he might be

from India or Pakistan or somewhere on the subcontinent, as I thought of it. He was my age, I supposed, and had short, straight hair and a thick mustache. He wore old gray pants and a tan sweater vest over a plaid shirt. I smiled and nodded at him, and halfway said hi to him, but it sounded more like "Huh" or "Ha." He didn't smile back but nodded at me once, not unfriendly, just serious. I didn't want to dither, because I knew I looked sketchy. I had never bought my coffee or my cigarettes here and although I was a native of Enon, to this man I was a stranger who could have been from anywhere. I figured I'd buy three or four of the largest coffees they had, black, and take them back to the house and keep them in the refrigerator and heat them up in a saucepan each morning. I looked at the cashier again and smiled.

"I drew the short straw, man," I said, surprising myself by the lie. A sudden, made-up story sprang into my mind, of me being on a painting crew and somehow having lost some kind of bet to determine who had to fetch and pay for coffee before work. I could even see the guys I was working with, and imagine the cramped pickup truck cab we were all stuffed into, bleary, smoking, irritable, one or two of the guys already draining nips of vodka and tossing the little plastic bottles out the window into people's front yards.

"I'm the sap who has to get the joe today. And pay for it," I said. The man at the register did not change his serious expression.

"Yes," he said. I lifted a twenty-four-ounce coffee cup from the top of the stack.

"This the largest size?" I asked. "These guys are coffee freaks."

"Yes," the man said. The urge to fling the cup and run out of the store seized me, and the cup did skitter out of my hand, across the counter, and drop onto the floor. I stooped to pick it up and dizziness swept through my head. I was suddenly mortified by the fact that I had not spoken to another person for nearly a month, and that I was high and drunk every waking moment, and that I was so discombobulated all the time that what I considered to be my relatively clear-headed state at the moment might seem to any normal person the brink of a coma. I grabbed the edge of the counter and took a breath and pulled myself up.

"Mondays, man," I said to the man at the register. He frowned and stepped down off the cashier's island and came toward me. I was placing the cup I'd dropped on the floor under one of the carafes. As the man took the cup from my hand and tossed it into the plastic trash barrel next to the counter, I saw that I had been about to serve myself something called vanilla cinnamon hazelnut coffee. The man took a clean cup from the stack and put it under the coffee dispenser.

"No, no, man," I said. "You saved me. I don't want that crazy sweet stuff." I winced at myself for calling him "man."

"What do you want?" the man said. He was clearly anxious to see me out of the store. "And," he said, "it is not Monday. It is Sunday."

"Sunday," I said. "Sunday, Sunday." I tried to sound humorous, resigned in the way that people who have terrible jobs with too many hours and awful pay use to try to keep their spirits up. "Work so much I can't remember what day it is. Terrible that us stiffs have to work on Sundays, isn't it?"

"What would you like?" he said.

"Oh, four. Four large of whatever dark roast stuff you have, without any flavors."

"The French roast," he said. He lifted a carafe with a laminated card taped to it that read PARISIAN CAFÉ, NOIR! and raised and lowered it by the handle to test how much coffee was left. "There is not enough for four. You will—" I could not understand what he said after. I lost the English words in the accents and syntax of his first language.

"I'm sorry, man," I said, now so irritated with myself at saying "man" that I just wanted to storm off with neither coffee nor smokes; I didn't deserve them because I kept calling this guy "man" and I couldn't even understand what he was saying. "I'm kind of half out of it this morning," I said. "What?"

He repeated himself and I still could not understand. It sounded like he was saying something about how I would not find any of the sort of coffee I wanted available for my friends, but also like there wasn't any left in the whole world, or something like that, which I knew was wrong. It was upsetting to listen so closely and just not be able to understand the guy. I felt like I was insulting him. I winced and shook my head, trying to show him I was sorry, but it just wasn't getting through my thick skull, it was all my fault. He repeated himself, but I still could not understand a word he said. I felt like I was in a weird dream, like it was just a matter of paying closer attention, but that I couldn't get myself to concentrate.

Embarrassed as I was, I knocked on the top of my head and said, "Oh, brother, I'm so sorry; I just can't understand a word. You know, I'll just get four cups full of whatever's made and the guys can just like it or—"

He put a hand up and said, "No."

I said, "No—"

"No," he said again. He folded his raised hand so just the forefinger stuck up. "Wait."

"Oh, no, man; it's okay; it's fine. You don't need to—"

"Wait."

I nodded. He tested the other carafes in the rack and picked up three of them and walked into the back room. Although he was clearly irritated, he did not hurry. I looked outside, worried that someone would pull up and come in while he was out back. The weather was changing. The sharp, blustery cold from overnight looked like it was being pushed away by warmer, billowy winds that seemed to be turning the dew in the grass to fog before my eyes. The meadows behind the stone walls across the street, at the end of the Tucker estate development, seemed to be steaming. While he was rummaging around in the back I looked at the items for sale near the cash register—pens with lights in them, beef jerky, car air fresheners. The cigarettes were stored in an overhead rack, in push trays, above the counter. Taped to the rack, facing out toward where the customers stood to pay, were two photographs, one of a boy about two years old, one of a girl around eight, I guessed. I leaned in toward the picture of the girl. She was dressed in a blue sari and there was a white flower in her hair. Her hair was dark and braided and very long. The braid was draped in front of her, over her shoulder, and reached below her waist. I thought she must never have had her hair cut. From the size and shape of her hands and her cheeks, I decided that, yes, she was in second grade, or whatever the equivalent was in what I now guessed must be

India, given what I thought was her Indian sari. Kate had looked like that when she was eight, skinny, getting taller, but still almost somehow like not a baby or a toddler but what Susan and I had always called a little kid, as distinguished from a big kid. "Ooh, look at you!" I'd say to Kate and scoop her up in a hug and kiss her cheeks and ears and head. "You're almost a big kid!"

The man came from the back of the store, lugging four carafes of coffee. He hoisted them onto the counter.

"I made you an extra amount of the French roast," he said, slowly, as if speaking to a dull child. I was afraid that he was going to help me fill the cups, but he replaced three of the carafes in the rack and left the fourth one on the counter and returned to behind the register, beneath the racks of cigarettes.

I began to fill the cups. The pumps on the carafes squeezed out only a couple of ounces of coffee at a time, so I had to keep pumping—almost, I imagined, like the old well water pumps people used to have in their yards. As I pushed on the pump, I nodded toward the photographs.

"Are those your children?"

"Yes. Those are my children," the man said.

"They are beautiful."

The man said, "Thank you."

"How old are they? Two and eight, or so?"

"My son is now five and my daughter is eleven." The pictures were old, then, I thought.

"Do they go to school here?" I asked.

"They are in India, with my wife."

I finished filling the first cup. I put a cap on it and began filling the second.

"Are your kids finishing up the school year before they move here?" I asked.

"I am saving up money so that they can move here," the man said. I understood that the man's situation was bad. I felt terrible suddenly for trying to win him over with pleasing small talk about his kids and bringing up a painful situation instead. But, I thought, the pictures are facing out and that must mean that he wants people to know about his family.

"Are they coming soon? Have you been away from them long?" I asked. I figured that I might as well show concern. I *had* real concern now, in fact, and there was no reason not to show it, I guessed. The guy couldn't think any worse of me, anyway.

"I do not know when they can come. I have not seen them in three years," he said.

"Oh, man," I said. "That's awful." The second cup was full. I put a lid on it and placed it next to the other full cup and started pumping coffee into a third. The coffee was scalding hot, even through the paper of the cup, and I had to keep letting go of it to cool my hand off. It smelled sour and acidic.

"I'm sorry," I said. I took a step toward the register and offered my right hand toward the man. "My name is Charlie," I said. "Charlie Crosby." The man shook my hand, limply, not because he lacked backbone or character, which was what I'd always been told by my grandfather a limp handshake indicated. ("Don't offer a wet noodle," he'd say. "Don't try to break someone's hand, either, especially a woman's. But be firm, outgoing, confident. It makes a good first impression.") I guessed he offered such a poor handshake because it was not

something to which he was fully accustomed. I hoped that I
hadn't offended him. I felt like an idiot for worrying that I'd
offended him and for thinking vaguely ignorant things like
maybe in his culture people thought shaking someone else's
hand was unsanitary or demeaning. Too late now, I thought. I
might as well just plunge forward, in good faith.

"I am Manprasad," he said.

"Manprasad," I said. "What are your children's names?"
Again I cringed, for thinking both that maybe it was rude to
ask something so intimate of a stranger as the names of his
children and that I was pathetic for making up such possibly
insulting things about Indian culture, which I suddenly re-
gretted not having read more about at some point in my life.
Twenty-plus years as a *reader's reader*, I thought, and not a
page about India. It's only one of the most important cultures
on the planet, I thought. I've read libraries full of books about
Enon and New England and next to nothing about the experiences of the vast majority of other souls on this planet,
who have never even heard of New England, never mind this
insignificant self-important spot of a village, as I suddenly
thought of it. I imagined how this guy would have never
heard of Enon when he'd been a kid, either, and yet it had
always been where he was going to end up, stuck behind a
cash register, scrounging for enough money to be with his
family. I wondered what the opposite would have been like
for myself—what obscure little village somewhere in the
middle of India waited for my miserable and astonished arrival? None, of course, I thought, since what had always
awaited me was the loss of my daughter and the suffering
afterward.

Manprasad leaned forward and ducked his head under the cigarette rack and pointed up at the picture of his son. "That is Swapnil." He pointed to the picture of his daughter. "And that is Anandita."

"What beautiful names, Mansaprad," I said.

"Manprasad," Manprasad said.

"Argh! I mean, Manra—"

"Manny," Manprasad said. "I am called Manny."

"Manny," I said. "Your children have beautiful names." I finished filling the last of the cups and brought them in pairs to the counter. "Can I have three soft packs of Reds, too?" Manny pulled three packs of cigarettes down from the rack. I was about to ask Manny more about his kids, but I felt strange, as if he might wonder what my motives were. I wanted to show him that I was just interested as a fellow parent. Before I thought it out, I said, "I have a daughter a little older than your daughter's age."

Manny said, "That is very nice." He tapped the prices of the coffees and the cigarettes into the cash register.

"Well, had," I said, wanting nothing more at that moment than to be safely back on my couch, smoking, savoring the flood tide of the next dose of pills, savoring the anticipation of narcotic peace. "I had a daughter. Kate. But I lost her about a year ago. About"—I counted—"about seven months ago, actually." I was shocked that it was only seven months. It felt like years already, like I'd been in mourning for years.

"I am sorry for your loss," Manny said.

"Ah, it's all right—" I almost called him "man" again, which seemed as if it could have been a further contraction of his name in a different life—Manny truncated to Man after, say, years of cordiality had deepened into a real friend-ship between us. The image of Manny and me sitting on milk crates across from each other, behind the cash register, play-ing cribbage all day and talking in the shorthand we'd settled into over the years, and laughing and breaking whenever he had to ring up a customer.

"That is thirty-one dollars and fifty cents," he said, and instead of the picture of us being friends and him helping me get through the grief of losing Kate and me helping him wait out the arrival of his wife and children, I found myself irri-tated at his reserve. Good for you, Crosby, I thought. So now he's the inscrutable Indian. All the better; he's not even that kind of Indian. You've managed a two-for-one special on bigotry. I pulled the plug of old, dirty ones and fives I had in my pants pocket and started to count out the money. I felt awful for ruining both of our days. What knowing creature, passing overhead, able to see the two of us through the roof of the Red Orchard, standing there, face-to-face, exchanging money and coffee and tobacco, wary, suspicious, provoked, could look down and see us for our better selves?

I had only twenty-two dollars and thirty-five cents.

"I'm sorry, man—Manny," I said. "I thought I had more. Or the stuff would be less. Um, how much are the generic cigarettes, the red ones?"

"Four seventy-nine. Five for twenty."

"Okay, I need to give you these other smokes back and can I get three of those?"

"Yes, very well."

I noticed the piles of newspapers. I realized I had lost track of all current events—local, national, international, all of it. Next to the Boston papers was the latest copy of Enon's weekly newspaper, *The Daily Bread*. The cover story was about the prizewinning garden owned and tended by a local woman whose yard I had taken care of for a brief time several years earlier. Her name was Wallace. I had the urge to study the paper, to read all of the local tidbits and details about town meetings and library events and bake sales and the police blotter—all of the current village minutiae, attached to familiar names. I took a copy of the paper and put it on the counter.

"This, too," I said. "And can I get a box or something to carry the coffees in?"

"Yes, they are there by the counter," Manny said. I hurried to the counter and picked up one of the flimsy cardboard coffee caddies and snapped it open and put the coffees in each of its four corners. I gave Manny the money and put a pack of cigarettes in each of my back pockets and wedged one in between the coffees. Tears started out of my eyes and I wiped them off with the back of my shirtsleeve.

"Phew," I said. "I'm, ah—I'm just sorry for bothering you today, man." I slid the box of coffees off the counter and cradled it onto my forearm. The bottom of the box was too thin to support the coffees and they wobbled.

"You have not bothered me, Mr. Crosby," Manny said. "Let me get the door for you." He came around the register and opened the door. He didn't say anything about the fact that neither my supposed coworkers nor their pickup truck were anywhere to be seen.

I wiped my eyes and my nose and said, "Argh, my crew must've gone on to the job. Nice guys. It's just up the street, though." I lifted my chin in the direction back toward my house. "Little walk back will do me good. A few deep breaths."

"Yes, Mr. Crosby, a few deep breaths will be quite good, I think," Manny said. "And thank you for asking so kindly about my family."

"I do hope they come soon, Manny," I said. I stepped off the curb in front of the door, onto the parking lot. "Okay. Have a good day." Manny nodded and went back into the store. I walked across the lot, the coffees tipping in different directions. Halfway back to my house one of the coffees tipped out of the box. Instead of letting it drop, I tried to catch it and all the coffees dropped onto the sidewalk. Three of them popped their lids when they hit the ground and the coffee spattered across the sidewalk and steamed in the cold. The fourth cup stayed sealed and coffee pulsed out of the small opening in the lid, the way blood would come out of an animal or a person, I thought, because it looked like it was being pumped through the hole, as if by a heart. I stooped and picked up the cup, which was still three-quarters full, and the pack of cigarettes I'd stuffed between the coffees, which was soaked but which I figured I could dry out by putting the cigarettes on a cookie sheet in the oven, if I could find one, if they'd gotten wet with coffee. I left the other cups and the sodden box and the spilled coffee steaming on the side-walk and walked back to the house as fast as I could without breaking into a run.

9.

IT IS THE CASE IN PARTICLE PHYSICS THAT WHEN TWO PHOTONS are collided together in a particle accelerator, new particles are created in the collision. As I marched home along the old railroad tracks in the western part of Enon Swamp one freezing dawn, after another night of labored and aimless roving, I thought about Kate on her bicycle and the car hitting her. Instead of her and the bike being pulled up underneath the car and mangled, I imagined an explosion and a burst of light out of which three cars and three bikes clattered, and three Kates tumbled, too, each dressed in the same cutoffs and polo shirt over the same bathing suit, wearing the same Red Sox cap. One Kate somersaulted onto the sidewalk. Another sailed into the brush. The third vaulted over one of the newly minted cars and landed on her back across the hood of another. Each girl lay dazed for a moment, then sat up and looked around, frowning at the scene, fizzing with electricity.

Then the Kates saw one another. They gasped and said in unison, "Kate?"

The girls approached one another, this one limping, that one nursing an elbow, the other patting a goose egg on her forehead, and met in a circle. It looked like a girl in a funhouse mirror except that all three images were really girls, not reflections. They touched one another's faces, and patted

one another's hair, and asked if the others were okay, and said,
"I guess so, but who *are* you?"

Instead of the woman who struck Kate on her knees,
wailing, and her three kids screeching in the back of the
minivan, there were three of her and twelve kids rioting all
over the road at seeing one another's mirror images stamped-
ing around them. There was mayhem when the police and
ambulances and fire trucks showed up, but eventually all the
Kates checked out and, after agreeing with the cops what a
bizarre coincidence it was that identical triplets with identical kids driving identical cars had struck identical triplets riding identical bikes, we all went home, where I was able finally
to distinguish the original Kate from her two new selves,
because both new Kates still had the moles on their chins
that the real Kate had had removed. I imagined us laughing
and joking about bunk beds and how money was going to be
really tight now, but how wonderful it was to have three
daughters.

"My embarrassment of Kates!" I imagined myself saying.

If you stood the three Kates in line, the original Kate first,
and looked at them left to right, you'd see that their eyes
went from nearly stark white to anthracite black, in an even
gradation, from eye to eye, girl to girl. The original Kate's
iridescent right eye had no color in it except for the faint
shadows created by the traceries of its iris and glowed when
reached by even the slightest source of light. Her left eye was
mostly white as well, with just a reflection of blue in its left-
most curve. The next Kate, we called her Katie the Second,
had a right eye the color of a robin's egg, with speckles of
moss green and brown in it. Her left eye was brown but for a

speckling of blue along its right rim. Katie the Third's right eye was dark brown with a grain or two of gold, and her left eye was pitch-black. It seemed as if either the original Kate's white eye was a shooting star with a white-and-blue-and-green-and-gold tail trailing across the girls' eyes back to the blackness of space, or as if Katie Number Three's obsidian eye was a black hole pulling all the color and light toward itself through the others.

When the three Kates came home, we turned on the radio and danced in a circle around the living room and sang and cheered at our great fortune. By the next morning, though, there were signs that something was wrong. The girls awoke with headaches that got worse by the hour. They began to have nosebleeds. The original Katie was cold all the time, even though it was summer. She sat by a sunny window wrapped in wool blankets. She made me turn the heat up to ninety and spent the morning shivering and sipping hot, milky tea. I found Katie Number Two in the kitchen eating spoonfuls of salt and sucking on a handful of coins she'd scooped from the change jar. Katie Number Three could not stand the heat or the light, and I found her in the basement, lying in the deep freezer, which she had lined with a sheet so she wouldn't stick to the frost. All three girls died as the sun set, and instead of mourning one daughter, right away, I gained a night of fraudulent joy at the cost of losing three the next day.

10.

It was the middle of April and I hadn't been able to find Frankie for two weeks. I was nearly out of drugs. I had only a dozen painkillers left and a few muscle relaxants. I could string along what was left with whiskey, but even being as parsimonious as I could manage, I would be out of stuff within two days. My hand no longer hurt, I just wanted the drugs. The only solution I could think of was to go out that night and see if I could find houses without alarms and maybe some prescription bottles on kitchen counters or bedroom dressers or nightstands. It occurred to me that Mrs. Wallace, the woman whose lawn I'd cut and whose award-winning roses I'd read about in the Enon *Daily Bread,* might have drugs in her house.

Mrs. Wallace and her husband were a prosperous, retired couple, the parents of five prosperous grown children, three of whom, according to the article, were lawyers, like their father, the other two consultants. The children lived variously in Manhattan; Washington, D.C.; London; and on Beacon Hill in Boston.

I had tended the Wallaces' yard for a summer, when Kate must have been eight or nine. Mrs. Wallace was then already fully wrapped in a serene counterpane of Valium more or less every waking moment. Her youngest child, a daughter

named Libby, had moved into a townhouse Mrs. Wallace and
her husband had purchased for her in Georgetown. I knew
this only because, even though my impression was that the
family had never been what I would have called close, Mrs.
Wallace had had some sense that the family had always been
so, and that the departure of the last of the children she had
borne marked the end of something vital and essential in her
life, and she managed to convey this indirectly during one of
a handful of lectures about my poor landscaping skills, which
culminated in her firing me at the end of the summer, before
the fall leaf cleanup season (right when I stood to make good
money from her, since her property consisted of eight acres,
on which there grew twenty-six mature maple trees, a nice
mix of sugars, which dropped their leaves early, and silvers,
which always held their leaves anywhere from a week to
three weeks later than the sugars and always meant a second
cleanup). On the afternoon when I realized she was on some
kind of sedative, she was chastising me for not mowing the
lawn short enough.

   "I don't like my lawn to look like a shag carpet, Mr.
Crosby," she said. "For reasons that I should think you might
find obvious." She had the plodding humorlessness of someone who got what she wanted through sheer will rather than
intelligence or grace. I scarcely ever saw her smile or heard
her laugh, and when she did laugh it had a tone of mirthless
superiority. She was dressed in what I always called to myself
her yard-work clothes, which consisted of an immaculate
white, short-sleeved sort of oxford shirt tucked into a pressed
pair of high-waisted women's khakis that ended above her
ankles and a pair of old, scuffed brown leather loafers. She

was a slight, trim woman and had let her hair go white. She
also wore a pair of white gardening gloves and as she lectured
me, she had one hand on a hip; in the other she held a fistful
of zinnias she had tugged up from one flower bed or another,
surely to the dismay of Suki, a Japanese guy who took care of
a bunch of gardens in Enon at the time, including Mrs. Wallace's. (It was said that Suki had been a fisherman in Japan but
had jumped ship during World War II, somehow ending up
in Stonepoint, and that he lived in an old tackle shed next to
a pier under the Stonepoint Bridge. I don't know if any of
that was true. He spoke no English, although he must have
understood some, and absolutely refused to have anything to
do with us landscapers. The most I ever managed to get out
of him once, when I needed to know if I could spread fertil-
izer on a patch of lawn I'd reseeded near some especially
delicate-looking flowers, was "Fucking *Yankee!*" and I left it
at that, because that made me like him.)

I said, "Certainly, Mrs. Wallace. I usually keep the grass a
bit longer this time of the summer, because it's so hot and
there's so little rain and the grass can end up burning out."

Mrs. Wallace stared directly into my eyes and hesitated a
moment before answering me, and that was when I realized
she was on some kind of prescription that, as the guys in the
crew used to say, smoothed out the choke.

"I had the *idea* that it was your *job,* Mr. Crosby, both to
keep the grass short and to make sure it did not burn out, as
you put it."

The article in *The Daily Bread* had quoted Mrs. Wallace as
saying that it was going to be hard for her to tend properly to
her flowers because her husband was coming home from the

hospital. If she still used Valium, and if her husband had had surgery, which no doubt meant a prescription for painkillers, theirs would be a likely house to visit. And even though it had been several years since I'd tended their lawn, I knew the property and I knew that they did not have any sort of a security system, that that was something in which they'd have taken pride, since their home and their village were places where one did not need such things. This was a sentiment shared by many of Enon's older citizens. And it was true that no public transportation ran to or through Enon, nor any major roads (and there were no signs on those roads indicating Enon's existence), and that no one from outside the village—and, in fact, not many inside it—would even be aware of homes like the Wallaces', which were not visible from the street nor indicated by mailboxes. The way to their home was a seemingly untended dirt road at an opening in the woods along a country lane off Main Street. I realized, too, that I could approach their home from the back if I went through the woods that began past Wild Man's Meadow.

I set out at midnight. It was Thursday. I dressed in black jeans and a dark blue hooded sweatshirt and wore work boots. I brought a pair of orange rubber dishwashing gloves so there wouldn't be any fingerprints, a nearly corroded can of 3-in-One oil from one of my grandfather's old toolboxes, for oiling hinges so the doors wouldn't squeak, and a roll of duct tape for taping up deadlatches. The night was damp and chilly, but mild for April. Pools of ground fog had formed in the depressions in Wild Man's Meadow, and mist flowed across the road between the field and the swamp. There was salt in the pith of the wind. I climbed over the stone wall bordering the field along the road and walked abreast of it, toward Cherry Street. The wall and the branches of the white pines planted at intervals of fifty or so feet along its entire length gave me cover in case any cars passed. Only one vehicle—a truck—drove by, very slowly, and in the fog its headlights made it seem like a submarine probing along the floor of a black ocean trench, searching for signs of life at such unsettling and inhospitable depths. For a moment, I was a frowning fish with a mouthful of serrated teeth, straining for a better look at the metal animal pushing along behind its starry lamps.

When I reached the back of the meadow, I cut into the woods at the Tucker family burial plot, which consisted of four headstones enclosed in an iron-railed fence. The woods felt strange and oddly open. I kept having the sensation of being approached from behind. I wanted to turn back, but I felt ill from the lack of drugs and so I continued picking my way through the dark.

When I reached the edge of the woods, at the border of the Wallaces' property, I knelt for a moment, steadied my breathing, then put on the rubber gloves and scuttled across the lawn. A mudroom off the kitchen led to the inner door. I oiled the door's hinges and handle, opened it, and stepped inside. The room smelled like clay and cold mud and sweet, damp newspapers. There was a shallow bench and a coat stand, from which hung a flannel shirt worn through at the elbows. Three kitchen trash barrels were lined along the wall opposite the bench, labeled, GLASS, PLASTIC, and CANS. A plastic tub stacked with copies of *The Wall Street Journal* and the Enon *Daily Bread* stood next to the barrels. Just inside the threshold was an iron doorstop shaped like a bullfrog wearing a footman's coat and black shoes with white spats. He had one arm tucked behind his back and the other extended in front of him. I picked the frog up and propped the outer door open with him.

My head and hands and legs buzzed and trembled worse than ever, and I was nauseated enough that I worried I might begin retching. I could barely concentrate on anything other than the need to stuff my mouth with handfuls of pills and I nearly sobbed out loud at being so strung out, sweating and scuffling at some poor, rich old couple's back door. I still had enough sense, though, to know that I fully deserved being brained with a poker or perforated by buckshot. In fact, the only way I'd gotten up the nerve to commit the crime in the first place was to have half-convinced myself that I would be caught and that would be justice, and that getting away with the drugs would be an absurd, almost malevolent turn of events.

I imagined Kate standing at the top of the hill, under the occluded sky, drawing her hair back because the wind kept blowing it across her face, looking across Enon to where I crouched at the door.

"Mr. Wallace had an operation, Dad. He needs those pills."

"I know, Kate. I'm sorry."

The moon shone above the hill for a moment and Kate turned away and disappeared down the back slope.

I pushed on the kitchen door with my left hand and pulled on the doorknob at the same time, so the door would not swing when the deadlatch cleared the strike plate. My hands sweated in the rubber gloves and felt clammy.

This is all just so ridiculous, I thought. The cool, fresh air gusting into the room smelled minerally and wholesome, and I wished that it contained all the nutrition I needed, that the spices distilled into the wind from the water and salt and rocks and earth and foliage of Enon could be the food that sustained me and the medicine that healed me. I cursed my loopy imagination and my weak will, the cramps knotting and unknotting in my guts, and inched the door open a crack.

Even in the dark, the kitchen glowed white. It was a large, tiled space, full of large white cabinets and old industrial-grade white appliances. The white enameled-iron sink was practically the size of a bathtub. I tiptoed over to the kitchen table. My eyes acclimated to the dark, and the objects on the table resolved themselves against the tablecloth, which had a blue-and-white alternating pattern of springer spaniels, mallards, and cattails. A gold pair of wire-rimmed spectacles had been placed on top of a couple of garden catalogs. There was a lined notepad, with a pen laid next to it and a note written in clear, elegant handwriting: *Amanda and kids, Fri., 1:30, grapes for Arthur.* I felt like a ghost, listless and confined, wandering in a house that had been mine a century ago, relegated to examining the details of the lives of strangers.

The refrigerator motor started with a clank and a man's voice called from deeper in the house, "Joan?"

Adrenaline burst inside me, and the cravings that I'd forgotten for a moment rang and buzzed again, and I nearly screamed and began rampaging through the house, knocking over vases and chairs and smashing through cupboards, so whoever had spoken would know for certain that he had

heard another living person in the house, a stranger, an in-
truder, and not have to wonder whether he'd heard a ghost.
But then I saw a lazy Susan on the countertop next to the
sink with twenty or thirty prescription bottles on it. Nothing
moved, and the voice did not call again. Euphoria swelled
over me and, after peering through the telescoping doorways
and rooms beyond the kitchen, I treaded to the bottles in a
kind of antic half-fit. There was also a small silver tray with
another dozen of the white-capped, brown plastic bottles, a
sheet of paper on which a dosage schedule was printed, and
a large diamond ring. I checked the bottles on the tray first.
There was a prescription for fifty muscle relaxants and, a miracle, a prescription for seventy high-dose instant-release
painkillers. I stuffed the bottles in the pockets of my sweatshirt. They rattled like little maracas and I shook them in my
pockets, once, twice, three times, and whispered, "Cha, cha,
cha, I'm *Car-men Mir-and-a*." I didn't recognize the other
drugs, so I gave the wheel of the lazy Susan a quick quarter
turn and looked at the next batch. There was a bottle with
forty Valiums, past their expiration but still potent. I picked
up all the bottles from the middle of the wheel and lined
them up along the counter, as if they were on a production
line in a factory. There were more muscle relaxants, a couple
dozen more Valiums, and another forty less potent and, as I
thought of drugs past their expiration dates, somewhat stale
painkillers. I opened the cabinet directly above the pills. It
was full of expensive vitamins and supplements and a bottle
of cough syrup with codeine, which I pocketed. Some inexplicable, pathetic, giddy sense of respect seized me and I
began to put the other medicines back on the wheel. I was

shimming the last couple of bottles in among the others when the man called out again—"Joan?"—directly behind me. I startled and the bottles scattered across the table.

"Joanie, hon? The dressing is all messed up again."

I turned around, terrified, certain the police must already be pulling up to the house. An old man—Mr. Wallace—stood, bowlegged and bent forward, with his two hands holding his stomach under his pajama top. He seemed so much older and thinner and frailer than I had remembered him. I hadn't seen him in six or seven years, since I'd taken care of his lawn for that one summer. His mouth hung open, slack, and a last few wisps of white hair stuck out from the sides of his head. When he saw that I was not his wife, his expression didn't change.

"Are you my brother?" he asked.

"No," I whispered. "No, I'm not your brother." His expression remained the same.

"Are you my son?"

"No; no, Mr. Wallace. I'm not your son."

"Are you my neighbor, with the barking dog?"

"No, Mr. Wallace," I said. "I'm Charlie."

"Oh. Charlie. Huh. Charlie, I'm awfully sorry, but I don't remember you. It's the old noggin; goddamned screen door."

"Water through a sieve, Mr. Wallace," I whispered, and tapped the side of my head with a forefinger.

"Say, Charlie, could you help out an old fellow airman? The woman who lives upstairs is out, and I've got this damned dressing messed up again, and these staples."

Mr. Wallace lifted his pajama top, and I could see a large bandage that he had managed to peel half off. There seemed

to be fresh blood on the bandage and blood soaking the elastic waistband of his pajama bottoms.

"I think you need to sit down, Mr. Wallace," I said. I
peeled off the rubber gloves and wiped the sweat off my
hands, took Mr. Wallace by an elbow, and guided him to the
kitchen table. I helped him onto a chair. The bandages smelled
sour.

"It's these staples. I don't know how they got here, but
they need to be out," he said. A line of staples held together a
black incision along his gut. Blood seeped from the cut and
some of the staples looked crooked, as if Mr. Wallace had
been trying to excavate them.

Why the hell is this guy home, I thought. There must be
a nurse here, or somebody. How the hell is this guy sitting
here alone in his study or whatever it is back there, picking
at these staples? It struck me what an awful thing it was to be
stealing this man's drugs. Worse, it struck me that it hadn't
struck me before, that I was so caught up in the undertow of
narcotics and alcohol and grief, I hadn't even thought about
the actual person in actual pain, from whom I was stealing.
I'd imagined Kate thinking of it, and reminding me, but I'd
even ignored that. I made a quick calculation that Mrs. Wallace would call the police no later than, say, seven or eight in
the morning, if Mr. Wallace didn't wake her after I'd left, and
that she'd be able to get a new prescription by no later than
noon, and probably earlier.

"Oh, no. No, Mr. Wallace," I whispered. "You can't pick
at that. The doctor says you have to keep the dressing on. You
won't get healed if you keep pulling at it." (I'd said the same
thing to Kate many times, when she'd been a little girl and

had had a hysterical, irrational terror of bandages, and had preferred to let her cuts bleed, no matter how bad they'd been, rather than cover them.) I grabbed around in my pockets and found the bottle with the strongest medicine. I tapped eight pills onto the table. I opened another of the bottles, poured the remainder of the strong prescription into that, plinked the eight pills back into the first bottle, and placed it on the table.

"Are those the vitamins?" Mr. Wallace asked.

I said, "Mr. Wallace, if you pick at those staples, you're going to get an infection and that'll be twice as worse, and you'll have to deal with all that mess even longer."

Mr. Wallace took one of my hands in his, squeezed it, nodded, and said, "You've always been such a good son."

A woman's voice called from the top of a servants' staircase I hadn't noticed at the back of the kitchen. "Arthur? Ms. O'Keefe? Arthur, are you *down* there?" Footsteps started down the stairs.

Mr. Wallace answered, "Joanie, I'm here in the kitchen. Kyle's here. He's helping get these staples out."

The woman, Mrs. Wallace, called from halfway down the stairs, "Arthur, *stop!*"

Mr. Wallace looked back at me. His confused, uncomprehending look vanished for a moment, and he cradled the back of my head with his free hand, squeezed my hand even tighter, smiled, and said, "You were always such a good brother, Warren."

Mrs. Wallace reached the bottom of the stairs, saw me in my dark hood crouched next to her husband, and began to scream.

I raised Mr. Wallace's hand to my lips and kissed it and said, "You were a good brother, too, Art." I ran across the kitchen, through the mudroom, and bolted across the lawn, back into the trees.

After crashing through the woods for ten minutes, tripping over fallen tree limbs and getting my hands and face lashed with thorns, I stopped to catch my breath and listen for anyone pursuing. The sirens and shouts and barking hounds I feared never came. Except for my own gasping, the night was quiet. Clouds still covered the sky, and the temperature had cooled almost to freezing. It took me a moment to figure out roughly where I was. I'd often daydreamed about the earliest beginnings of Enon, before there were roads, the general sense of direction or proximity to a homestead indicated by marks carved or burned into some of the trees. There must have been few trips at night, through the dense, original forests, the world so quiet back then that the open space above the lake a mile away could be heard. The first glimpse of light from a house through the trees would mean a return to food and warmth and shelter that would not have been taken for granted. But as I imagined myself a man returning to his home through the woods in the cold four centuries ago, I understood that those comforts were given meaning only because Kate and Susan were in the house, Kate perhaps already in her bed, which had been placed nearer to the fire than usual because of the terrible cold spell that had gripped Enon since the New Year, Susan sitting in a plain, hard chair placed on the other side of the hearth, darning. Susan and Kate in the home catalyzed the potencies of the light and warmth and food. But with Kate

dead and buried in the hill across the village and Susan gone
back to her ancestral home, and me stumbling away from
robbery, light and warmth and food lost their meanings, and
there was no reason anymore even to try to find that Puritan
home in the darkness. There was no reason to prefer that idea
of home to a cleft in an oak or a hollow beneath a granite
boulder. The house fell dark. It went cold. Rats ate the apples
in the basket and the wheat in the sack. The house became a
dark box of wood in a dark clearing and it was best to look
at it from the dark trees. Raising the house had been auda-
cious and the blessings it had been meant to preserve—to
hoard, it seemed in retrospect—had not simply vanished but
decayed into cursedness. The house had not merely lapsed
back into the equilibrium of the woods but was blighted, as
if inside it did not contain a hearth and a chair and a bed but
my cankered heart. Or I carried the blackened house inside
myself instead of a heart. The idea of entering the house and
walking over the dark threshold and sitting in the dark room,
on a dark chair, by the dark hearth, and looking through a
window with broken panes, back out at the perimeter of
dark trees, seemed like damnation.

By the time I arrived home from breaking into the Wallaces', I was in a state that felt close to the onset of real withdrawal. Damned or not, I entered the house and went straight
to the living room and sat on the couch and emptied all of
the treasure I'd found from my pockets and laid it all out in
front of me across the coffee table. I opened the bottle of
cough syrup and took a large swig from it. I lit a cigarette and
took a swallow of whiskey from the bottle. I took a muscle
relaxant and ground two of the instant-release painkillers

with the bottom of a highball glass. I rolled up a dollar bill and snorted the pills. I emptied the rest of the pills onto a magazine and ground them up, too, and put the powder into a small plastic bowl and added a couple teaspoons of tap water to it and mixed it together and put it in the freezer.

I went back to the living room and sank back on the couch and had another pull from the whiskey and surveyed my take. The drugs began to take effect and I did not think about the poor Wallaces or the dark house or my dark heart but only about how set I was for a while now. I thought about that in wholesome terms, as if I were for the time being out of danger of something like malnourishment or from a debilitating disease for which I needed a great number of powerful and usually prohibitively expensive drugs. I compared myself to an innocent, sick child while I finished the whiskey and took a couple more pills and had another shot of the cough syrup. I compared myself to an impoverished, desperately sick orphan and I did so with the purest sincerity and charity toward myself until I lost consciousness and fell off the couch.

I woke up on the floor the next afternoon, vomiting. I lurched to the bathroom and finished being sick and drank water out of the bathtub faucet and stuck my head under the water. Volleys of pain exploded through my head, and my stomach felt as if it were knotted full of writhing eels. Shame overwhelmed me, and a line from a poem I could not recall, about remorse being the adequate of hell, repeated itself over and over.

11.

RUMMAGING THROUGH THE GARAGE ONE NIGHT SOMETIME later in the spring—one morning, really; it must have been around four—for what I no longer remember: a monkey wrench I had suddenly been convinced I needed, an orange extension cord—I found the old fishing gear we used to take up to Maine when my grandfather was alive. The equipment had been my grandfather's, and when he died I had held on to it, intending to take Kate up to the camps we stayed at and to teach her how to fly-fish for brook trout. There was a mustard yellow tackle box, full of reels and leaders and small folding knives and needle-nose pliers, line cleaner and fly dressing and the metal tins in which we kept our fishing flies. There was an old cardboard file box, full of survey maps of where we fished, which were so detailed that we could even find the cabins we stayed in on the pond, and outdated Maine atlases and rain ponchos and a pair of wool socks and a couple of flattened baseball caps, and the fishing vest my grandfather had always used, which was fitted with a carbon dioxide canister so that, if he ever fell out of his boat into the pond, he could pull an orange rip cord at the front and it would inflate into a life jacket. The inside of the garage felt cool and clean. It gave off a clean, chaste smell that I attrib-

uted to the whitewashed drywall and the smooth concrete
floor. The backyard was still draped in darkness but pitched
just on the bevel of sunrise. I stepped over boxes full of old
clothes and dishes to the front corner of the garage, where
the fishing rods in their aluminum tubes leaned in a pile.
There were ten tubes, each about chest-high. Each had a
screw-top cap. I pulled the tubes toward me in a bundle and
looked at their caps and found the one etched with the words
To Geo. W. Crosby, from "Skunk" Morell, 1983. My grandfather's closest friend, Ray Morrell, had made the rod for my
grandfather, out of graphite, with which at the time both
men had been enthralled, and for which both immediately
forsook their older English and Scottish cane rods. I leaned
the other rods back in the corner and unscrewed the cap of
the case and drew out the nylon sheath in which the two
pieces of the rod were bagged (my grandfather and Ray had
both been smitten, too, by nylon, although I always liked the
faded brown, quilted, cotton rod bags in which the older rods
were stored). I slid the halves of the rod out of the sheath. The
rod was a green so dark that it looked black unless it caught
the light at a certain angle. My grandfather had taught me to
always take the ferrule at the base of the top half of the rod
and place it alongside the outside of my nose and give it a
couple of turns because the oil from your skin helps the
pieces fit together and prevents the bottom half of the rod
from splitting when you join it to the top half. Rolling the
ferrule upside our noses was, I imagine, as practically useless
as it was religiously observed every time we fished.

I rolled the end of the rod against my nose in the dark

garage bay and fitted the rod together. I held the rod at arm's length and flicked it up and down a couple times. I laid the rod across the top of an old dresser and found my grandfather's favorite reel in the tackle box. It was still fitted with a fly line and leader. I tightened the reel into the reel seat at the base of the rod and balanced the rod and reel in my open hand. A grainy, chalky light came into the garage from the back window, and I could just see the overgrown yard, beneath a chest-high layer of mist. The mist hanging over the yard looked like the mist we often found hovering over the pond we fished in Maine in the morning. The mist in the yard seemed aqueous and the high grass just beneath it like weeds in an outlet. The grass in the yard had clumped and braided and was all brushed in the same direction, as if it were being combed through by currents. No doubt wind had made the patterns, but with the mist billowing over it in the near dark, the yard seemed like a phantom body of water.

I drew the line leader through the eyelets along the length of the rod, the reel clicking out its length. I pulled the line through the tip of the rod and yanked a couple more yards of line off the reel and set the rod back on the top of the dresser. My skin felt tacky and I suddenly felt as if I were contracting inside my skin, or as if my skin were dilating, I couldn't really tell which, in a way that I have felt many times near dawn, after having been up all night, when the adrenaline of nocturnal wakefulness suddenly burns off, and whatever energy it is that holds your muscles to your bones and your skin to your muscles evaporates and you suddenly feel as if all your tissues and organs are made from soft lead, and you falter under the sudden burden of exhaustion. Whatever combination of drugs

and alcohol had sustained my late-night foraging disinte-
grated. The cool grainy, plastery smell of the garage suddenly
felt like sleeping gas, a perfume no longer tonic but now sedative. I had a sudden urgent need to get back into the house
and onto the couch, under a single, cool quilt, and feast on
sleep. But, oddly, along with the necessity of sleep, there came
the succinct, imperative thought—which the instant before
had not existed and in the next permeated my entire mind, to
such an extent that it seemed as if my brain had never been
made for anything other than to contain it, and which I experienced not as a thought but as a newly acquired but no less
deep-seated instinct—that before I could sleep I had to wade
out into the early dawn mist and weeds in the backyard and
cast. Just as suddenly as I had been transformed into a new
species living in a new world, the implications of that new
world began to elaborate themselves, and my first thought as
an angler of rivers of grass was that, whatever fly I chose for
fishing the yard, I had to clip off its barbed hook, so that it
would not snag in the fibers of the grass-water. I selected a
yellow grasshopper from a tin of flies and snipped off the
hook. I tied the fly to the end of the leader and stepped out
the back door of the garage into the mist and the snarled
flow of long grass. I waded out into the yard and stepped up
onto the old oak stump in the middle, slightly above the fog.
Reflexively, I let go the fly on the end of the line and began
to flick the rod back and forth over my head and yank arm
lengths of line out from the reel, pausing a bit longer between
each back-and-forward cast to allow the longer and longer
lengths of line to uncoil behind me and roll out in front of me
properly, so that when I finally laid the line out the fly would

plink onto the surface of the water with no more disturbance than an actual bug. I threw the first cast toward the tree line at the end of the yard, near a tree that had fallen out of the woods and just into the yard. The line rolled out and dropped the fly down into the mist, just to the right of the tree. I meant to lure any fish that might be hovering among the tree's submerged branches. Because I was casting into a meadow, for wicker fish, I had to jerk and haul at the line to retrieve the fly. I realized that I was using the same sort of fly that I had when I'd taught Kate how to fish, and that I had clipped the hook off that fly, as well, so that neither of us would get hooked on the ear or the back of the head, should Kate have trouble with the pace and timing of her casts.

After five casts at the same spot near the tree without a strike, I turned forty-five degrees to my right and presented the fly out to what looked in the gloom like it might be a clump of locust saplings. I listened for rising fish and by habit focused on where I knew the fly rested under the surface of the fog, waiting for the sudden grab of a fish at the bait. Light rimmed up against the horizon behind me and sparkled inside the dark mist. As I beat at the fog-submerged yard and the line sizzled above my head, and, when I mistimed a cast, the fly snapped like the frayed end of a whip, and I turned a few degrees at a time on the stump, presenting the fly along the circumference of the yard, and the light slowly rose up into the world, and I could see the large, dark roots of the trunk radiating out from below in every direction, it seemed for a moment that I was standing on the hub of a great spoked wheel suspended in a cloud and spinning at breathtaking speed and that the force of my centrifugal casts and centripetal retrievals acting on its axis might just create some kind of torsion where, for a fraction of an instant, I might find myself standing next to my daughter in a wooden rowboat at dawn.

Instead, the light increased, the mist shimmered and rainbowed and began to lift away. The lawn appeared, neglected and literal. Exhaustion overtook me again, this time along with the humiliation of being high and drunk, fly-fishing off a tree stump in my backyard. I began to crank the line back onto the reel and the fly snagged in a hump of weeds. I pulled the rod and it bent into a U, but the line would not break. I checked my pockets, but I had nothing with which to cut the line. The first heat of the day coated my skin, and sweat began to run out of my hair, along my jaw, down my nose, along the nape of my neck. My eyes and my head ached. I dropped the rod and reel where I stood and hurried back through the garage, across the driveway, and into the silent, arrested darkness of the house, where I rummaged through a plastic food container full of prescription bottles, found some sleeping pills, popped four of them, curled up on the dusty couch, among the old newspapers and books and bottles and ashtrays, and tried to keep thoughts about Kate away from myself in my decrepit state, holed up in what, as I passed out, struck me as the kind of nest in which a rat would live.

KATE HAD A PART-TIME job as a tennis instructor at the Enon playground the summer she died. She had taken lessons at the playground for six years and become an excellent player. She was co-captain of her middle school team and certainly would have made the high school varsity squad her first year. I knew Sylvia Black, the woman who ran the summer program at the playground, from my grandfather, so I talked to her and she agreed to let Kate teach some lessons, even though she was only thirteen. I never mentioned it to Kate because it would have embarrassed her. Anyway, she was thrilled to have a real job. She took it very seriously and sometimes was a little too intense with the kids, I thought. The first lessons she gave were at eight in the morning, and she biked to the playground by seven-thirty every day. The playground was located behind the Enon Tea House, where mostly women went every day for tea and cucumber sandwiches. The tennis courts were located below the playground, down among a stand of trees, near a vernal swamp the fire department flooded every winter for skating.

I tried to visit Kate at the tennis courts a couple times a week, when I had the chance to take a break from my job. There were two tennis courts, side by side, surrounded by a cyclone fence and a long bench outside the gate, made from two long planks nailed down to three evenly spaced sections of telephone pole that had been sunk into the ground. The planks had been painted a dark green, but much of the paint had worn off over the years, exposing the smooth, bare, purplish-gray wood. The courts radiated a kind of coolness that early in the morning, as if they absorbed the night's cold and released it with the rising sun. Kate's job was to give lessons to the littlest kids, and they showed up at the court bleary and mussed, dragging their rackets behind them. Before she started the lesson, she gave them a pep talk and made them run around the court twice and do ten jumping jacks, to get them going. They seemed like little animals that had just uncurled themselves from dens hidden in the woods. The lessons amounted pretty much to half a dozen kids chasing a bucketful of fluorescent green tennis balls around the courts, and usually Kate yelled encouraging things at them. I loved the sound of the tennis balls pocking off the rackets and the jangle of the chain-link fence every time a ball hit it. She taught six twenty-minute lessons every morning, from eight until ten-thirty, and I mostly made it to the courts by the fourth or fifth lesson. I sat on the bench, trying to be quiet because, although I thought Kate liked me being there, I knew she was self-conscious about being independent with her first job, too. She wanted to show me how hard she worked and how competent and dependable she was. I always brought her a bottle of orange juice and a corn-bread muffin, and, after she finished her last lesson, we'd sit together on the bench and she'd drink the juice and pinch little bits off the muffin and eat some of them and throw some of them on the ground in front of us, for the sparrows.

Sometimes Kate's competitiveness overtook her and she became too intense with the kids. She barked once at a girl that she had a crummy backhand.

"Come on, Emma. You *had* that! Put some effort into it!" She turned away from the girl and shook her head and muttered, "*Jesus.*" I had to stop myself from yelling at her to cool it. It was the first time I'd ever seen her turn her temper like that toward anyone but Susan or me. It was the first time I found myself angry with her in a way I might have been angry with an adult. My anger burned off immediately and transformed into shame, then into that sort of sorrow you feel when you see that time does pass and that you and your children really will perish. I stopped myself from telling Kate to knock it off because her emotions were new and raw and complicated and of course I had felt the same kind when I'd been her age. As much as I wanted to tell her to knock it off I also marveled at her seriousness and at what that seriousness might mature into, at what an intense, amazing woman my daughter might someday grow to be.

After the lesson I told her that she'd seemed harsh with her student and she replied that the kid had some talent and needed someone to push her to get better.

"But she's like five years old."

"Exactly. If she's going to be any good, she needs to get rid of her bad habits now."

"Okay, okay. I guess that's a good point. Just try to go easy on the tykes, all right?" Kate picked at the muffin I'd brought her. She rubbed her fingertips together to get the crumbs off and wiped her hand on the side of her tennis skirt.

"Sure, Dad."

"What's up for the rest of the day? Want to go for a walk in the sanctuary or go over to Gull Harbor and look for sea glass?" I knew she wouldn't want to do either of those things, but I hoped that she'd still like that I'd asked her.

"Carrie and I are going to the beach."

"Who's giving you a ride?"

"We're going on our bikes."

"Wait. Did you ask Mom about this or anything yet?"

"No. It's okay. We'll be safe."

"Ah, no. Sorry, kid. But no. I don't like the idea of you riding around the lake there and down Grapevine. It's too winding."

"But *Dad. You* did it! You used to do it when you were *younger!* Come on. That's not fair. Why not?"

I wanted to tell her that I didn't care if it was fair, or if it was thoughtful or mean or capricious or bad parenting or anything. I wanted to tell her, *Because I just don't want you to, and I'm the parent and that's why not.* Instead, I closed my eyes and frowned and feigned an exhausted sigh and said okay, she could go.

"But be careful, especially around the lake and along the shore road," I said.

"*Especially* there, Dad," she said. I stood up to go and she grabbed her racket and a bucket of balls.

"Home by six," I said.

"Seven," she said, and kissed me on the ear.

"Not a minute later. I'll make you guys dinner."

"Get corn."

"Okay. Love you."

"Love you, too, Dad."

THERE WAS A HEAT wave in July. I had no working air conditioners, only two fans, one a large, dust-caked window fan and the other a small, plastic desk fan. I put the window fan on the floor near the couch and the desk fan on the coffee table by my head. Frankie had come through with all of the drugs I'd asked him for the week before, and I was set up for a while.

I drank a glass of grapefruit juice mixed with the extraction from four pills and lay on the couch in my boxer shorts and a sleeveless T-shirt, with a rolled-up washcloth soaked in cold water across my forehead. A book about Enon's history lay on the floor near the couch, so I picked it up and leafed through it. There was a photograph of Main Street in July 1890, taken from the middle of the road, facing east, with the caption "Beating the heat with Conant's grapes." The elms on either side of the road look parched and papery. The photo is overexposed and light floods out much of the detail that would otherwise be visible. A single white house sits behind the trees, on the apparent verge of evaporating into pure light. Two children stand hand in hand across the street, on the right. One is a small boy wearing short pants and suspenders and a wide-brimmed straw hat. The other is an older girl in a plain white cotton dress, black socks, and ankle-high leather shoes. They are nearly swallowed in the light.

I closed my eyes and imagined what it must have been like standing in the center of the road, directly in the sunlight and heat, which was so intense that it seemed like liquid, difficult to breathe in and out, scalding, nearly asphyxiating. The boy and girl are both looking at me standing in the middle of the road, and the boy, young as he is, perhaps four or five, is wondering in a straightforward, practical way why I am standing out in the middle of the road, where it's so hot. The girl wonders the same thing but with a twinge of suspicion about me that the young boy is too young to have. Her suspicion does not frighten her, but it makes her cautious and curious at the same time. The unpaved road is smooth and dusty in the heat. The dust seems nearly to hover just above the ground, in a sheer plane, and twists up into dervishes when a molten gust of air coils down the road, and spins off out of the frame, into the backyard behind the house, and dies somewhere among the hot red pines and oaks. I am aware that there's a good chance that the children will disappear, that the photograph itself will dissolve if I try to approach them. Some kind of boundary exists, one familiar from dreams. The girl is Kate, but not quite Kate. She is obviously who I want to approach and have turn into Kate, but not deliberately, not by an act of my will, but by hers or some other, external accord, because whomever we most want to meet in our dreams always vanishes the moment we intentionally try to preserve her. I stand in the wide, open middle of the blazing road, suspended. If I take a step closer, the boy and the girl I want to be Kate will evaporate in the heat. If I turn away, the entire picture will give way. It seems that the best I can hope for is the preservation of my desire for the girl to be Kate, which is not quite but very nearly as painful as her not being there at all. Just as I feel a kind of prevenient, atomic ripple approaching the threshold of my awareness, which will scatter this fragile notion and replace it with, say, a coarse, literal thought about the washcloth on my forehead, the girl speaks.

"These grapes are as big as apples." I notice for the first time that she and the boy are standing in front of a yard to another house. The house is invisible, but I see that the near corner of a grape arbor is discernible beneath the canopy of elm behind the children. The details of the boy's and the girl's figures are mostly blurry, but now I see that each is holding what looks like a large, translucent, deeply colored purple apple. The girl holds her piece of fruit out, as if to give me a better look.

"It's a grape," she says. "I always think they should be heavier, like apples, but they're not."

Although I cannot see them, I can feel, almost as a pressure inside my chest, the weight of fist-sized grapes clustered on stems as thick as ropes in bunches the size of bodies hanging from the vines in the arbor. It must take a buck knife to cut them off and wheelbarrows to move them. When the grapes are ripe, Benjamin Conant, the man who owns the house and the arbor, and two of his neighbors, Jonah Fisk and William Dodge—Joe and Bill—harvest them. Benjamin sets a stepladder under the arbor and wriggles up into the vines. He cuts the clusters free with a whetted knife. The largest weigh close to sixty pounds. Joe and Bill stand beneath the grapes, holding between them a small, round mattress filled with goose down that Benjamin devised and sewed himself. When Benjamin cuts a stem, the cluster begins to sink. As it does, Joe and Bill position the mattress so that the cluster will lower onto it like an infant laid in a crib.

Just before he makes the final pull of the knife, Benjamin says, "Hup," which signals the coming weight of the fruit. He draws the blade back and the grapes tear free from the vine and are delivered onto the pillowy mattress.

The men at either end of the mattress each bark out a terse, "Yep," and spend a moment adjusting it to make sure the grapes are properly bedded. As he does every year during the hottest months, Benjamin has the men take the clusters of ripe grapes to an underground stone bunker in his backyard, in the coolness of which he has stored half a dozen one-hundred-pound blocks of ice, cut from Enon Lake the previous winter, in piles of sawdust. He has the men lay clusters of grapes over the blocks of ice and chills them for two days. Then he has the men bring the grapes out to his front yard, where most of the children and younger people of the village have gathered. The men hang the clusters of cold, nearly frozen grapes, spitwise, in the crooks of two upright poles. Benjamin Conant then makes a brief, explicitly religious speech.

He declaims, "Dear children, our righteous root has yielded fruit again! So long as our ground is good and the thorns do not choke it, the root shall not cease such yield, but each year become pregnant again with sweet bounty."

Two elderly women who have stopped on their way to the Tea House and stand behind the children gasp a little at this reference to pregnancy. They and a number of other especially prim souls in the village find Benjamin Conant's speeches impious. Perhaps it is because they associate grapes with paganism. But because he is such a civic treasure, they merely tut-tut and continue to listen.

When he has finished his invocation, Benjamin Conant invites the children to approach one by one, the littlest first, please, if they would like a cold, sugary, luscious grape. The children manage to order themselves and behave despite their excitement, and everyone who wants one receives a piece of the fruit after a brisk little ritual wherein the child asks, "May I have a grape, Mr. Conant?" and he answers, "Of course you may, my dear child," and solemnly but with great pleasure selects a grape, unscrews it with a single twist of his callused hand, turns, and presents it to the boy or girl with a slight bow. The child says, "Thank you, Mr. Conant," and bows or curtsies, according to custom, and returns to the general congregation.

The skins of the grapes are dark and too thick for most of the children to bite through, and taste bitter anyway. So each grape is peeled and the tannic skins tossed into a wheelbarrow to be carted off into Conant's back meadow, to rot in what the children all find a mesmerizing and horrific wasp-covered pile. Before the older girls peel and eat their own grapes, they help the younger children peel theirs. The girl I think of as Kate peels the little boy's grape. He takes the slick globe and bites at it. The blinding sun catches some of the grapes hanging from the spit and illuminates them with a dark green light beneath their purple skins. The children spit the pips into a pile. Some of the older boys start to see who can spit them farthest into the street, but Benjamin Conant puts a stop to that, insisting that spitting of any sort besmirches the village. The little boy with the girl I think of as Kate drops his grape. He gasps and picks it up. Half of the fruit is covered in grit. The other half is still clean and sweet, until the boy turns it around in his gunky hands to inspect it. He tries a bite, spits, and sobs. Kate turns to him and scolds him a little. She hands him the rest of her grape. I take a step toward the girl and the picture begins to flare out, like a sheet of photographic paper bathed too long in developer. The conscious thought of being on the couch with the washcloth on my face pierces the dream, and the image of the girl and boy and the grapes and Main Street, Enon, July 1890, bursts into white and disappears in the solvents of mere waking.

12.

I PUSHED DEEPER INTO THE SHADE, FURTHER TOWARD THE BOR-der between this life and what lies outside it, and became something closer and closer to a corpse myself. My hair was thin, my bones stuck out, and my skin stretched across my skull. I needed to be careful and not step over the boundary, because the thought that her own death caused her father's suicide would be too awful for my daughter to bear. And I did not want the word I craved to hear from Kate when I met her there in the murk—murk to me, as a living person, trespassing in realms that might well prove to be brimming with a nutritious light not visible to our own, colloquial eyes—when I finally reached her on my tether concocted from the strongest medicines; when I might have only a split second before being yanked back up and landed into the bay of an ambulance or a hospital bed, at the surface of the waking world; I did not want the possibly single word she uttered to be No. I found myself weeping many times at the prospect of my daughter's face cresting for a moment out of the gloom, looking directly into my eyes and smiling, and saying, in the half girl's, half woman's voice that I practiced every day to remember, Yes.

ONE MORNING IN LATE July I woke up and took a cigarette from a pack sitting on a dirty plate on the floor. I swiped around through the litter on the coffee table, trying to find a lighter. I found a box of matches on the floor, under the skirt of the couch. When I held a lit match to the cigarette in my mouth, I saw that my hand looked gray and withered. Some of my fingernails were long and grimy. Others I'd bitten down and spat on the rug. I realized that I must look like a castaway. I hadn't bathed in a long time. I tried to figure out how long it had been; I couldn't. The closest I could guess was five weeks. I must have changed my clothes sometime, though, I thought to myself, but I couldn't recall having done that, either, although I did remember rummaging around in Susan's closet and finding one of her old belts for my pants, which had gotten too loose to stay up on their own. Susan's belt looked like it was forty years old, as if she must have bought it at a thrift shop. It was made of white leather and had a big, medallion-like buckle on it, with a fish that looked like it was swimming after its own tail and the word PISCES in block letters. The certainty that I looked terrible and the urge to see just how bad struck me at the same time, so I went into the bathroom to inspect myself in the mirror. At some time in the previous few weeks, I had draped a pillowcase in front of the mirror over the bathroom sink. I had also turned the full-length mirror so that it faced the wall. I think I had covered the mirrors because I had been embarrassed by how I leered at myself when I washed my hands or managed to brush my teeth before passing out late at night after I had taken so many pills or drunk a bottle of cough syrup with the usual whiskey. But that morning I wanted to see my actual appearance. I suppose I had some hope of being frightened into repentance.

I looked distressingly bad. My hair had grown up into a tangled pile that listed off the left of my head. I hadn't shaved in at least two months and had a sparse, stringy beard on my face and neck. Most upsetting, though, was how thin I had become. At the time of Kate's death, I'd been trying to lose ten or fifteen pounds because even though I still got plenty of exercise landscaping I guess my metabolism had slowed, and I still ate steak twice a week and pizza and snacks and pretty much anything I felt like, especially late at night after Kate and Susan had gone to bed and I was watching sports or reading. When I looked in the mirror, though, it seemed as if I'd lost fifty pounds or even more. My face looked pale and gaunt, my neck like a bundle of ropes. I was lost in my T-shirt, which had food and drink stains on it and was yellowed at the underarms. When I'd first found Susan's belt and put it on, I'd thought it might look sort of hip, sort of charmingly disheveled, but it looked ghastly cinching my pants. I resembled someone I'd have expected to find on a park bench, under a Sunday newspaper, sleeping off a bottle of fortified wine. When I thought that, I felt bad for whatever poor soul had to suffer my comparison with him.

THE OBSIDIAN GIRL MOVES through the trees at night. She moves across the fairway of the golf course, near the road, by the stone wall that acts as the hood for the footlights to the stage. She is all but invisible, the girl of black glass, appearing only as a wobbly blur. She is a dark lens. Through her, the dark underpinnings of the world are visible, but they turn whoever might see them to stone, or to ice, or to salt, or to marsh grass. Every night, just before dawn, she climbs down into the hill through a hidden trap door. She sounds like a crystal decanter rolling along the granite seams that lead down to the heart of the hill, where a furnace burns all day and all night and dark, vague men shovel coal into its white-hot mouth. When the girl made of black glass appears, the men lean their shovels against the walls of the chamber and retreat into the shadows. The girl steps in front of the furnace and the heat roars out and over her like a shimmering hurricane. She tilts her head back and holds her hands out at her sides. The heat blasts at her, and the tips of her fingers begin to glow. The outlines of her face and arms and legs begin to buckle and kink. Her legs give at the knees, and the rest of her slides off them and drops in front of them. She remains upright for a moment on the stumps of her legs, but then she topples face-first onto the dirt floor in front of the open furnace. It appears as if she is sinking into the dirt at first, but she is actually melting. The glass girl is melting.

The glass held the shape of a girl only while it was cool. But now it is molten and pools over the floor. There is no way to tell if the glass leaks out of the girl or if the girl leaks out of the glass.

There is a sound that no human ear can hear, coming from a place no human eye can see, from deeper within the earth but also from deep in the sky and the water and inside the trees and inside the rocks. The sound is a voice, coming from deep inside the throat of the world. The sound is a note from a register so low that it cannot be heard, but many people throughout the town are disturbed from their sleep by it. It is a note from a song the shape of which is too vast ever to know. It encompasses and sustains all that is human but is not loyal to the human, only to what is latent within the human. It terrifies. The awakened clutch their hearts and gasp and groan and press their hands into their temples. They fuss over their problems and feel in their guts that if they had not been born to trouble they would not have been born at all, and that their troubles are the only sign that they still cast shadows above this earth. The note is a part of great, vaulted cathedrals of chords that keep the universe speeding out from its own genesis. It is sensate, and down in the chamber of the hill it sounds both like weeping and like laughter, and both are at the grief of the glass girl, who throws herself in front of the fires every morning just before dawn and who, to her unending despair, is remade every evening, in a deeper foundry, and evicted from the depths of the hill, back to the surface, where the cool air flowing through the grass cools and sets her glass eyes and her glass brow, her glass brains and her glass heart, and she begins another night as the brittle memories of a man who is the father of a girl she never was.

I SPENT SO MANY nights sitting in, stealing through, crawling over, and sometimes passing out in, the cemetery, and always behind Kate's stone, so she'd be spared, that I came to think of it and the hills and the adjacent golf courses as a large, elaborate set, constructed on a rotating stage. The stone wall served as a hood for the footlights, and the putting green was the apron of the stage. The hills were counterweighted with enormous granite boulders and cylindrical lead weights the size of small towers and many tons of magnetic iron and other ballast. They were held in place during the day by brass cogs the size of Ferris wheels, which in turn were held in place by black iron pawls on pinions, deep, deep in the earth. Late at night, levers released from capstans and gears began to turn, and the top-heavy hills upended into their nocturnal arrangements in perfect silence and with such smoothly ma-chined precision that it was almost impossible for the human eye to perceive, even on the brightest night, under the bright-est, fullest moon. The hills shifted and recalibrated all night long and only the most alert, vigilant observer, exactly aware of what it was for which he watched, could sometimes sense just the finest tick of a shift in the corner of his eye. When he looked over, he would see nothing. But he would have the distinct feeling that the rise he was looking at was not quite in the same place as the last time he had noticed it. Only he could not quite remember clearly, already, and would doubt himself for a moment, until his attention was diverted again by what appeared to be a new seam in the silhouette of the crown of the hill, and so on, for the rest of the night, as the stars rotated up from beneath one side of the hill, arced over it, and sank back down into the other side, until the whole set finally arrived back at its fully upright, daytime position, in the instant before dawn, and the first light of day crested the hill and the observer would see that the land was as it always had been, and would think how odd it is, the mind's tricks, and what a strange trance he must have been in to think that the topography moved around at night, and he must really have been half—or more—asleep for much of the night, although he was certain that he had been fully awake the whole time. But after all, he would think as he rose to leave, that is how sleep always does overtake us.

Some early mornings I could almost hear the echo of the last gears of the stage clicking into place as the swoosh of the first sunlight ignited across the fairways and rushed down toward me at the outskirts of the golf course on the near side of the cemetery. I had the feeling of some familiar soul having just fled out of sight, that I had just caught a glimpse of the back of someone's heel as she dashed offstage. It unsettled me, and I even had the notion that all the dead in the cemetery had just closed their eyes again, as they were compelled to do, but that they were telegraphing their irritation at a breach of address I had committed and at the indignity they felt at so nearly being caught up and about. I dreaded the notion that to the dead being awake was perfectly normal. I even began to feel not so much that the dead disapproved of me nearly catching them about on their own accounts—such a predicament might delight them, even inspire them to mischief—but on the behalf of just one of their members, whose hurried flight they may have even protected by distracting me by tumbling back into their bunks, and their stagy, tight-lidded feigning of sleep. I sometimes had the sense that, in the instant before I caught sight of them, all the winged skulls on the headstones and all the statues of angels throughout the cemetery had had their eyes shut, too, as if their usual, unblinking vigilance over the dead was something from which even they, slate and marble that they were, needed rest, that the dead and the stone carvings on their headboards all rested hardly in peace and in truth led lives more hectic than those of the living.

I had cast Enon's dead in the vignettes I made up for Kate, but as I became more and more unbalanced, they seemed to act of their own accord. Certainly, it was the drugs and my exhaustion and my sorrow producing these phantasms, but they haunted me nonetheless, and with increasing frequency and vividness. I understood how dire such hallucinations were becoming late one early summer night when I sat down to rest at the edge of one of the putting greens on the Enon Golf Club, near the street. I sat on the grass, put my legs out in front of me, leaned back against the stone wall, closed my eyes, and took a deep breath. I opened my eyes and felt suddenly as if I were awaiting the beginning of a performance of some kind. The grass was wet and smelled vegetal for the first time in weeks, not like hay, not like thatch. Wind swelled and ebbed like a surf, and broke against the foliage in the rows of trees running up the hill between the golf course and the cemetery, sizzling through it and rushing across the open fairway in front of me. The green slope of the hill was only just still green, lowering into black. A low, dark, nearly green band of thunderheads, in front of a scrim of solid, lighter gray clouding that held the very last of the day's light, a suffused luminescence that seemed without source, not even light, not even a sight, receded behind the hill, so swiftly it made the hill appear to loom up above me, ready to topple onto my head. I rubbed the tops of my arms, chilled. The streetlamp in the parking lot of the golf course club-house flickered on, halfway up the hill, to my left, behind a break of beech trees, figuring their branches and leaves into a hive of citrine light. Ocean fog poured across fairways from the cemetery, salting everything in a cold mist. Caverns under the hill and granite shelves and the water in the water table vibrated beneath me, voicing an unnerving basso profundo. The wind funneling through the stone walls sounded a strange descant in the hollows. My bones and bowels and breathing slowed and fell into cycle with this dark solfège and I whis-pered the note "La."

The heel bones of a pilgrim or cobbler ran across my flanks from beneath, and an arpeggio of ribs, and the smooth curve of someone's skull.

Places, everyone. Please take your seats. If you please.

The key of the overture is disturbing. I shift on my haunches and shiver at a coldness that has descended across the landscape, and feel a little nauseated. I have a sense that there is something telescopic about this production, as if I am actually on a stage, in the foreground, and not in the audi-ence. The music I hear is not for me but for an audience on the far side of a proscenium, watching me watch for the en-trance of other actors deeper in the stage. I put my head between my knees and breathe deeply. My stomach is sour and my vision fizzy.

There is a cavernous open space behind me, stalls and vertically stacked galleries and state boxes filled with rowdy old phantoms and spooky pilgrims, elbowing one another and leaning over and whispering, *Look, he doesn't feel so good now!*

Mockery and laughter ripple through the audience, across the orchestra, all the way from the grand circle to the loge to the gods near the cloud ceiling. I look behind me and see only the empty street. This elicits a frank, unabashed guffaw from the hidden spectators, who find my inability to see them hysterical. This is at my expense; their laughter is delight not at how well I play the fool, but at the fact that I am one.

Then the hill does loom up, blotting out everything behind it. It teeters, splits down the middle, like a curtain, and crumples into two heaps on either side of a dim gray pillar glazed in the faintest yellow light and set in relief against a background of sable darkness. Bones rise from the dark earth. There are clavicles and ribs, femurs and tibias, hands and feet. There are claws and great spines as thick as tree trunks that taper into tails, and rings of vertebrae that once encased marrow the size of pot roasts, and heavy garlands made from the gut-strung skulls of tens of thousands of rodents, draped over horses' skulls that have been fused onto the delicate skeletons of human infants. The riot of interlocking bones turns and forms a towering girandole. I try to concentrate on the writhing, clicking, tapping, grinding, clunking monument, to get a clear view of individual bones, especially skulls, because when I look at it as a whole, it increasingly seems composed of animals that could not possibly have ever existed, and that it is assembling into some horrific machine dedicated to manufacturing my deepest terrors. But then the middle of the machine spirals open like the aperture of a camera shutter, and Kate steps out.

She is fitted into an outrageous, gigantic emerald green polonaise. The dress is verdant and oceanic, mossy and Atlantic green. The bodice is constructed of willow branches, stripped to the green wood, girthed tight with eelgrass. Will-o'-the-wisps halo Kate's head. Her hair is suffused and golden, flaring, solar.

Well, well, now.

My, my, *isn't that interesting?*

What fantastications are these?

I ignore the insults and the jeers from the balconies that continue to rise higher behind me, across the road, in the darkness of the cornfield. Kate is magnificent and beautiful, if not a queen then a princess, repatriated into the wood and the water and the starry sky and the cold ocean abysses broiling beyond the continental shelf, just beyond the rise, through the trees, not presiding but naturalized. Yes, I think, this must be her first pageant, an equinoctial communion, restoration after a satisfactory yearlong trial as a member of the deceased.

A menagerie of horse and pony skeletons prance around the stage in exaggerated, ambling gaits, draped in caparisons made from their own former hides.

A pillar of fire erupts from the top of the hill and towers miles up into the night until it breaks against the invisible ceiling of the atmosphere and fans out across the sky in flaming traceries. A great crown of fire burns miles above Enon, bejeweled with Ursa's stars.

Kate watches the fire from her mark onstage, in front of

the whirling shutter of bones, which seem to rotate within
their revolutions, alternating between the reliquaries of leg-
ends and dinner-plate leftovers, one instant the remains of
leviathans and saints, the next drumsticks and short ribs. Kate
cranes her neck to follow the fire up into the heights and I
see that the rest of her does not move, that beneath her gown
she has been clamped into some sort of frame. Her arms are
raised to shoulder height and bent at the elbows so that the
tips of her fingers nearly meet in front of her chest. She cannot move her arms. They are confined by some kind of ar-
mature beneath the gown and only her hands are free at the
wrists. This confirms why there is stiffness in how she moves
her head to look up at the fire. She cannot rotate her shoulders or her torso or her hips, or turn on her feet to get a
better look at the braided column of flames roaring behind
her. I can feel its heat from where I sit. She is much nearer to
it, and although I have the thought that she is no longer subject to burning, I also have the sense that she is burning, and
that she cannot move herself back from the heat. I can see
now—not actually see with my eyes, but see in my head,
know—that Kate has been fixed to some kind of rigid frame
made of wooden strapping and hammered iron rivets, not so
much to restrict her, perhaps, but to insulate her from the
weight of the costume, a lesser kindness within a greater cru-
elty, sponsored by an ultimate benevolence, possibly if not
probably, which I now see is laden with clots of gems and
strings of pearls and made from bolt after bolt of silk brocade
and lace, douppioni and zibeline, and trussed and knotted
with leagues of silk ribbon, and mounted on a series of con-
cealed panniers that spring out and upward, elevating Kate to

a preposterous height just as it occurs to me that they are present beneath the fabric. Kate rises and the skirts of her dress cascade from beneath her and across the green. I can hear pulleys and winches turning and squeaking. Kate's ascent illuminates a system of fine silk threads, tied to the tips and the joints of each of her fingers, which rise above her and disappear in the upper darkness and lift and lower her fingers according to elegant but predetermined pattern. I squint to get a look at the darkness above Kate's head, certain there must be a scrim of black velvet, perfectly lit to blend in with the real night, that conceals a rotating brass drum bristling with stubs that pluck the tines of a metal comb. Each of the threads connected to Kate's wrists and fingers is looped around one of the tines. As the drum revolves, her hands perform an intricate set of poses. I am terrified that Kate is going to be immolated. I panic and try to rise but I cannot move. The crowd roars with laughter.

The music accompanying the spectacle is stilted and fractured. It lurches from wheezy calliopes to pennywhistles to ground-shaking brass to sour, scraping strings to air-raid sirens. At one point, I catch an oompah pattern sounding on an accordion deep inside the din. I tap the triplets on my thigh with my ring, middle, then forefinger, grateful for something recognizable, almost reassuring. I begin to sway my head back and forth in whole notes behind the rhythm. When I look back at Kate, she is raising and lowering her right arm and her right leg and tilting her head to the right, along with the beat I'm playing. I frown and stop tapping my fingers and Kate's arm and leg and head stop, too. I tap my right ring finger once. Kate's leg raises and lowers. I tap my middle finger once and Kate's arm raises and lowers. I tap my forefinger and Kate's head nods. I repeat the pattern with the fingers of my left hand and Kate's left limbs rise and fall and her head tilts left. I look up into the darkness above her and see that the brass drum and the metal comb are not the mechanisms that control Kate behind the curtains but props, meant to be seen, meant to be seen within the play on the stage. I tap my fingers in a little march and Kate jerks along with it.

I gasp when I realize what is happening and a wall of flames bursts behind Kate and her grotesque costume ignites. She is enshrined in fire and the entire production gives way. All the staging and framing and cables and gears and winches collapse in an instant, with Kate disappearing underneath it all, and the wreckage is yanked back behind the hill without a sound and without a trace. The last I see of Kate is her pale face before it is gulped into the fire and collapsing rubble. The whole spectacle has the appearance of being staged to look like a disaster, as if the beautiful girl perishes in a catastrophe, but that, of course, is always a part of the trick. I cry out for her.

That's right; chuck your girl into the furnace, palooka!
Huzzah!
Hip, hip, hooray!
He burns her at the stake every single night!
And look at him crying over her—what a baby!
Boo hoo hoo!
Just wait until we get ahold of you!

13.

A HURRICANE STRUCK THE EAST COAST AND SWEPT THROUGH Enon in early August, right before the anniversary of Kate's death. I would not have known that it was coming if I hadn't walked to Stonepoint to try to find Frankie Shuey at the Ironsides Tap Room, so I could buy more drugs. When I arrived at the bar, Frankie and another guy were the only ones there. The guy sitting next to Frankie looked vaguely familiar, as if maybe I'd seen him on other landscaping or painting crews over the years. He was thin and his shoulders so slouched it looked like he might snap in two. His complexion was pale gray and the sharp bones in his face looked like they might split through the skin. He had thin black hair and a black mustache up under which a burning cigarette had been stuck. I could tell by how sunken his cheeks were that he had no or very few teeth left. Overall, he had the appearance of a body long abused but not especially strong in the first place. I had a sense that he was always sick, always had a cough, always had asthma or bronchitis, always needed bed rest and hot soup and a good drying out. He and Frankie sat side by side, each with a boilermaker. The already dim bar darkened more and I looked over at the two high, wide, narrow, smoked windows in the wall that faced the harbor. One window was already blacked out and I watched as someone outside fitted a sheet of plywood over the other and began pounding it into place with a hammer and nails. The guy Frankie was drinking with sat on his left, so I pulled out the bar stool to his right.

I said, "Hey, Frankie." Frankie turned to see who I was and turned back to the bar.

"Hey," he said. The guy on the other side of him looked at me and crunched up his nose.

"The fuck's this guy?" he asked Frankie.

"It's Charlie Crosby," Frankie said.

"Who the fuck?"

"He's a guy named Crosby," Frankie said.

"'Scuse *me*," the guy said. "He smells like shit. Tell him to get out of here. Hey, you, Charlie Crosby; you look and you smell like shit—get lost." I remembered stories about how sometimes the guys on the fishing boats that worked out of Stonepoint would stage fights on a pier or in an alley behind a bar at night. They'd make some crew member fight the toughest guy in the fleet, and threaten to beat him half dead if he didn't. They'd get him drunk and riled up and show him a little wiry guy they said was talking shit about him and say that if he didn't beat the guy up they'd beat *him* up for being a punk. They'd always snare a new guy into this trap, the bigger the better, because he'd always think that he could take the little guy they pointed out. I remembered stories guys to whom this had happened told about how all the other fishermen made a circle and got the little guy and the dupe in the middle and started taking bets about how long it'd take the little guy to put the big new guy into a coma. Every version of the story I'd heard was about how unbelievable it was what a ruthless and tough fighter the little guy had been and how the guy he'd beaten had woken up in his own apartment three days later packed in ice, so battered that he couldn't see or eat or nearly move just to get a sip of water for a week. In all my time working on painting and landscaping crews, I'd never been in a fight and never seen one as bad as the ones they described (sometimes guys took a slap at each other, but nothing really brutal). I could see the guy sitting next to Frankie being sick and drunk and high and underfed and never getting any sleep and hauling fish or lobster traps up into a boat in a T-shirt with bare hands in roasting sun and drenching rain and freezing snow, every day that the seas weren't too high, for twelve, fourteen hours a day, looking every second as if what he was supposed to do was die, as if it was his real job to die, young and viciously, whether through ignorance or orneriness or hatred born of destroying himself in revenge against whatever it was that brought him into this world from his mother's womb just so that it could watch him suffer his dad's fists and his friends' fists and after die back out of it, ground down and broken.

I didn't know whether the guy with Frankie was tough like that or one of the guys who weren't strong, weren't tough, but were the wretched of the wretched and for that reason left alone by the brawlers, or not left alone but let be by them, allowed to be a kind of mascot. He made me feel sick and frightened but also guilty. Part of me felt like I'd like to grind him right up and out of this world, like a roach, because he was so bereft of anything like human kindness or intelligence or light. But for the same reason part of me felt defensive of him against that very same sentiment of disgust and contempt.

I stepped back from the stool I was about to sit on.

"Hey, hey; okay; I don't need to stay. I just want to ask Frankie something," I said.

"*Oh,* well, fuck *you,*" the guy said, in a high voice, like he was trying to imitate a little girl.

Frankie snorted out a laugh and looked at the guy for a second and looked again at the bottles lining the back of the bar and shook his head. "Jesus, Scruff," he said. "You're a white-hot little leprechaun today. It's business, man."

"I *bet* it's business," Scruff said. He looked at me from my shoes to my hair. "Fucking *gimp.*"

"Sorry. Don't mind Scruff. He gets all fucked up whenever there's a storm."

"When there's a fucking *gimp,*" Scruff said.

"I don't got anything right now," Frankie said.

"Nothing?" I said. "Oh, man—I was hoping—you'd been to New Mexico." I meant to come off as nonchalant, to keep it sounding light.

He turned from the bar toward me and dragged on his cigarette and squinted at me. "Nah. I don't go to New Mexico no more," he said.

"Last time you *ever* say 'New Mexico,'" Scruff said. *"Ever."*

"Okay, okay. Sorry, sorry," I said. "But I'm kind of in a jam."

"I got twenty Vickies, twenty-five each," Frankie said.

"That's kind of steep," I said. He was gouging me because I was clearly starting to fray.

"How about fifty each, gimp?" Scruff said.

"I only have three hundred," I said. "Can you do it for that?"

"Nope. A dozen for three hundred."

Scruff swigged at his beer and tucked his chin in to swallow and get his next insult out as fast as he could. I wished I could dash his brains out on the bar top. The whole predicament was so lurid and so cartoonish, so almost diabolical, though, that I just repeated, "Okay, okay, okay, okay" as fast as I could, to stop Scruff from saying anything more, and yanked the money out of my pocket and handed it to Frankie.

Scruff looked at the dirty hank of cash. "How much dick you have to—"

"Oh, *man*," I groaned. "Just shut *up*, would you? *Jesus,* you're a grim pain in the ass."

Scruff leaned back on his bar stool and blew smoke up at the ceiling and laughed and slapped his knee. "Ha! You're worse than *me!*" he coughed. "You're some kind of sad *shit,* Kemo Sabe."

Frankie opened a plastic bag and removed eight white pills from it and put them, loose, back into his pocket. Instead of being glad for the bag of twelve pills he handed me, I could only think about the eight he'd put back in his pocket. The pills were strong but full of acetaminophen I'd have to extract, and that made me all the angrier. I slid the pills into my pocket.

"All right, Frankie," I said. "Thanks for everything. Will you have some stuff by the end of the week?"

"I don't know. Check in if you want to."

"Okay. Thanks for everything." I turned and walked toward the door.

Scruff called out behind me: "I hope a tree falls on you

and you *die,* fuckwit." I bowed my head and waved and left
the bar.

OUTSIDE, THE WEATHER IN front of the hurricane made it feel
like another planet. Moisture saturated the air, insulating
sound and making it feel as if I were moving through liquid,
almost as if I could lean forward and gently push off the sidewalk with my feet and do the breaststroke floating half an
inch off the ground the rest of the way home. The light behind the ceiling of low, dark clouds seemed to come down to
the earth through water and not air. I swallowed two of the
pills dry, and by the time I reached the bridge that connected
Stonepoint with Barnton, across the harbor, it felt wholly as
if I traveled through an underwater kingdom of refracted
light and quiet. Even though there was no wind or rain yet,
everyone already seemed to have made their probably need-
less, I thought, dashes to the supermarkets and hardware
stores for batteries and bottled water and plywood and mask-
ing tape.

When I crossed the town line from Barnton into Enon,
the quiet and stillness seemed to deepen even further. I felt as
if I were the only man on earth, as if I were floating through
some uninhabited, primeval realm. Only jellyfish and I would
watch the vast nets of lightning being cast across the sky
above and the rains churning the ceiling of our watery kingdom into sizzling, unmappable topographies, and hear the
muted roaring of the winds over the face of the water, and
watch with our simple eyes the atmosphere cooking and
boiling and synthesizing itself so that when the storms qui-

eted and passed and the sun shone back down on us, we
would step onto the sand with our brand-new feet and walk
out of the carbonated surf onto the fern-littered shore. What
was that first clot of plasma not merely cooked by lightning?
What colloidal smudge shivered and convulsed at the charge
for an instant? What Adamic fleck of aspic was that? What
first, shocked self that then became the first corpse?

The clouds looked like fiddleheads of oily liquid curling
across the watery sky.

I took two more pills when I reached home and poured
some whiskey in a coffee mug that read, SOMEONE AT AYERS
MIDDLE SCHOOL APPRECIATES ME. I crushed the eight remaining pills in a decorative mortar made of green onyx that I'd
bought Susan for Christmas the first year we dated. I ground
the pills with the pestle until they were a fine powder. I
tapped the powder out of the mortar into a ramekin and
added a teaspoonful of water and mixed it with my finger
until it made a smooth, consistent paste. I put the ramekin in
the freezer.

My daydreams about floating in primitive oceans gave
way to fairy-tale equations, like spells or the sorts of drawings
to which I imagined the girls drinking wine and reading
tarot cards in the cemetery might at some point be or have
been attracted and drawn in chalk or spent a long windless
night rendering in colored sand on the lid of a crypt, enchanted that someone might come along before a breeze
scattered the sand and look at the beautiful, apparently diabolical but in fact harmless design and feel a worried thrill,
but perhaps even more delighted at the possibility that no
one besides the owls above in the trees would ever see it be-

fore it dispersed. The bookcase at the back of the kitchen was still stuffed with old tapes of movies and kids' shows, and with the plastic containers in which Kate had kept her felt markers and crayons. There was a round bucket full of fat, rainbow-colored sticks of chalk. I took the bucket to the living room and drew a stick of bright red chalk from it. I stepped up onto the couch and lifted the mirror hanging above it from its hook and threw it across the room in the direction of the armchair, half-hoping it would land quietly in the seat, half-hoping it would fall short and explode all over the far side of the room. The mirror landed on one of its corners a foot short of the chair. Its glass broke with a single crack, almost like a gunshot or an isolated detonation of thunder in the middle of an otherwise peaceful snowfall, and the frame tipped onto the chair and stopped dead. I stood up on the back of the couch and leaned against the wall and reached up and over as far as I could to my left.

I wrote on the wall, *Let the world be* W.

Below that, I wrote, *Let Kate be* k.

Below that I wrote, *Therefore, let Kate's death be* (W − k). *Let* I *be me. So* I *is now* (I − k).

I was never good at math or logic. My thoughts quickly became confused as I tried to demonstrate the calculus of grief, to draw up a circuit or graph or model written on the wall that captured the function of loss. I could barely figure out a long division problem, though, so my variables and function signs, sigmas and trigonometric equations quickly gave way to hieroglyphs, because I had to find a way to factor in the gothic girls in the graveyard, and Aloysius's voice box (a *v* inside a rectangle), narcotic vectors (skulls and crossbones, color-coded, according to the pill) and blood alcohol (the old *xxx* from cartoon jugs of moonshine, plus or minus a number from one to five, based on degree) and the tame birds in the sanctuary and the pattern of the paths there and the shifting lights of the constellations of my sorrow. I had to attempt to fold hope (H) into the emotional tectonics, too, as subtle and rare a particle as it was, because even if at any given coordinate its value was statistically equal to zero, even if at any given moment it was no more than the hope for the return of hope, a single grain of it still contradicts a universe of despair. I drew mandalas and particle accelerators and calendars made up of concentric moving circles and ox-turn algorithms.

At a certain point in my calculations I realized that I could no longer merely draw symbols on the wall, that to catch Kate on the wing, to contrive a machine that could hold something like a part of her absence, I had to bring the figures I was making out into the space of the room.

It was night by then. Daylight had drained from the house. I tossed the piece of chalk in my hand into the bucket and switched on the three lamps in the living room. Their light seemed not bright enough, so I removed their shades. Still their light did not seem bright enough for me to get a proper look at my drawings on the wall, so I moved them closer. Still there was not enough light, so I brought in four other lamps from other parts of the house and plugged them all into a power strip, and the light was not enough still. I stood back from the wall and looked at my drawings. They began on the upper left part of the wall as straight lines of equations and veered downward in anticline toward the center of the wall into primitive-looking pictures and icons. It seemed almost as if the characters were being pulled by some force toward the middle of the wall, and as the strata of letters and numbers drew closer to the center they spontaneously turned into the little animals and stars and bottles of cough syrup that they really were, right before they were vacuumed into a black hole.

There was no hole in the middle of the wall, though. There was nowhere for the drawings to be pulled into, no crucible, no alembic inside of which they could properly react. I could see the dead center of the wall, where it was still white and unmarked, right where a hole needed to be made to break the plane to allow the numbers and letters and animals and people to spin, move, whirl into the hole, be transformed, and possibly reemerge.

I need the hole saw, I thought.

"You are a ragpicker," a voice said.

My grandfather's toolbox was in the garage. I stepped outside. The hurricane loomed, bearing down toward Enon, out over the dark ocean, where fire-breathing whales plunged into valleys and breached from the peaks of the mountains of water it raised and overturned within the eons of each moment. The heavy wind sounded like waterfalls cascading in the trees. I opened the bay door of the garage. The streetlamp across the road projected pendulums of light through the trees in front of it and against the back wall of the garage, where they swung in an arc, in a steady rhythm. The wind on the serrated edge of the hurricane spun for the moment in strict tempo, and I thought that if the storm stopped traveling, and just remained, hung high above the village, spinning in place, and if it were fed the same diet of pressure and water and temperature, at a constant rate, it would be like a great, single-geared clock turning above us in the sky. We could set our watches to it. We might learn to make little hurricanes ourselves, to wear on our wrists to tell time.

"Doesn't it sound like waterfalls, Kate?" I said. I stood before the open bay of the garage. I pretended Kate was standing just behind me, to my right.

"Some of the first clocks made were powered by water. Clepsydras, they were called. Water clocks were called clepsydras. Grampy told me that."

I carted the toolbox into the living room. I plugged my grandfather's drill into an outlet and fitted the drill with the hole saw. I measured the exact center of the wall with a tape measure and marked the spot with a pencil. I pressed the drill against the wall and pulled the trigger and leaned into the drill and the drill opened a hole in the middle of the wall. It felt like a seal breaking when the hole opened and I stopped panting and drew a deep breath. It felt as if the air in the room were being vacuumed into the hole. I stepped back and surveyed the wall. The hole was too raw, too inelegant, too small. I traced a larger circle around the hole, using the mouth of a mop bucket from the basement. The house moaned and sighed under the weight of the gathering wind. I cut the larger circle out of the wall with my grandfather's reciprocating saw. The air filled with plaster dust that rippled and turned like liquid. It made paste in the back of my throat and glue in my nose. Standing back, I thought it looked like the hole gaped and gulped down everything I'd drawn, with blind, deaf, and dumb appetite. It simply devoured. So I yanked out a couple yards of aluminum foil from the roll in one of the kitchen drawers and tore it into long strips and folded the strips over three times each and pressed them flat and stapled them around the rim of the hole in the wall. That looked funny and ham-fisted, too. I wanted a whirlwind, a vortex, the eye of a storm, the crater of a volcano. I wanted the hole to spin and churn and vomit light and gulp it back up again and transform it into something I'd never seen and the light to have a voice and to speak a word that said Kate was okay and showed her well and transfigured and became the heart in my chest and the love welling up behind my ribs and the anger seizing my throat and the murder churning in my eyes and the sulfur burning in my nose and the hurricane howling in my ears and the fury in my cup and I wanted the hole to be the rent veil and even in my stupor I could see that the machine I was dumbly improvising out of candles and copper wire and brass leaf and teakwood and tiger's teeth and heavy coins and blue pearls was a grotesque demolition of my own home and not the beautiful altar I intended.

The paste in the freezer had crystallized. I put it in a coffee filter and squeezed the liquid from the filter into another ramekin and drew it up with an old children's medicine syringe I'd found in a plastic food container in the back of one of the kitchen cabinets, among old inhalers and droppers and thermometers. I had given Kate medicine with the syringe when she'd been too young to take it from a spoon. I stood at the kitchen counter and stuck the syringe into my mouth and pushed the plunger about halfway down the barrel. The liquid was cold and acrid. Before any time elapsed for my better self to argue with my lesser self, I pushed the plunger another quarter down the barrel. Just to make sure because that first squirt wasn't quite halfway, I thought.

"Three-quarters of eight pills; that's, what? Jesus, it's like five pills—no, six. Wait, is that right? And those four others. Charlie, you're going on a *ride*."

I shuffled back to the living room. The floor was strewn with tools. The couch was covered in plaster and dust. I tried to read what I'd written on the wall and to follow the equations and improvised ideograms as they drained toward the hole in the plaster which looked pathetic now, fringed in aluminum like a kid's attempt at a special effect for a home-made science-fiction movie. The first wave of the drugs swelled over my brain and I cursed myself for making such a wreck of the living room, especially the couch, where I wanted to lie down and float away.

"Ha, you just signed up for some housecleaning, Charlie Crosby," I said. "Ah, Kate, your dad's as big a jackass as he ever was. Bigger, in fact. Your dad's a big, stubborn, born-and-bred chump." I smiled. Kate loved the word "chump." I used it once to describe someone I'd done a job for and when she heard it she clapped her hands and threw her head back and laughed out loud. "Chump! What's that?"

"Kind of a jerk," I said. "Kind of a numbskull. You should look it up in the dictionary." Kate hauled out the dictionary I kept in the living room next to the couch.

"It's the sawed-off end of a log," she said, holding the dictionary up to her face and squinting. Why don't I get my act together and make an appointment for her at the eye doctor's? I thought. "It's like 'chunk' and 'stump' stuck together! Like a block of wood."

"A blockhead," I said. "A block of wood for a head."

Now I dragged the vacuum cleaner out of the closet and

plugged it in and turned it on and yanked the hose from the body and began to drag it back and forth across the top of the couch and the cushions. The white dust was so heavy and fine that the hose just made lines in the fabric.

"Attaboy; make it worse. Good show, old boy," I said. I teased myself in the cheerful tone of voice I'd used when I was mad at myself but trying to contain my anger in front of Kate.

"Your daughter's *dead, old boy*—you stupid shit," I said. "And you are a wreck of a man with a block for a head." I sighed and tipped over onto the couch and lay there with the metal vacuum cleaner wand across my chest, listening to the motor whine, feeling its revolutions through the wand. "A block of a head soaked in ether, a stump soaked in turpentine."

The wind roared and buffeted the house, the vacuum motor whining harmony over it. Somewhere upstairs a storm window rattled in its frame. I felt as if I were spinning head over heels. At some point, I lost consciousness, with the vacuum still running and the storm rolling over Enon like a great, kingdom-sized turbine, tilling up its trees and hedges and fences, toppling tombstones and tearing shutters from their hinges and weather vanes off barn roofs, all while I dreamed my opium dreams.

I came to the next day at noon, already bolting dizzily off the couch, nearly stumbling over the books and bottles. The vacuum cleaner was still running from the night before and its canister burning hot to the touch. I switched it off and the sudden silence made me aware that the noise from its motor had been driving me mad in my sleep for hours. My ears rang in the quiet and it seemed as if I could still hear the vacuum the way that you still see the sun in front of you when you blink after you've turned away from it. A bitter, cooked smell wafted up out of the machine.

From what I could see outside the living room window, the yard was strewn with fallen branches and leaves and shingles from the roof. Something like the actual world began to resolve itself out of the oneiric morass in my skull and I made my way to the kitchen. I put on an old pair of sneakers that sat on top of a pile of old newspapers and mail and opened the back door and stuck my head out. The cupola from the garage roof lay splintered on its side in the yard. The trotting-horse weather vane that had been set on top of the cupola was speared upside down in the grass a few yards away. Four of the windows in the garage doors were broken. Glass and bricks and shingles and tree limbs were scattered across the driveway. I stepped outside and walked around the back of the house. Pillars of sunlight burst down from between the speeding clouds, swept across the landscape, and swung back up into their billowy bays. The wind ran smooth and strong behind the storm and smelled clean and sweet and invigorating, as if it were cleaning up in the hurricane's wake and not the tail of the hurricane itself, or as if it were a signal that the hurricane trailed behind itself that said the violence was over and calm and safety and order were spreading back over the world. One of the maple trees had toppled and glanced off the back corner of the house, where Kate's room was. I stepped back from the house into the yard to get a look at the roof. Half of the shingles had been blown off. A dozen bricks had broken loose from the top of the chimney, giving it the look of a crenellated castle tower. The yard smelled rich and earthy. Sparrows flew around and chirped and found food and grass and twigs to repair their nests with. The stark blue sky and the churning, retreating clouds and the cascading sun and the bright green grass and livid blond pith wood gleaming from the broken ends of fallen limbs and the wounds in the sides of the maple trees and the silvery-gray clear rainwater collected into a wide pool in the middle of the backyard corrugating in the wind were all overwhelmingly beautiful and I smiled at it all and sat down in the soaking muddy grass and wept.

THE HOUSE AND THE yard were such messes from my abuse and neglect and from the hurricane that I could not stand the idea of them remaining in that state while all of the other homes and yards of Enon were cleaned and repaired and brought back to their properly cared for conditions; nor could I bear the idea of following along in order not to be noticed and cleaning and repairing the house and yard myself. There was some irony in the fact that I felt certain I could not do the work because I actually knew how to do it and so I knew how much energy it would take, energy I knew I did not have anymore, in my condition. The idea that I neither could leave the house as it was nor fix it made me feel more hopeless than ever. On top of that, I imagined Kate standing at my side, surveying the damage, looking to me for resolve and optimism. Had she been alive, I'd have put my arm around her shoulder and squeezed her against me a couple times and said something like "Piece of cake, babe. We'll have the farm up and running again in no time flat." As it was, I sighed and said, "Ah, the hell with it, all of it." I grabbed a backpack from the front hall and filled an old plastic soda bottle with tap water and started away from the house. When I was almost to the Red Orchard store, I took the backpack off and scratched around in the bottom to see if there was any money. I thought I might buy a pack of cigarettes or a candy bar if there was only a little change. I wanted to see how the store had weathered the hurricane and to say hi to Manny. I hadn't been to the store in several weeks, maybe a couple months even—longer, in fact, I realized, not since I'd met Manny the first time, or talked with him anyway. I had a spontaneous hope of maybe helping him tape up a broken window and mop up the flooded floor and afterward sitting on milk crates and sipping cold colas and commiserating about all the work we'd accomplished. The store looked fine from the outside, so I stuck my head in the door to say hi and ask Manny how his kids were and to apologize for not having dropped in for a while, although in truth I was sure he couldn't have cared less that I hadn't been back in, and might have been glad for it, given the state I'd been in. There was a guy I didn't recognize at the register, a tall kid with long hair and a bad slouch.

"Oh, hey," I said.

"Hey," the kid said.

"Sorry. Is Manny around?"

"Who?"

"Manny. The guy—" I almost said, *with the kids.* "His full name is Manprasad, I think. Works here every day."

"Oh, that dude. He split."

"Split?"

"Moved back to China or something. Couple months ago."

"No kidding. Well, um, thanks."

"No thing, man."

Manny having moved back to India felt tragic, like the end of a sad movie, with me the guy walking away, dismayed and crushed as the credits roll. Damn, crummy little village, I thought. Crummy little footpaths and crummy little sanctuary. It's all such a bunch of bullshit, and I'm its sorry-ass mascot. The Idiot of Enon. *Fuck* it.

I walked around for the rest of the day and late into the evening. It seemed I had no possible place left on this earth to go. I could not go back to the house. I did not want to spend the night in the wet, storm-tangled woods. A hotel was out of the question. I stopped walking and looked around. I was near the road across from Mrs. Hale's estate, where I had spent summer nights stalking through her meadows with Peter Lord and my other friends, and where Kate and I had rested on our way home at dusk and watched the sun set and the beautiful, grand house settle into the dark, and where my grandfather and I had seen the amazing and for all purposes apocryphal orrery, with its ivory planets and moons and brass sun, and I had turned the wooden-handled crank and made the entire arrangement of spheres spin on their axes and around one another and the sun in perfect symphony.

I decided to break into Mrs. Hale's house and find the orrery. Nothing in the world seemed more important suddenly than turning the crank and feeling the perfectly machined resistance it offered and the perfect ratio of force applied and degrees that the crank turned to the various periods of the celestial bodies, from the almost imperceptible orbits of the outer planets to the smallest little moons, which spun as quickly and neatly as tops. I walked in a straight line across the road and across her meadow, right toward the few lights on in her gigantic house. I made no attempt to conceal myself or to be quiet. I did not think about looking for any drugs. She's an old Yankee nanny goat anyway, I thought. I bet she's never even swallowed an aspirin.

"Your old pop may be headed for a stretch in the joint, kid," I said. "But it's time, way past time. There're some things in this place you just have to see." I thought about the James Cagney and Edward G. Robinson gangster movies we'd watched together, which, unlike the old westerns we'd seen, she had genuinely loved. I drew a deep breath and shook my head and smiled in disgust at myself and said, "Made it, Kate—top of the world. Anyway, what I'm about to show you is something *else*."

I walked up to Mrs. Hale's broad, oak front door, the one my grandfather and I had stood before, what, I thought, twenty years ago, waiting for Mrs. Hale to let us in. I grabbed the brass door handle and pushed down on the leaf-shaped lever with my thumb and it went down all the way and I pushed on the door and it swung open inward and I walked into her front hall. The hall was lit by a single, dim, candle-shaped bulb set in a wall sconce. It was wide and deep and receded into the darkened depths of the house. Dark paintings in gold frames lined the hall. All were portraits of men and women I took to be Mrs. Hale's ancestors. The floorboards creaked and echoed as I walked down the hall. It turned left at the back of the house and continued lengthwise. I came to a large stairway that rose eight steps to a landing on which stood the Simon Willard tall clock I'd fixed with my grandfather. I peered up at its austere dial.

"Come along. I'm right in here," a voice barked. I startled and turned to run but remained on the landing. It was Mrs. Hale, and she sounded exactly the same as when she'd told Peter Lord that we sledded like girls and when she'd asked my grandfather what she owed him for fixing her clock. Her voice was clear and strong, her words as composed as if set in sharp, indelible black ink on cold, blue-white paper. I went up the rest of the stairs and crossed a wide landing to an open doorway. If running into Mr. Wallace wandering around his house at night had been like finding a puzzled half-ghost, half-man, fuzzy and vague from fumbling around between realms, Mrs. Hale seemed like the pure concentration of all the light and air and earth and people of Enon, from every lap it had ever taken around the sun, not merely from its relatively brief and no doubt fleeting career as a village of colonists but from its centuries as home to more original souls and a tract of forest, and its millennia under glaciers and at the bottoms of unnamed oceans, all taken in by her ancestral house and focused through the precisely configured windows, aligned and coordinated with the clocks and orrery and rendered into the small, prim, neatly dressed figure sitting on a plain wooden settle beneath an electric candle, in the middle of the room, the temple, the dim penetralia, everything else shrouded in darkness, as if she were an artifact in a museum or a prophet in a pew.

I stood at the door dumbfounded and already abashed to the point of reform, the forthcoming speech I imagined already a formality, already perfunctory if not for the agonizing, extra efficacy of having to hear in full the details of the charges of which I already knew I was guilty. Mrs. Hale sat

with her hands folded in her lap, looking straight at me, with
perfect poise—with what both of my grandparents unhesi-
tatingly would have called character. I had the impulse to
check the bottoms of my shoes to see if I had tracked dirt
into the house, to smooth my hair down, to tuck my shirt in.
My shame doubled, trebled. It struck me how repulsive it was
for me to be inside her house, the outrageousness of it made
all the starker by her sitting there with such patience and self-
possession that to judge by her it was as if I were prevailing
upon her tact in some small matter of manners.

I tried but could not suppress a gasp at my idiocy. "Mrs.
Hale," I said.

"Do not speak, Mr. Crosby," she said. "I know who you
are and why you are here. You will find none of what you
came for in this house. I am sorry for your loss, but it is time
you stopped this carrying on. It is disgraceful."

Tears brimmed in my eyes and ran down my cheeks. I
was humiliated and in awe of the woman. She possessed the
majesty of plain speech.

"Mrs. Hale," I said. It would have been foolish of me to
tell her I had not come for drugs. That was somehow imma-
terial to her.

"I know what you are doing out there at night, Mr.
Crosby," she said. "It is not a mystery. With all your crawling,
you'll soon be going on your belly. You'll spend your days
swallowing dirt and hoping for bare heels to bite."

"Mrs. Hale," I said.

"Yes, Mr. Crosby."

"I am sorry."

"Well and fine, Mr. Crosby, but your sorrows are selfish.

You are a maker of dismal days. You burn your daughter in strange fires when I should think you would be grateful for the blessing of having had a lovely child. Enough is enough."

I understood as she spoke that Mrs. Hale was not going to call the police. She was not going to report the break-in, or call the offices of *The Daily Bread,* or speak any more sternly than she already had, or, as a matter of fact, speak any more at all. I had been dismissed.

She sat still and erect on the settle, looking at a point high on the opposite wall, toward whatever it was that moored her to her convictions, clearly finished with the affair, clearly weakened and frail and, worst, frightened, another victim of my violence. The hardness of her consideration toward me was so nearly unbearable that I almost offered to help her lie on her bed or to make her tea or to care for her lawn for free for the rest of her life, gestures that themselves would have been violent, would have demonstrated that I had missed her point precisely, that I rejected precisely the straightforward responsibility she had extended to me, enacted for me.

For an instant I thought of murdering Mrs. Hale. She seemed so impossibly decent. But her dignity provoked me into humility and silence. After bowing my head and standing mute before her for a moment, I turned from the door and walked back down the hall, the wide pine floorboards creaking. I descended the dark, narrow staircase. The grandfather's clock on the bottom landing read one-thirty. I paused in front of it for several seconds. The silence of the house was so deep that each tick of the clock seemed to enfigure in sound the brass works rotating behind the dial. The clock seemed a device for preserving and telegraphing the heartbeats of my grandfather and my grandmother and my mother and Kate, and a coffin, and a reliquary, and finally just a plain old beautiful clock. Somewhere I could not remember the orrery sat in its room, still, latent, potent in the darkness. I descended from the landing and followed the hallway back to the front door. I stepped outside into the dark night and closed the door behind me.

I WALKED ACROSS THE meadow and into the woods, into the Enon River sanctuary near where my grandfather and I and Kate and I had fed the birds from our hands so many times. I imagined the birds dropping dead from the trees until the ground was covered in a tangled mass of corpses, the beak and broken wings and soiled feathers and needle-thin bones of one animal interlaced and looped with those of the next and all the bodies knitted together. And I imagined that the plaited bodies might be lifted in a single pane and draped over my shoulders and clasped together at my throat with claws and worn like a cape or robe. It would be very light, made as it was from feathers and hollow bones. It would be very long and I would wander from the tame boundaries of the sanctuary out into a real wilderness with a great train following me that would comb up insects and grass and bark and snag on stumps, and that would constantly force me to stop and turn to gather or yank free or untangle, only to have it catch again a moment later on another barb. Bones would snap and wings unscrew from their sockets and I would leave a trail of looping feathers and scattered limbs. My thrashings would knot the garment as much as they rent it. The garment would attract living, wild birds as I passed below their nests and they would alight on it and become entangled. Over time, the garment would be transformed, expelling those first, tame birds and accumulating dark pheasants and crows and elusive little songbirds. After many years, the cape would no longer contain any of the birds from which it had been originally formed. It would become more and more gruesome as it metamorphosed from entirely dead birds to a mixture of the dead and the living. It would writhe and twist with black and brown and flutter scarlet and yellow and purple. The snared birds would peck one another bare and pick out one another's eyes and preen themselves and eat one another and defecate upon one another and couple, all while they screeched and sang and made nests and brooded over eggs that were not theirs but had boiled up beneath them through the thickets of bones and plumage, even as their own eggs had sifted away to hatch somewhere else or fallen from the cloak onto the ground or in cold puddles, where their quickening yolks would cool and cloud to mere jelly. Sparrows would raise waxwings and crows beget finches and there would be generations of birds that were born, lived, sang, struggled, and died wholly ensnared in that monstrous cloak.

When I came to the creek that ran from Enon Swamp to the lake, I stopped and filled the backpack I had brought with me with as many stones as I could shoulder. I walked through the woods to Cedar Street, crossed the street, and marched through more woods to Enon Lake.

The night was moonless and lidded with clouds so thick that they were invisible within the darkness they made. The clouds seemed low enough that I had to hunch down not to crack my head on them. My mind blazed with ravishing lies. I thought, I cannot accept this gift of myself, myself as a gift, of my person, of having this mind that does not stop burning, that deceives itself and consumes itself and immolates itself and believes its own lies and chokes on plain fact. Mrs. Hale is right, but I cannot stomach it. My grandfather always told me that whether or not I believed in religion or God or any kind of meaning or purpose to our lives, I should always think of my life as a gift. Or that's what he told me his father had told him and that *his* father had told *him,* in a tone of voice that suggested that such a way of thinking had seemed to him as remote and as equally magnificent and impossible as it did to me, even as he passed it along as practical advice. But it's a curse, a condemnation, like an act of provocation, to have been aroused from not being, to have been conjured up from a clot of dirt and hay and lit on fire and sent stumbling among the rocks and bones of this ruthless earth to weep and worry and wreak havoc and ponder little more than the impending return to oblivion, to invent hopes that are as elaborate as they are fraudulent and poorly constructed, and that burn off the moment they are dedicated, if not before, and are at best only true as we invent them for ourselves or tell them to others, around a fire, in a hovel, while we all freeze or starve or plot or contemplate treachery or betrayal or murder or despair of love, or make daughters and elaborately rejoice in them so that when they are cut down even more despair can be wrung from our hearts, which prove only to have been made for the purpose of being broken. And worse still, because broken hearts continue beating.

But that was only how I'd felt since Kate died. I felt as if it was always true and that I was merely deluded before, that I believed in, was enchanted by, a lie of love and goodness, simply because I had it so good for a time. But it was not a lie while I lived it. It was true. It was as true as my despair after her death. I would never have called myself an optimist, or even happy in the sense of being satisfied. I was always restless and ill at ease, running too hot. But Kate gave my life joy. I loved her totally, and while I loved her, the world was love. Once she was gone, the world seemed to prove nothing more than ruins and the smoldering dreams of monsters.

I WALKED INTO ENON Lake with the intention of drowning myself. My idea was to sink myself with the rocks in the backpack. The water was cold and pure and clean. It washed my filthy hands and my filthy face and my filthy hair. I was exhausted and scorched and the water quenched me. I could practically hear the water hiss as I immersed myself in it. I unshouldered the backpack full of rocks and it sank behind me. I waded out until I was up to my neck. My clothes weighed me down but I still had to half-tread with my arms and hands. I exhaled the air in my lungs. I ducked under the surface and sank into the cold quiet water.

There had been so many times when I had felt embarrassed for my daughter that I was her father, mostly times when, after I'd been fired by a client or had failed to make enough money to last the winter without having to dip into the money from selling my mother's house, Kate would hug me and kiss me and tell me, "It's okay, Dad," and I'd have to act comforted by her while being overwhelmed by what a wonderful kid she was and how humiliated I felt at having put her in the position of consoling her own parent. I realized that what I had been doing since Kate's death was nothing short of violence. It was not grieving or healing or even mourning, but deliberate, enthralled persistence in the violence of her death, a willful preservation of the violence imparted to her and to our family by that car battering her and dispatching her from her self and from this world, and my perversity—that was the word for it, I realized in that instant, under the cold water—my perversity was perfected by the fact that I knew better, that I had known all along that the drugs and punching the wall and breaking my hand, on purpose, of course, of course, of *course,* I thought—and ravaging my family's home and digging around in the dark and ruining the peace of other people's homes and terrorizing them was the deliberate cultivation of the violence of the instant of the collision of the car with my girl and, worse, the deliberate, angry sowing of it on neighbors and strangers and worst of all Kate, whatever that name now meant—memory, angel, voodoo doll. And yet I knew better. I had known every second of every day that what I was doing was wrong and I had done it anyway.

The water's mercies were brief. My breath gave out. The foreign, submarine world suddenly alarmed me. I surfaced and gulped at the air and scrambled back toward the shore, reaching the edge of the water on my hands and knees. When I attempted to stand, I tottered under the weight of my soaked clothes and sprawled on my back, my legs still in the shallows. I unzipped my sweatshirt and peeled out of it like I was shedding a bloated second skin. Exhaustion overtook me and I lay panting and freezing on the sandy gravel. The last tatters of storm clouds streamed across the bright summer stars. I barked a laugh.

"Mercy, mercy me; this is *sad,*" I gasped. "Enough is

enough is right. Charles Washington Crosby, you have got to get your *shit* together." I would have curled up and fallen asleep where I lay if I hadn't been so cold and dismayed with myself. Instead, I got to my feet and started back toward home, dragging my heavy, limp sweatshirt by the hood over the ground behind me.

When I had crossed the golf course and reached the top of the hill behind the cemetery, I paused and looked down at the irregular ranks of headstones. From where I stood, Kate's stone was obscured behind the maple tree. No matter, I thought, glancing at my dark, dirty sweatshirt. I look like an old ghoul dragging around some fawn I snatched from its mother's bed. I'll get some dry clothes and some sleep and come back tomorrow.

Directly in front of me, halfway down the hill, maybe seventy-five yards away, a spark of light flashed and backlit two or three large rectangular headstones, so quickly that had the afterimage not pulsed its way across my vision, I'd have been convinced that it hadn't happened. I squinted at the dark. The light sparked again, and again, and blinked into a tiny flame. A young girl's voice laughed and another shushed at it. I realized it was the two girls I had seen drinking wine and reading tarot cards and talking about boys. I could just make out a cigarette and a face in the light for a second before the lighter went out again. One of the girls laughed again and the other tried to hiss her quiet but started laughing, too. They hushed each other but I could still hear them talking in delighted, hurried undertones and it was charming, how happy they sounded to be together, raising a little hell, acting up a little. I thought about the nights when Peter Lord and my other friends and I used to range all over Enon, not really even a little truly feral after all, maybe, but boisterous and happy. And I thought about what fun I'd had with Kate hiking all over the village, too, and how when she'd been younger, how thrilling it had been for her whenever we'd wandered off a bit too far and had had to walk home in the dark.

I started back across the hilltop, intending to sneak away without the girls noticing me and maybe getting scared, ruining their good cheer. I must have grunted or something, I'm not sure what, but I made a noise and the laughing stopped. I froze and the girls froze.

"Carl?" one of the girls called. "Carl, is that *you*?" For all I'd been through in the past year, I felt more petrified than at any other time. Christ, I'm going to jail tonight after all, I thought, imagining the girls shrieking and being frightened half to death at the sight of me, soaking and strung out and wretched.

"Carl, cut the shit; I'm *serious*."

As idiotic as I felt, I croaked out, "Um, no. Ah, hi. It's not—Carl. I'm—"

The girls got up on their knees. I dropped my sweatshirt and started walking toward them, with my hands out at my sides, almost like I was approaching a skittish animal. I didn't know what else to do.

"Who's that?" one of the girls asked.

"Sorry," I said. "Sorry. I didn't mean to sneak—I mean, I didn't know you guys were there."

"Who *are* you?" the girl repeated.

"Well," I said, "I'm Charlie." It sounded so strange to say that. It felt so odd that there was nothing else I could say to these young girls, girls near to my daughter's age, that the only appropriate thing for me to say seemed to be nothing more than my name.

"Charlie, huh?" the other girl said. They both stood up. One of the girls was noticeably taller than the other, very slim, with dark eyes. She wore a black sweatshirt with the hood pulled over her head. Her long, snaky, jet-black hair cascaded out from the hood and down the front of the sweatshirt. She stood a step in front of the other girl, who was fairer, with lighter eyes. The other girl's hair had been dyed black, too, but she'd let it half-revert back to its natural red color. She wore a black leather jacket that had a white skull with a Mohawk and the word EXPLOITED spray-painted across the front of it. She wore a black skirt with black leggings and high, heavy black leather biker boots. They were trying to be cool, but they were nervous. I thought of Kate and felt like they were not being nervous enough. I walked toward them until I stood about ten feet away. I deliberately kept my body turned a third away from them, to show that I wasn't going to move any closer in their direction.

"Sorry, guys," I said. I looked down at my soaking, muddied self. "Sorry. I'm not having"—I wasn't sure what to say—"such a good night."

The shorter girl elbowed the taller girl and the taller said, "Ohh; it's *you*."

"Sorry—" I said. "It's me?"

"Yeah, it's you—Kate's dad."

I knew they knew. It was as simple as that, but I still feigned a little. "'Kate's dad'? What are you talking about?"

"Kate's dad," the girl said. "You're Kate's dad. The kid—

the girl—that died last year. The eighth grader. You're her dad, right?"

"Right," I said. "Yeah, that's right, but—"

"Don't worry, man," the girl said. "It's okay. Kind of everyone knows."

"Everyone knows what?" I said.

"Yeah. I mean, the guys know. I mean, these older guys we kind of know, at school, and some girls; they've seen you walking around at night a few times. Everyone kind of knows about you. I mean, not the cops or the parents, just some of us. No one told them it was you that did that break-in. We know you walk all around at night. Everyone kind of thinks it's cool."

The other girl said, "We know right where Kate is, right down there. We talk about her sometimes."

"Talk *to* her sometimes."

"Yeah, to her."

"We saw her once."

"Right down there, by her stone."

"She was, like, made of the shadows."

"Yeah, or like inside the shadows, but we knew it was her."

"We could tell from her hair."

"Yeah. Her hair was really pretty. Really, *really* black."

"But black because of the lights moving around in it, kind of."

"Yeah, it was really weird. But she was so beautiful. I mean, really, *really* beautiful."

"Yeah, we really kind of fell in love with her."

Just like Kate fell in love with the idea of Sarah Good, I thought. The taller girl took a drag of her cigarette. She took a half-step forward and offered it to me.

She said, "Dude, you look like you need a *smoke*." But then she stepped back and dropped her face a little, as if suddenly remembering her manners in front of an adult.

I said to her, "Your name's not Sarah by any chance, is it?"

"No, I'm Lilly," she said.

"And I'm Caroline," the other girl said.

"How many times did you say you've seen my daughter?"

"A bunch—"

"A couple—"

"Once for sure."

I thought: Jesus, these kids *know* about me? I thought: Jesus, Lilly and Caroline, in the cemetery, drinking some white wine you pinched from your moms, playing with tarot cards, probably getting okay grades, probably going to decent colleges in a year or two, trying to work things out, trying to be good kids, really.

"Lilly and Caroline," I said. "What a couple of lovely"— I wasn't sure what to call them: girls, women?—"souls you are." I felt mortified, too, though, soaking wet and strung out, talking and sharing a cigarette with teenage girls in the cemetery late at night, with evidently half the kids in the village aware of what I'd been doing for the past year, and these two not as frightened by me as they rightly should have been. But it felt like a spell had been broken, too.

I stammered a vague thank-you, suddenly not wanting to explain the facts of the night, charmed by these kids but suddenly wanting nothing more than to be home. So I told them that they didn't know how much they had helped me and I didn't know what else more to say but thank you.

"No problem, my man," Caroline said.

"That's what we're here for," Lilly said.

"Well, your secret's good with me, you guys. Just—ah—be careful, okay? Take it easy with the booze and those smokes, all right?"

"Okay, Mr. Charlie."

"Okay, *Dad*."

I laughed out loud at that. As ridiculous and reduced and outrageous as the whole situation was, it was nice to be called dad, and in that funny, smart, sarcastic girl's voice.

"Bye, guys," I said. I turned away and limped down the hill toward the road.

Lilly called out in a loud whisper, "Hey, Mr. Charlie?"

I stopped and turned around and whispered back, "Yeah?"

"We're really sorry Kate died."

Caroline whispered, "Yeah. We bet she was a really good kid."

14.

KATE AND I SHARED A LAST MEAL IN THE TWILIT REALM I HAD invented for her. The meal was the same meager supper I had provided when she first arrived in that other world, but reversed. I had imagined the world, colonized it, and come ahead of her in order to build a stone-ringed fire pit and a

wigwam of lashed saplings covered over with bark and insulated with straw, and to make a sooty fire and to toast some
meal cakes. She sat on a bench made from a planed log,
wrapped in a shawl, pale, gray even, ill from the rise and drop
of the ocean. The wigwam was smoky and dark and cramped.
The floor was covered with dirty straw. Kate nibbled at her
empty fingertips until a pinch of crumbs appeared kneaded
up between them. A corner of tasteless cake grew in her
hand. Once it formed into a square, Kate removed it from in
front of her mouth and handed it to me. I placed it back into
a pan resting next to the coals and traced its outline with a
knife and it joined back into the rest of the cake behind the
blade. Kate stood up and stepped backward toward the doorway. I shuffled back from the hearth and stepped behind her
and we both left the house, watching it recede into the trees.
We struggled for a mile and a half, through trees and meadows, scrub and dune grass, our backs to our destination, Kate's
seasickness getting worse along the way, until we arrived at
the shore. When we reached the smooth stones and clotting
seaweed and the first waves soaked our feet and curled back
up into themselves, I turned around to face Kate and the
ocean. We embraced and I turned her over to a lean, half-
starved, sunburned sailor, who stood in the water up to his
knees in front of a dinghy. A small, battered, and dark caravel
with tattered lateen sails lay a hundred yards offshore. The
sailor took Kate's hand and she, watching me, backed up over
the side of the dinghy and onto one of its two benches. The
sailor pushed the boat into the water by the bow, leapt into
it, took up a pair of oars, inserted them into the tholes, and
began to row the boat backward toward the ship. When the

dinghy reached the ship, I could see Kate stand and be raised up to its deck by two men on board. The sailor who rowed her to the ship climbed up a rope ladder. The dinghy was pulled up with a windlass and stowed. The ship raised anchor and began to draw back across the ocean, stern first. I backed up across the sand slowly until I stood on slightly higher ground, near the edge of the dune grass. I watched the ship for hours, as it receded and diminished, until its small sails sank and disappeared beneath the horizon. I watched the empty ocean for hours afterward. The sun dropped through the sky and followed the ship off the eastern ledge of the world. The sunlight spread across the far line of the flat earth and dimmed into full night.

IF THE DAUGHTER OF the son of a daughter of a son of a mad tinker who was the son of a mad minister perish beneath the wheels of a passenger car conducted by a distracted mother of three, her father shall be liable to death by slow poison from his own hand, during the long administration of which he shall wander bare and wooded hills, open and choked meadows, thickets and swamps, day and night, befreckled with ticks and beknotted with burrs, burned by the sun and frostbitten by the snow, making acquaintance with all the dead of Enon, be they recent or remote, and luring himself toward their society with flimsy, elaborately constructed decoys of his daughter.

I returned to the walk-in health clinic and told Dr. Winters I was afraid maybe I'd developed a little dependency on the pills. She took mercy and humored my euphemism and wrote me a prescription and gave me a list of vitamins to take and food to eat and phone numbers to call. I did everything she told me and sweated and ached and wept and shit myself and bid my farewells to all the exhausted effigies, the poor hapless understudies, with turnips for brains and empty birds' nests for hearts. Once, during withdrawal from the drugs, which was hardly terrible in terms of real withdrawal but grisly and horrific nevertheless, I had a vision of all the versions of Kate I'd invented since her death lined up along a shelf on a wall, like old dolls in a dark, dust-choked room in the back reaches of the oldest basement in the village. They were made of rags and hay and grain sewn into little sacks, disemboweled by mice and rats. They had mismatched eyes of marbles or buttons. Their heads were scavenged gourds or cracked porcelain skulls that whistled in the drafty night.

Poor manikins; poor mandrakes; poor, innocent potatoes. What grass-stuffed rag dolls of my daughter I made. They were grotesques. Any flicker of beauty to be found in them had to be discovered only during the most merciful moments, by the kindest eyes, in order to perceive the source of human grief from which they had been conjured. They were fetishes, cobbled together by a mind clumsy with drugs and sorrow, and shaken in terror like rattles at the immense and exact unfolding of my daughter's true absence elaborating itself in the world.

THE NIGHT BEFORE KATE died, I woke up from a dream about an immense house, filled with relatives from a dozen generations. It was the beginning of September and there was a heat wave and we didn't have any air conditioners. Susan's and my bedroom was located at the front of the house. There were two windows in the room, one facing the side yard, which looked out into the foliage of a large beech tree, and one facing the front lawn. I had opened both windows, hoping for a cross breeze, although the air was completely still, and I had angled an oscillating fan between the stool and sash of the side window, so that it would draw in air that had been cooled by the tree and push it through the room, over our bed. I think I knew that the tree did not cool the air, but the idea was appealing. When I awoke, the fan had tipped back against the screen in the window and was making a sound like an animal trying to claw through the screen as it tried to rotate back and forth. I sat up and gulped at the glass of water on my bedstand. Susan did not stir. She flourished in the heat and slept deeply. My T-shirt and my hair were damp with sweat. My pillowcase was sticky from sweat on both sides. More like a sponge than a pillow, I remember thinking, groggy, grumpy. It struck me at that moment that the room in which I'd last been in the house in my dream was a vast conservatory, with high, vaulted ceilings made of glass and aluminum, built-in bookcases full of old leather-bound books, and lots of red leather chairs and couches, like in the lobby of a grand hotel, all of which seemed to have immense potted ferns looming up behind them, shading them with green canopies of fronds. I crawled forward to the end of our bed and propped the fan back up on the windowsill and stuck my face in front of it. The currents of air broke against my damp skin and made the hair on my neck and arms prickle. Torpid, I crawled off the bed and knelt at the back window and looked out into the night. The air was perfectly still. Not so much as a leaf on a tree rustled. The yard seemed timeless, and it struck me that the wind moving the trees and the grass and the clouds was what usually gave the sense that time was still moving, that the world was still moving, that the wind was a mechanism something like a clock. Or the trees and the clouds were the clock and the wind the power released from some immense solar springs uncoiling in space. I thought my grandfather might have liked the idea of a clock made of clouds and wind. The display on the alarm clock flashed, so the power must have gone out at some point while I'd slept. I had no sense of what time it was. I knew that I would not be able to fall back asleep again anytime soon, so I tiptoed down the dark hall, past Kate's room. She mumbled something when I passed the open door. I have noticed that sleepers will stir when the air in a still house is disturbed by a moving body. I scooted to the stairs and braced myself on the railings running down both sides of the stairway and eased my weight onto each step slowly, so that I would not wake Kate. She could be a tense, light sleeper, easily startled and easily frightened. It took her a few minutes after being jolted awake by thunder or a tree branch breaking in the yard or the wind toppling a garbage barrel into the street to realize where she was and that she was not in any danger. Being startled was something she especially hated; it was one of the very few things I ever saw her become really angry about whenever it happened, even if by accident.

I reached the bottom of the stairs. I remembered that the Red Sox were on a West Coast trip, so that their games did not begin until ten o'clock at night, and if the games were slow

or went into extra innings they lasted deep into the night. I
loved the Red Sox series on the West Coast. I loved baseball
during late summer nights. The clock on the cable television
box read 3:30. I clicked the TV on to see if I could get a score
from the game. The sound came on first and I heard the mono-
tone hum of a sparse crowd and the voice of the Red Sox
play-by-play announcer. The screen kindled, and instead of re-
runs of the sports highlights show, the game between the Red
Sox and the Seattle Mariners that had begun five and a half
hours prior was still being played. The score was tied at one
run to one, and the game was in the fifteenth inning. This
seemed like a small treasure, something to help me deep in a
mildly strange, half-asleep night. I went to the kitchen and
poured myself a glass of orange juice and returned to the living
room and sat on the couch to watch the game.

At some point I became aware that Kate was up and
looking at me from the darkness of the hallway beyond the
dining room. I wasn't sure what to do. I didn't want to turn
and call her name, for fear of frightening her, even though it
might seem as if she were the one who was liable to frighten
me. So I watched the game for ten more minutes, self-
conscious when I clinked out a little march on my juice glass
with my wedding band, or cursed, Shit, shit, *shit,* at a diving
catch the Mariners' right fielder made to end the inning,
aware of Kate watching me and thinking that she was looking in on a person who thought he was all alone, unobserved,
when she was in fact watching a performance. It was that
idea, that I was in some sense defrauding her, that caused me
to finally sit myself up straight at the end of the inning, stretch
my arms over my head, say Ay yi yi, shake my head, reach for

my cigarettes and lighter on the end table next to the couch, and rise, as if I were innocently getting up to go have a smoke on the back porch before the game resumed.

I heard Kate skitter back to the staircase and pad up to the third or fourth stair and turn around and thump back down, as if she were just coming down from the second floor. She came out of the dark hall into the doorway of the living room.

"You okay, Late Kate?"

"Fine, Dad. Just peeing. It's *roasting*. The game's still on?"

"Seven*teenth* inning," I said.

"Did the power go out? My clock's blinking. What time is it?"

"After four."

Kate went to the bathroom and I stepped out to the back porch and lit a cigarette. I took a drag or two, but when I saw Kate coming out I tapped the ash off the end and palmed it.

"Perfect way to ruin a beautiful summer night," I said as Kate stepped outside.

"It's okay, Dad. I don't care if you smoke." She'd told me once that my smoking made her worry about me getting cancer or having a heart attack, but that there was also something comforting about it to her as well. She was used to the smell, she said.

I said, "But *I* care if *you* smoke."

Kate looked up and said, "Wow—look at all the stars."

The night sky was saturated with oceans of stars, with the maples and beeches in the yard making inky black continents among them. The clouds of the Milky Way were visible behind the stars.

"Weird to be lying on a couch watching a game called baseball on a thing called a television set, of all things, with all that out there," I said.

"Hey," Kate said. "There're no crickets."

I cocked my head and listened and, after a few seconds said, "That *is* strange. *Really* strange."

"Too hot, maybe?"

"I really haven't got the slightest idea. But it makes the night extra spooky."

We stood for a moment, watching, then Kate said, "Dad, when you came downstairs, did you stop and look at me sleeping?" I turned to her and arched my eyebrows.

"I plead the Fifth," I said.

"I don't care—just wondering." She stared at her feet and raised one off the ground and pointed her toes and made a little figure eight with them in the air, like a dance exercise.

"Well, I don't need this stinky thing," I said, and stubbed out the cigarette on the driveway and flicked the butt into the planting pot I kept tucked against the corner of the house for spent smokes. "Let's go see about them Sox."

We returned to the living room. I dropped myself down on the middle of the couch, rested the orange juice on my stomach, and flung an arm behind my head. Kate sat on the edge of the end of the couch nearest the doorway to the dining room. I waggled my fingers and Kate leaned over and took my hand in hers and kissed it.

"My dad, the vampire," she said.

"Some vampire, lying on the couch watching baseball," I said back.

"How long's this thing going to go?"

"I don't know. Maybe forever at this point. The game that never *ended*," I said, in a silly, sinister voice.

"They could make a special channel for it on TV."

"Nah, well, this guy who's pitching is a bench player. Someone's going to knock a cream puff down the right field line and end it any second."

"A cream puff right down Pastry Alley."

"Exactly."

Kate gave me a last, hammy smooch on the back of my hand, like in the cartoons, where the rabbit gives the hunter who's stalking him a long, wet *Mmmmmwah!* before he yanks the hunter's cap over his eyes and dives back down the rabbit hole.

"Night, Dad."

"Night, Kates."

Kate hiked back up to her room. I watched the game for another quarter hour and fell back asleep and again took up my dream, which had switched location from the house to a vast, curved aluminum frame, like a zeppelin's, suspended in the clouds, along which I crawled, terrified. As I slept, the Red Sox finally beat the Mariners, and an hour later the sun rose over the last day of my daughter's life.

15.

I PLACED A SMALL BOUQUET OF BLUETS AND BUTTERCUPS ON Kate's stone on the first anniversary of her death. I placed a spray of chicory and hawkweed that I saved from the summer on her stone, on what would have been her fourteenth birthday. The stone is a dark gray, flecked with chips of what look like quartz or mica. It is next to my mother's and my grandparents' stones. I sometimes imagine a quiet, clean, hidden bower for Kate, with little ornaments made from twigs and leaves and elaborate mobiles made of branches and cordgrass and even handmade bird feeders tucked into hollows, which I'd keep filled with black oil sunflower seeds, and evenly balanced and weighted by pebbles wound in twine and suspended from the corners, and slim glass flutes wound into the twine, in which I'd put droppers full of sugar water, so that there would be a watchful aviary above my girl, attended by birds whose ancestors were the ones Kate and I used to feed from our hands in the sanctuary.

I sold our house after I repaired the damage I had done to it and cleaned the yard. I sent Susan half of the money and put the rest in a savings account. I rented two rooms at the back of a large house half a mile from the center of Enon, from an elderly widow named Trowt. I received her permission to paint the rooms white (they were an antique salmon color when I first moved in). One room is my bedroom. I have a twin bed and a nightstand with a lamp on it. I keep my clothes in the closet, either hanging from hangers or in one of two inexpensive plastic three-drawer storage containers that have transparent fronts. The other room has a small electric stove, refrigerator, and sink along one wall. There is a high table with a butcher-block top in front of the appliances and sink, where I prepare my meals. Without any conscious decision, I have stopped eating meat. Most of my meals consist of rice and vegetables, which I chop with a dull old chef's knife that has a magnet stuck to its handle that I found on the side of the refrigerator when I moved into the apartment. There is a narrow chair in one corner of the room, and a small table, on which sits a goosenecked lamp and a putty-colored rotary telephone. In the remaining corner of the room there is a large wingback Queen Anne chair that Mrs. Trowt gave me after checking in on me a week after I moved in and finding the apartment so spare. The chair is upholstered in fabric that has sun-faded poppies on an ivory background. The arms are slick and threadbare and stained with loops and dashes of ink that has browned with age. There is a standing brass lamp with a gold shade next to the chair that Mrs. Trowt also gave me.

I no longer drink bitter potions, or whiskey. I own an old green-and-blue pickup truck that I bought for twenty-five hundred dollars from a retired landscaper I knew years ago. I use it to transport a used ride-on lawn mower and a weed trimmer and a rake and a big broom and a shovel. I tend fourteen lawns in Enon. The truck breaks down regularly and I am happy to work on it during the weekends with some of my grandfather's old tools, which I keep in a large plastic gray toolbox just inside the door to my rooms. My hand still hurts at the end of most every day and I take aspirin before I cook dinner every night.

I still smoke a cigarette with the pot of coffee I drink early every morning, and another after dinner. My rooms give out onto a circular courtyard formed by the turnaround of the gravel driveway. There is a barn opposite my rooms. It has a large door that slides open and shut on an iron roller. I open the barn door and sit just outside the opening on an old iron garden chair painted white that has blisters of rust erupting all over it. I am comforted by the feeling of the large dim open looming interior of the barn behind me. I smoke my cigarette in the morning and watch the light unroll across the yard and illuminate the gardens. I smoke my cigarette at the end of the day and I watch the evening advance and the light retreat and the gardens fold back up into shadow. When it's hot I sometimes pull the chair just behind the threshold of the barn door so I can sit in the shade. The barn timber smells sweet. There's a trace, too, of the hay once stored there. The big interior of the barn mutes the hissing of summer. When it's cold I sometimes pull the chair just inside the barn so I can sit out of the wind or the snow. In the cold, the barn smells like the iron nails that hold it together and the iron pulleys above the loft. I sit in the chair and smoke and look at the light and the colors and think about things like trying to paint the same view in different seasons and how I could never translate the colors I see into paint, or how I don't know what colors I'm actually looking at. I am a connoisseur of the day. Sometimes I sit in tears. Sometimes I sit in a wordless, inexplicable kind of brokenhearted joy.

At night, I am tired from work. I sit in my white room in the chair and look at a library book under the lamp. Sometimes I fall asleep in the chair. Sometimes I dream about Kate. I wish the dreams could be us sitting together in the garden, talking peacefully, with me kissing her forehead at the end and promising to see her again soon. But my dreams are the usual bizarre, fractious affairs and Kate always shows up just as I am about to slide off a steep roof, or when I am wrestling a wild dog in the desert, or when I've forgotten that I had a daughter and am enjoying the inexplicable admiration of a beautiful woman at a party in a majestic house. The timing is always terrible and I am always caught off guard by her sudden appearance. I try to tell her not to move because the tiles on the roof are loose and she will plunge to the cobbled street below if she does not stay still, or I yell to her to run before the dog notices and turns its fangs from me to her, or that I am sorry for flirting, and that I miss her so much, every single day, everywhere, all the time, and that I love her so much, and this is all a dream, and she knows how dreams are, and that I didn't mean to let her out of my thoughts for even a moment. As upsetting as these meetings are, there is consolation in them, too—real joy at seeing my daughter—whether they anticipate an eventual reunion or are just figments that comfort me once in a while until I, too, simply cease and there isn't a soul left in Enon or anywhere else on this awful miracle of a planet to remember either of us.

About the Type

This book was set in Bembo, a typeface based on an old-style Roman face that was used for Cardinal Bembo's tract *De Aetna* in 1495. Bembo was cut by Francisco Griffo in the early sixteenth century. The Lanston Monotype Company of Philadelphia brought the well-proportioned letterforms of Bembo to the United States in the 1930s.